FILL THE SKY

FILL THE SKY

Katherine A. Sherbrooke

(sixoneseven)BOOKS

Boston, Massachusetts
2016

Permissions requests may be addressed to:

SixOneSeven Books
21 Wormwood Street
Ste. 325
Boston, MA 02210
www.sixonesevenbooks.com

Publisher's Note: This is a work of fiction. Names, characters, places, and incidents are a product of the author's imagination. Locales and public names are sometimes used for atmospheric purposes. Any resemblance to actual people, living or dead, or to businesses, companies, events, institutions, or locales is completely coincidental.

Cover design by Whitney Scharer. Interior by Eliyanna Kaiser. Author photo copyright Melissa Forman.

Boston / Katherine Sherbrooke — First Edition
ISBN 978-0-9848245-3-3

Printed in the United States of America

For Patrick, Henry & George

Look deep, deep into nature,
and then you will understand everything better.
Albert Einstein

Tell me who you walk with,
and I'll tell you what kind of person you are.
Ecuadorian Proverb

Fill
the
Sky

ONE

Tess

*T*ess hung up the phone and fought against an overwhelming sense of powerlessness. She wasn't willing to accept her inability to help, to *do* something. She had pulled it off four years ago, the last time Ellie was sick. She'd done the research and found just the right medical team to blow away the odds and usher Ellie into remission. But that same team had now told her friend, her dearest friend, that she would be lucky to get another six months—nothing much they could do. And in her desperation, Ellie had already decided that flying off to Ecuador to work with shamans, or medicine people, or whatever they were called might be her only chance at survival. How had she failed her friend so completely?

"Jonathan!" she yelled from her chair.

"At your service." He appeared so fast, she sometimes wondered if he just stood outside her office waiting for her command.

"Cancel everything for this afternoon," she said. "Tell Rafferty I'll look at his data first thing tomorrow. Then I need you to call Parker and tell him to meet me at Il Fornaio at eight."

Jonathan's eyebrows went up at this.

"Jesus, Jonathan, it's not a date." He did have a point. "Make sure he knows that. But tell him it's urgent." She closed her laptop and grabbed her phone and keys off the desk.

"Um, can I give him any context for this extremely demanding, in-case-you-forgot-you-dumped-him request?" He tilted his head to the side with a mock smile. Jonathan loved to remind her that at forty-six, she couldn't afford to break up with guys he called "a dream and a half."

She gave him a *not now* look and slung her bag over her shoulder. Halfway through the door she stopped.

"Oh, and just in case," she said, "you better clear my calendar for the week after next. I might need to be out of the country."

"Did an alien sneak past me somehow and possess you? You just told everyone at the staff meeting to prepare for a lock-in for the next month, and now you're going, where exactly?"

The timing sucked, no doubt about it. Her company was on the line. The convergence of all this would crush most people, but she couldn't afford to collapse. People were depending on her.

"It's Ellie," she said.

"Oh, no." All his puff deflated with just two words.

"Go home tonight and give Daniel an extra hug," she said. "Life's too damn short."

She knew she was in trouble as soon as she saw Parker's reflection in the mirror behind the bar. His hair had gotten a little longer, and he was wearing his trademark oxford tucked neatly into the same pair of jeans that had been left in a heap at the foot of her bed so many times. He didn't try to contain his smile when he saw her. As he walked over, a pair of women at the maitre d's podium followed him across the room with their eyes.

"Hello, stranger," he said, and leaned in to kiss her on the cheek. "What's wrong? Jonathan was pretty vague."

Tess had handled Ellie's news all day like a crisis manager in charge of contingency planning, but telling Parker was different. She clasped her hands together and tried to find the courage to speak.

"Please don't tell me you're getting married," he said, with true alarm on his face.

She told him about Ellie, everything she knew about her condition, how she had called everyone she knew who worked in the field and the prognosis was definitely grim.

"God, you must be devastated," he said. "I'm so glad you called."

"Here's the thing." She took a sip of her drink. "I know your work is confidential, but I need you to tell me if any of your clients are working on any under-the-radar trials that might help her."

"You called me for my research?" He leaned forward in his seat. "Listen, you know I would tell you in a minute if there was something on the horizon that could help Ellie, but how are you, Tess? How've you been? I've missed you."

"So you don't know of anything."

"I'm sorry." Parker put his hand on hers.

This was proving harder than she thought. He was looking right into her, and she knew he was trying to determine if the spark was still there between them or if she was only after information. She should have emailed him. She needed to stay focused on her purpose. This had to be about Ellie. She pulled her hand back.

"Joline wants to take her to Ecuador to see some medicine people or something. She's got Ellie's hopes up they can actually help. It's crazy, Parker. Ellie's going to die, and I can't do one thing to help her."

Parker understood this dynamic. Joline was Tess's and Ellie's other roommate at Stanford, and while Tess loved her, it was hard not to be exasperated by thirty years of introductions to the latest new-age solution for health and wellbeing. Ellie bought into it every time. It all drove Tess a little nuts.

"Maybe going to Ecuador isn't such a bad idea," he said.

"How would it possibly be a good idea?"

"Well, the research on the placebo effect I've studied is pretty clear that a patient's chances of recovery are most highly correlated with their own belief about whether or not they will get well." Tess loved hearing him talk research. "If Ellie believes going to Ecuador will help, maybe it will."

"She wants me to go," she said.

"Then maybe that's the single most important thing you can do for her."

Tess stabbed the lone olive in her glass and considered ordering another drink.

"Tess, let me drive you home. You must be running on fumes."

She knew she wouldn't resist inviting him in. As soon as they shut the door behind them, he unclasped the hair clip at the base of her neck, hitched her up to his hips, and wrapped her legs around him. In the space between the front door and the bedroom, the year they had been apart dissolved like sugar in a boiling beaker. Gone.

The morning of her flight to Quito, Tess felt the warmth of Parker's body next to her before she opened her eyes. Every morning since Ellie's news, he'd been there. It had been a relief to dive back in without any questions, without rehashing old issues. There were already too many top priorities in her life right now without worrying about that.

She had to get moving. She'd have only a few hours at the office before heading to SFO. Forcing herself to open her eyes, she found Parker watching her.

"God, don't do that," she said. "What are you doing?"

"Can I drive you to the airport later?" he asked, brushing her hair off her face.

"That's okay. The driver will pick me up at the office," she said. "Shit, I still have to pack."

She tried to swing her leg out of the bed, but his hand was on her thigh.

"Are you ready for this?" he asked.

"For jumping into Joline's crazy healer world? What in God's name would make you think I wasn't ready?" she said.

"Ready to behave, I mean."

Tess rolled her eyes.

"I told you," he said. "Casting doubts won't help Ellie. You have always been the one she can lean on. She's going to need that from you more than ever."

Tess felt a tear threatening to surface. She shut it back, under a long blink.

"I know," she said.

"And when you need somewhere to lean, I'm here," he said.

"Oh, I'll be fine."

"How can you possibly be fine, Tess? Your best friend is dying and your company is on the brink."

"What choice do I have?" she said, feeling anger rise. What good would it do to sit around and whine about the shit-show her life was at the moment?

"No, you're right. You've always been a force of nature, Tess. I get that. You've never needed help from anyone in your life." He sat up on his side of the bed, his back to her.

"What did I say?" she said.

He put his jeans on and wandered around the room in search of his shirt.

"This doesn't work for me if you don't let me in," he said. "These last two weeks have been. . . It's been amazing to be with you again. But I need more than that. I want to be needed. I need to know that I am the one you count on—"

"I can't do this right now," Tess said. Could anyone give her a break?

"I know. But I couldn't let you leave without telling you how I feel. I love you, Tess, like it or not. And I need to be loved back. Otherwise there's no point."

She wasn't sure what she was supposed to say.

"You get packed. I'll make you some breakfast," he said, and left her clutching the edge of the cool white sheet.

As the plane banked toward Quito, the rising sun pushed a yolk of light across Tess's screen, making her spreadsheet unread-able. She hadn't slept. She still couldn't believe she was actu-ally headed to Ecuador. The idea that a group of people with no medical training could possibly help Ellie was ludicrous. But as hard as she'd tried, Tess had found no better option to offer. Not yet, anyway. After they got through their week of "healing ceremonies," as Joline called them, Tess would continue her search for a new drug or new trial or new procedure that could save her friend. There had to be something.

She glanced over at Joline, still asleep in the aisle seat, the static from the paper pillowcase pulling at her graying spikes of hair, her bare arm hanging into the empty seat between them. Her silver rings encircled almost every finger, and an arc of bangles hung on her wrist. With her dark brown eyes closed, her face lost its usual warmth, the hollow of her cheeks emphasizing the crest of her cheekbones and edge of her jaw. Her wiry frame, tightly wrapped in her skinny jeans and tank tops, made her look a little older than her forty-seven years, or maybe it was having a teenaged boy under her roof while getting no help from a deadbeat dad.

Tess sighed and tried for the umpteenth time to stretch her legs out under the seat. She re-clipped the jade barrette at the base of her neck, then pulled up the shade and squinted into the sun. Not far below, multiple mountain peaks surged toward the sky, some still covered in snow, their ridges rough and strong. She hoped Otavalo would have plenty of trails, the steeper the better. A long run was all the healing Tess needed.

She couldn't stop thinking about Ellie's kids. She loved to be in that house, where dinner was allowed to go cold in favor of a good snowball fight. It reminded her of her own childhood, back before her mother had died, when life was a carefree orbit around her mother's warmth. Tess couldn't bear the idea of Ellie's kids having to endure the pain of losing their mother—it was too much to expect of a child. She shook off the thought. Ellie just couldn't die. They all needed her too much.

Tess spotted what looked like the mouth of a volcano. She knew there were dozens of them around Quito, now dormant, mountains that had molded their inner roiling into something strong and reliable, immovable. One was even taller than Denali, all of them now playgrounds for hikers trying to conquer obscene altitudes. She admired the sculpted cliffs and slants, every angle representing a challenge of mortal strength.

Just beyond the peaks, patches of dark green and brown land sloped down toward Quito, its buildings tilted in haphazard groupings, as if they had slid down from the hills and bunched up at the bottom, like slush on a windshield. A lone cell tower stood above the city, and Tess wondered just how backwater a place they might be headed for.

The pilot's announcement of their final approach woke Joline.

"Looks like we're going to be early," Tess said, looking at her watch. "If we hurry we can get to Ellie's gate before she gets off."

"Good morning to you, too," Joline said, rubbing her face. She slid into the middle seat and leaned over Tess. "What magical mountains. How amazing that we're all going to be here together."

"I can't believe it either," Tess said.

"Give it a chance. Nature will support."

Her favorite phrase. Joline always managed to boil the most complex issues down to her belief that whatever should happen will happen, that nature was a divine force that found the best solution on its own. Nonsense. Ellie was an amazing mother, devoted wife, the best friend Tess had ever had. How could "nature" possibly justify any of this? Ellie simply didn't deserve to be sick.

Tess wondered if her friends would say the same if she were the one to get sick. Or would they think she had brought it on herself with her endless hours, her drive, always pushing for one more mile, one more bend in the trail? It was the one thing she knew Joline and Ellie would never quite understand. Life as a solo warrior was different. She did what she had to do to survive.

Tess put away her laptop and fastened her seatbelt.

"Just tell me they make martinis in Ecuador," Tess said.

"Oh, they make better than that," Joline said.

Tess was too tired to ask what she meant.

TWO
Ellie

W alking into the boarding area, Ellie immediately spotted Tess, taller than most of the crowd by six or eight inches, her auburn hair a beacon in the sea of jet black heads. She was thumbing her phone while leaning on her roller-bag. She never did check her luggage—too inefficient. Even after a red-eye, Tess looked beautiful. Her long lean legs, turquoise eyes, and the shiny ponytail draped over one shoulder gave her an elegance that belied her tenacity. There was no one Ellie would rather have beside her in a crisis. *Crisis.* The reality of how different this week would be than their usual girl's week-ends made her want to drop to her knees and sob. She stopped walking to compose herself.

When she looked up again, Joline was only steps away. She engulfed Ellie in a hug, holding on through three or four deep breaths that rose and fell against her chest. Ellie relaxed into the embrace, knowing she could crumple if she needed to and not fall to the floor.

"I'm so glad to be here with you," Joline said into her hair. Then Tess added her arms to the reunion and Ellie swallowed hard. This is what would give her strength, these two amaz-ing women. She held onto them for a few extra beats before untangling herself.

"You know I could never do this without you," Ellie said.

"We would never let you," Tess said.

"Everyone who loves you will be with you this week, Ellie B. You need to remember that," Joline said.

"Now, shall we do battle with baggage claim and get something to eat?" Tess said. "I'm starving."

Joline squeezed Ellie's hand. "Are you ready?"

Ellie nodded. Tess was already in motion.

"We'll have to grab something to eat on our way. We don't have that much time before we have to be at Don Emilio's," Joline said.

Ellie's stomach shifted. She wished she could have a little time to fall back into rhythm with her friends before seeing their first shaman, a chance to absorb the strength she felt when they were all together, the way their friendship refueled her, shored her up.

"Wouldn't it make more sense to go to the hotel first and settle in before Ellie has her first appointment?" Tess asked. "It's been a long trip."

"Don Emilio is right on our way to Otavalo," Joline said. "It actually works out perfectly."

Ellie forced herself to keep moving. This is what she had come for. No matter what the doctors told her, she wasn't about to give up. She had to do whatever she could, and Joline's plan, as unorthodox as it was, just might be it. She found great comfort in the fact that Joline had lived her life way out ahead of convention, and her discoveries often ended up going mainstream. Hadn't she started meditating before anyone knew what that meant? She'd been the one to try yoga when the rest of the country was learning aerobics, and drank green smoothies a decade before putting spinach in a blender was fashionable. She was one of the first people in the country to convert her masterful instincts for helping others into a formal practice, and the success of her life-coaching business was a testament to her gifts. Even Tess was impressed by that. Ellie hoped the idea of being cured this way—through ancient rituals and plant medicines— would be proven in time, the kind of thing that people would come to accept ten or fifteen years from now, and talk about freely at cocktail parties and say "of course" when told of miracle healings. She held tight to the hope that she could be one of those people. Lilly and Hannah would be all grown up by then. Connor might even be married.

By the time they cleared customs and walked to the rental car lot, Ellie was out of breath. She hoped the burning sensation in her chest could be blamed on the altitude, just as David had warned. Of the many reasons he hadn't wanted her to come, altitude had been near the top of the list—not enough oxygen, too much strain on her already compromised lung. She knew David just didn't want her going away as sick as she was, and overheard him arguing on the phone with Joline about this trip more than once. But Joline had a way of getting her brother to see her side.

Ellie reflexively put her hand on her chest.

"Are you okay?" Tess asked.

"I just need a second." She paused to catch her breath and broke into a hacking cough, leaving her friends looking on, frightened.

"I'm okay." Ellie steadied her breathing. "Honestly, this is one of my few symptoms. Other than some fatigue and my ribs feeling too tight sometimes, I've really felt fine." Nothing inside her proclaimed death, nothing except the three-week-old echo of her doctors' voices, calmly stating that they could only give her six months, as if her lungs were a pair of snow tires that had worn through. It all made her nauseous and angry. *Give her* six months? Where had that expression come from? This was all about taking—cutting off the second half of her life, ripping her children away from her, making her children motherless.

She could picture what she'd already missed that morning at home, those precious waking moments that gave each day its shape: Connor pulling the covers over his head, exposing his gangly ankles, begging for ten more minutes; Hannah not budging, her sleep so sound she would have to be gently shaken to be brought back into the light; Lilly pretending she was still asleep, but not being able to stop a smile from blooming onto her little face. How many seconds of daylight would her children be allowed to enjoy each morning before they remembered she was dead? How many times would they simultaneously crave the comfort of their mother and realize that they would never see her again? Ellie closed her eyes and steadied herself against the car.

"I'm going to get you some water," Tess said, and hurried back toward the rental building.

Ellie cranked down the window and hung her arm out, grateful for the warm breeze. She was happy to have the back seat to herself. Tess always drove, and Joline needed to navigate. They had left the city of Quito behind and were climbing a winding road. A wide valley quilted with squares and rectangles of different colors stretched out below a drop-off on the left, mountains standing watch in the distance. Tall trees poked through the thick brush on the edge of the road like frayed umbrellas that had long since given up offering shade, their frond parasols outlined against the deep blue sky. Ellie would have thought they were beautiful had she not been worried they might be dying.

"How did Hannah's science fair go, Ell?" Tess asked. "I hope my email about kinetic energy versus inertia made sense to her."

Ellie smiled. "A complete success, thanks to you, Tess. Oh, and Jo, you have to see this photo of Connor. All dressed up for David's birthday dinner," Ellie said, holding out her phone. "He actually wore David's loafers, if you can believe it. I didn't have the heart to tell him he should wear something other than his white socks, he was so proud."

"So grown up," Joline said. "He's gotta have a foot on Dylan by now."

Joline's son was almost a full year younger than Connor, but they had looked like twins when they were younger. Now Connor towered over his cousin.

"And you have to see this video," Ellie said. "One of Lilly's bunnies got loose in the back yard. It's hilarious." Joline watched the video, her nieces and nephew hopping around the lawn trying to corral the rabbit, and her face contorted with laughter.

"I get to see that later," Tess said. "Play one of Dylan's new songs for us, Jo. You brought them, right?"

"Where's he staying while you're gone?" Ellie asked.

"At Joey's," she said, grateful for the open invitation from his parents for Dylan to stay whenever she traveled.

Ellie was happy to dip into regular conversation, comforted by the idea that she had a whole week to chatter with her friends, to talk about all the little things that added up to something larger than any one big topic could contain.

They made one stop so Joline could pick up eggs and cologne for Don Emilio. Ellie wondered if they had some monetary or symbolic value to the shaman—could they not get eggs in their village? Was he paid in cologne?

While they waited, Ellie noticed two boys collecting rocks for a slingshot, while a third righted a pile of cans on a nearby wall. Another troop of kids kicked a ball made of duct tape in the street. Their faces were wide and round at the jaw, their skin a deep honey color. As Joline got back in the car, Ellie waved, and two of them happily waved back.

"Why aren't these kids in school?" Ellie asked.

"School is too expensive for most families. There are no free schools here," Joline said.

"Gosh, how sad," Ellie said. The boys cheered when the rock found its target and all five cans went flying.

They drove on, past a corrugated tin house with one gray wing of flapping laundry, past a cow tied to a tree, its tail swishing at the family of flies hiding in its ribcage. Eventually they turned down a dirt road with a jumble of shacks on one side, and a tall cement wall on the other.

"Park next to that wall," Joline said. "Don Emilio's house is just on the other side."

Oh boy. Here we go.

They climbed out of the car, and Joline put her hands on Ellie's shoulders.

"Before we go in, I want you to take a moment to set your intention," Joline said. "This is the time to free yourself from diagnoses and timelines and all the anxiety doctors have put in your head." Ellie nodded. "This is about your energy now, your desire to be healed. All week you are going to be surrounded by people who know that we already have inside ourselves everything we need to heal. You have it inside. Focus on that."

Tess rubbed Ellie's back. Ellie closed her eyes and pictured her happiest, healthiest self at home with David and the kids on a warm summer day. No sadness, no worry. Just joy.

"I love you, Ellie B," Joline finally said, and gave her another long hug.

Arms linked, the three friends walked through an iron gate into a concrete courtyard, crowded with two pickup trucks and ten or twelve dusty dogs lounging in every available splash of sunshine. Several baskets of corn crowded the main doorway of the yellow house, the only two-story structure in the town. They were greeted by a large woman who introduced herself as Don Emilio's wife. She grinned enthusiastically, her teeth outlined in gold. Joline explained that the heavy strands of beads wrapped around her neck like a scarf were a sign that she was married to the most important man in the village. Ellie was sure it took all of Tess's self control not to point out that the village was no more than a row of tilting shacks with a lean-to for a store.

Emerging from a side door, a middle-aged man introduced himself as Diego, the shaman's son, and vigorously shook Joline's hand. They followed him through the dark doorway and into a room that was no more than a basement. One lone bulb hung from the ceiling, and an opening cut into the far wall let in little light. An acrid smell drifted up from the dirt floor, an odor Ellie couldn't place. How could any kind of healing happen in such a dank space?

Diego motioned for the three friends to sit at a large wooden table across from Don Emilio. Only now did she notice the shaman—a slight man, half the size of his wife, with a pensive and deeply weathered face. Strands of beaded necklaces hung over his denim shirt, and the crown of brown and blue plumes he wore reminded her of something out of a school play. His white Nikes tapped the dirt floor in a nonsensical rhythm. She shivered, the dampness in the air starting to seep into her bones.

Diego stood proudly beside his father's chair. Two young women and a young man, perhaps all part of Don Emilio's family, sat behind them, whispering into their chestnut-colored hands, while a little girl skipped back and forth along the line of legs, touching each knee as she passed. Her curls bounced and bobbed as she went, reminding Ellie of Lilly's soft spiral twists. It made her ache for home.

Three candles had been lit and affixed to the table with wax. Don Emilio studied each flame, his gold pinky ring glinting in the light. He seemed to focus on one in particular, as if examining the details of a painting, and spoke first to Joline. Ellie was glad he hadn't started with her, as she was having a hard time concentrating. Diego translated the Quechua words into English, something about mother earth and the wings of a bird. He gazed closely at the next candle and then spoke to Tess. Ellie couldn't absorb his words. Her pulse throbbed in her ears, and she wondered if she had made a terrible mistake coming here. Could she really expect this man to save her?

Don Emilio circled his hand around the last candle, the one that was meant to be Ellie's. He looked deep into the flame and then spoke. Diego translated to the room. Ellie forced herself to focus.

"It is good that you have come here. Your energy is very low, and when energy is too low, it can make illness in us, even death."

Ellie swallowed.

"Think about those that love you. Breathe them in and hold them with you."

Ellie attempted a deep breath, and fingered the string bracelet Hannah had given her before she left. She closed her eyes and pictured each of her children, and David, and her friends beside her. She had to shut out everything else, everyone else. When Don Emilio spoke again, he talked for a long time before Diego translated.

"He says you need to be close to Pachamama, which means Mother Earth. She can help you. For you to have healthy life it is important to focus on the place where energy is blocked."

Ellie nodded. She put her attention on her lung.

"You must focus on your heart. Don Emilio says you have a problem in your heart. He will work on this today."

Her heart? What about her lung, the one lung she had left, the one that wasn't supposed to last?

"It is time for the ceremony. You please get undressed now and go to the end of the room," Diego said and turned away.

"What?" Tess half-yelled. "Did he just say *get undressed?*"

"We can keep our undies on. And bras. If you want," Joline said.

"You must be out of your mind." Tess stood up.

Ellie knew if Tess saw her waver she would pull her out of that room without a second thought.

"Tess. I know you think it's crazy, but this may be my only chance—"

"Don't say that."

"I need to. I need to give this a chance to work." Ellie lowered her voice. "You know chemo won't cure me this time." Ellie tugged Tess's hands. "You did everything you could possibly do for me back home. Everything. We simply ran out of options. I have to at least try this."

Tess closed her eyes. "Okay. I'm sorry," she said, remembering Parker's advice. "I'll do whatever you need."

Ellie turned her back to the spectators and slunk out of her shirt and jeans. She used to be proud of the long scar that ran up the right side of her ribs, proof that she had conquered cancer. Now it felt like a flaw. But at least Don Emilio wouldn't miss the location of her true ailment a second time.

She followed Joline down to the far end of the room, and stood between her and Tess. She put her hands over her belly, conscious of the softness there, and its contrast with Tess's board-flat stomach and Joline's bony form, her skin stretched over each joint.

All the spectators stayed in their seats and watched expectantly. She was used to being poked and prodded by a parade of doctors and nurses, but they were careful to look at just one part of her body at a time, and never into her eyes unless her hospital gown was safely closed. Her near nakedness seemed entirely inconsequential and yet essential to everyone else in the room, as if she were a steed being assessed by a family of ranchers.

Don Emilio's wife lumbered into the basement carrying the eggs and cologne. Diego put on his own feathers, shorter than his father's, and the two men stood together facing the three-some. Don Emilio's wife handed the men fans made of huge palm fronds. They started to chant in Quechua and took turns flapping the branches on the friends' heads, legs, and arms. They said the word "Pachamama" many times amidst a slew of other words. Ellie's hair swirled into a frizz each time the leaves grazed her head. The little girl swatted them with a smaller palm branch, unable to reach much higher than their waists.

Ellie couldn't quite comprehend what she was seeing when Don Emilio picked up one of the bottles of cologne, unscrewed the cap, and took a huge swig. He swept his hand over Joline's eyes, stepped back, and spewed the mouthful onto her. Ellie gasped. He spit the cologne down each of Joline's arms, across her bare breasts, onto her stomach. Joline kept the point of her chin high, her arms at her sides. The sinews running down her throat barely twitched. Had she known this was coming?

And then Don Emilio stepped in front of Ellie. She crossed her arms over her body and squeezed her eyes shut as he took a gulp and emitted a long spray at her chest and belly. Her whole body shuddered. The room reeked. She kept her breathing shallow. The cologne splattered across her shoulders and onto her face. The liquid stuck to her hair, her bra, and stung her skin. Time slowed as he sprayed her again and again. She had the urge to wave him off, push him away, but she was afraid to open her eyes.

Think of those that love you. She clenched her fists and pictured Connor, Lilly, and Hannah, playing together in the back yard. Would they be able to experience simple childhood moments anymore with their mother dead and gone?

Every day of the last three weeks, ever since hearing her doctor's cruel words, she had found herself picturing her memorial service, specifically the first row of the church, the girls clutching David on either side, pale with grief, Connor trying to be brave at the end of the row, swiping at his eyes with the back of his hand, David reaching across Hannah's hunched form to grasp his son's shoulder. She swayed, and then forced herself to banish the image.

A small yelp from Tess told Ellie that Don Emilio had moved on. She peeled open her eyes and tried to rub away the sting of cologne and the pixels of grief lingering in her thoughts. Tess's chest was pumping out short exhales. As each spray landed, Tess recoiled, but then straightened up again, like a soldier refusing to bow to the abuse slung at her from a commanding officer.

After Don Emilio put the bottle of cologne back on the table, Diego handed two eggs to his father. Ellie exchanged a wide-eyed glance with Tess, imagining cracked shells and smeared yolks. This was about to get worse. She could endure anything for her children, but she felt terrible that her friends were being subjected to this madness, too. Joline had insisted that all three of them should participate in the healing ceremonies, that they would be more powerful that way, and equally valuable for all of them. But this?

Don Emilio approached Tess and started to rub the eggs on her thighs, on the sides of her hips, her arms, her belly, and around her collarbone, chanting while he worked. *Shungo, Shungo, Shungo.* He moved the eggs so fast that Ellie was sure they would break open. He stood on tiptoe to rub the eggs on Tess's forehead. *Shungo, Shungo, Shungo.* After several passes up and down her body, he walked to the side of the room and threw the unmarred eggs out the window. Ellie felt some measure of relief that Tess wasn't dripping in yolk. Although, maybe eggs didn't break open on healthy people. The little girl fanned her again with her palm fronds, creating a breeze that chilled her skin.

A cell phone rang. The young man flipped it open and walked from the room.

Don Emilio rubbed two eggs on Ellie next, jiggling her stomach, the flesh at her hips. *Shungo, Shungo, Shungo.* He lingered at her cleavage, and she worried for a moment she might tip backward as he worked the area around her heart. *Shungo, Shungo, Shungo.* She willed him to see the cancer in her lung, to focus there instead. He scrubbed the rest of her with the eggs, but kept coming back to her heart. She braced for a cracking or crumbling sound, but it didn't come. He tossed the two orbs out the window just as he had before. Ellie let out her breath.

Don Emilio brought two new eggs over to Joline. He worked up and down her body, and even when he furiously rubbed the eggs on her bony sections, they stayed intact.

Scooting the little girl back toward the chairs, Don Emilio turned away, and Ellie started to relax. The ceremony must be over. But the two men busied themselves back at the table, and one of the spectators pulled the girl onto her lap and settled back into her chair. Diego raised two torches into the air, handed one to his father, and lit them. They both held bottles of cologne. Dread rippled through her.

The men tipped the bottles of cologne into their mouths in unison and blew onto the torches. Ellie turned her head to dodge the lick of flame that threatened to singe her hair. Joline didn't move. Tess jumped to Ellie's side as the blaze shot at them again. It stopped a few feet from them and receded, like a dragon breathing in. She took a quick sip of air before the heat rushed toward them again. The roiling yellow, blue, and white light blurred her vision. She could no longer see the door that was their only path of escape. The heat engulfed them and she felt a rising panic. What if their cologne-soaked bodies ignited? Would the women jump from the sidelines and smother them with their woolen shawls, save them from being cooked alive? Don Emilio moved closer, and Ellie clutched Tess's arm as he tipped his bottle up to his mouth again, and shot a wall of fire directly at them.

And then it was over.

The spectators stood, grinning and nodding, and clapped Don Emilio and Diego on their backs. Tess looked as relieved as Ellie felt. Joline seemed spent but satisfied, like someone who had endured a painful workout.

Ellie pulled her shirt on gingerly, as if she could save any part of it from her sticky skin. The two young women approached them and put hand-knit hats on Joline's and her head, each with a tassel on top and flaps at the ears. They motioned for Tess to bend down and pulled hers into place before she had a chance to corral the auburn wisps that had escaped her ponytail with all the swatting. Llamas walked the perimeter of Tess's hat; a string of little girls held hands on Joline's. Ellie didn't know what hers looked like.

Still grinning, Don Emilio's wife handed out shot glasses, holding up her own in the universal symbol of a toast. Ellie was relieved that the drink was clear, not the brown color of the cologne, but it scalded her throat when she downed it.

As soon as the toast was over, Ellie dropped into a chair with a thud.

"Are you all right?" Tess asked, squatting at her side.

"Are you?" Ellie tried to smile, but a wave of nausea washed through her. "Maybe I need to get outside."

"Good idea," Tess said. "I'll get your bag."

Ellie passed Joline counting out crisp twenties for Don Emilio's wife, walked outside, and found a smooth section of wall on the far side of Don Emilio's courtyard where she could lean and tip her face up to the sun. She put her hand on her chest and felt the pulsing against her palm, one beat after the next. Her heart. He had focused on her heart. A small sob escaped her throat as she realized that the shaman had been able to see everything she had hidden there. Her heart was compromised, soiled, and Don Emilio knew it.

It had all happened just after she went into remission, three years earlier. She was on Nantucket opening up the tiny cottage her grandfather had left her—she couldn't bear to sell it, and rented it in the high season to cover the cost. It was a glorious spring day. She was out for a walk on her favorite route, and all her senses were attuned to the sheer miracle of life. She wasn't prepared to come across Gavin Melbourne hanging a new sign outside the Sconset House—Gavin, the high point of her high school summers, her first love. The smile that erupted across his face when he saw her was full of spontaneous pleasure, and at the same time a deep knowing, as if he had been waiting for her all along. She was instantly transported back to a different time.

Over dinner that night, as they caught up on the last three decades of their lives, and he told her about his divorce and his plans for the inn, and how he had always known he would come back to the island one day, a longing inside her awakened, a desire that had been buried for a long time. And contrary to every logical notion of who Ellie Baker knew herself to be, she had let it envelop her.

She knew that being with him would steer her life off its course, and yet the gravitational pull was stunning, the way her body burned when he was near, the effortless rhythm of their entwined bodies. She fell back in love, like an unencumbered teenager, though she was anything but. She felt vibrant and passionate for the first time in years, and yet her life was filled with deceit. She didn't recognize the person she had become.

Ending it had been the right thing to do, a sacrifice she needed to make for her family. That she *wanted* to make. But she still didn't know how to erase Gavin from her consciousness. The loss of him had left her hollow with grief, her guilt for grieving the worst of it all. Maybe if she had been able to talk to Tess and Joline about it, she could have stopped herself sooner. Maybe they would have even understood the pain that had come with breaking it off. Maybe, if she had been married to someone else. But Joline wouldn't have been able to forgive her for betraying her brother. And it wouldn't have been fair to burden Tess with the secret. She had dealt with the guilt and the grief on her own. She didn't deserve their comfort anyway.

It had never occurred to her that her betrayal would be on full display to these healers. Perhaps her lies—her shame—were as much a part of her as her organs, her veins. She had never believed that love was a zero-sum game, but what she had done with Gavin belied that. Secret love stole its flame from existing fires, leaving the hearth at home sputtering, small embers desperate to find oxygen within the crumbling ash. She was the worst kind of thief, and the shaman knew it. The relationship, over or not, had taken something precious from David, from their life together, from their family.

She buckled over and retched.

Wiping her mouth with the edge of her sleeve, she moved away from the wall, hoping no one would see.

THREE

Joline

"Holy shit, what was that all about?" Tess asked as soon as they were all back in the car.

Joline knew she had taken a risk not telling Tess and Ellie much about Don Emilio's ceremony in advance.

"Okay, I know it was a little strange," Joline said, "but these medicine people have been practicing specialized rituals for hundreds of years. We're just not used to their techniques."

"That's an understatement. He wasn't even looking at the right things, Jo," Tess said.

This hadn't escaped Joline.

"Remember, it's not just our physical bodies they're looking at. They see our auras, the energy that runs through us," Joline said.

"Auras? Seriously?" Tess asked.

She ignored Tess and turned around to face Ellie. The green and white wool hat sat half-cocked on her head, the curls that fell to her shoulders frizzier than usual. Her hazel eyes were wary. Ellie had always been like an eager student with Joline, keen to soak up information about everything she had to offer. But now she looked worried.

"I know it might feel like he missed your issue, Ell," Joline said. "But try to have faith. Every ceremony is like a different piece of the puzzle. It will all fit together in the end."

God, she hoped she was right. Ellie and David had put their faith in her this week. She had to come through. It would be exhausting work for Ellie, for all of them, but if they could just focus their energy and believe in the gifts of the shamans, it could be undeniably powerful, all encompassing. She had seen transformative things happen down here. She dared to picture her brother's face after hearing that Ellie was healthy. Her nieces and nephew would be wild with joy. Crazy Aunt Joline had made it happen. Dylan would be amazed.

But she couldn't afford to have made a mistake in the shamans she had picked for Ellie. If she were honest, her own reading with Don Emilio hadn't resonated either. Something about being restricted from freedom, like a bird with its wings held down. That didn't sound much like her life. She had never felt freer—spending the last year understanding the world of shamans in the hunt for the best place to build an executive retreat center in partnership with her client, Bryce Gardner. She was finally making enough money to give Dylan a proper home and music lessons. It was like living out a dream, not to mention the flexibility she now had. Focusing on a single client and a significant, meaningful project had been an extraordinary gift.

Joline wondered if Tess's reading had been more accurate.

"How about you, Tess? What's the big decision?" Joline asked.

"I don't mean to be cynical, but don't they use that line every time? 'Standing at a crossroads?' It's like carnival tarot card stuff." Tess paused. "Except for all the spitting."

It would be a long time before Tess let her live that down.

"Can you imagine if you told David we willingly stripped in front of this old man and his whole family?" Tess said, laughing. "And he spit on us?"

"And then practically lit us on fire?" Ellie's words tripped on bursts of laughter. It was a relief to hear her laugh.

They were right. Her brother would have her head if he'd been there. It was a shame, in a way, that he wasn't. They'd been a great team the last time Ellie was sick, she and Tess and David. He was an undeniably reliable soul. When he and Ellie fell for each other, Joline knew with all her heart that David would never let her best friend down.

Tess and Ellie were still laughing.

"And your hat is so fetching, my dear," Tess said, bonking Joline lightly on the head. "But hot as hell. You're not serious about wearing it all day, are you?"

"I told you, it helps keep in the healing energy," Joline said.

Tess shot her a sideways glance just as Joline's phone beeped. She pulled it out of her backpack.

"You get service here?" asked Tess. "I haven't been able to get any since the airport. The lab must think I've gone AWOL."

"Satellite phone," Joline said. "So Bryce can find me no matter how far into the jungle I go."

She read the message.

"Damn. Bryce wants to meet early," Joline said. "He wasn't supposed to be in town until next week, after you guys left."

"What does he want?" Tess asked.

"I promised him analysis on which community I think is the best choice for the site for the center," Joline said. "I'd love you to look over my presentation, by the way." She frequently relied on Tess's business advice, and appreciated her effortless way of framing complicated topics. She was a natural at analysis, which was not Joline's favorite use of energy. "Although something tells me he has jumped ten steps ahead. Sounds like his real estate guys have him pretty convinced Otavalo is the place."

"I thought you loved Otavalo," Ellie said.

"It's probably the best location in terms of finding shamans, but there's lots of other issues to consider, and you can't just pick a village without doing a lot of relationship work first. I'm not sure he has that kind of patience."

"Bryce Gardner is certainly not known for his patience," Tess said. "Best snap decision maker out there. I hope you know what you're getting into."

Tess had no idea just how far in she was. She hadn't told Tess yet that Bryce had insisted she give up her other clients now that the retreat center was beyond the exploratory phase. That was a conversation for another time.

"He's come a long way," Joline said. Tess was acquainted with Bryce through her own investors, but Joline had worked with him intensely for two years as his coach before agreeing to work on the retreat center. Everyone in the business world thought of him as a shark, but she saw it differently. Bryce wanted to be a good guy, but lacked self-awareness. On top of that, no one in his life had ever had the guts to tell him when he was doing something wrong, so he'd never learned to self-correct. It was a common problem she saw with powerful people. She finished her thought. "His level of self-awareness has increased dramatically."

"I wish you could work on that with your father," Ellie said.

"Good luck with that one," Tess said.

"I lost that battle the minute I was born a girl. Apparently his order for a fourth son got lost," Joline said. "And he doesn't talk girl."

"But even David talks a different language than Graham. I suppose I have you to thank for that," Ellie said.

"I guess all those hours of forcing him to play psychiatrist with me when we were little must have rubbed off," Joline said. "But at least he can talk business with Dad. Real estate development is a great stand-in for actual conversation. The latest techniques in life-coaching, not so much."

"He must be impressed you have Bryce as a client," Tess said.

"I don't give him that satisfaction," Joline said. "I'm not in it for his approval."

She rolled down her window and tasted the flavors of eucalyptus and sage wafting on the breeze. She let the aromas infuse her.

"Breathe in, girls," Joline said. "The air here is healing."

"I can't smell anything but cologne," Tess said. "God, it stinks."

"I know this is all about as fun as a root canal for you, Tess," Ellie said. "But you're a serious trooper to put up with all of it for me."

"Nope. I'm 100% on the program. Don't you worry about me," Tess said. "Doesn't mean I can't give our fearless leader here shit, though."

"Promise?" Ellie said.

"Why would you egg her on?" Joline said.

"The day you two start agreeing on everything because you're worried about me is the day I know I'm doomed," Ellie said.

"Deal," Tess said and threw a satisfied look Joline's way.

"Great," Joline said, her sarcasm punctuated with a chuckle.

She drank in the explosion of color on the right side of the road—flowers in pink, purple, gold, and orange dotting a huge field, nature resplendent and harmonious. Each flower was a universe of its own, the stalk commanding water from the soil as the petals flapped open to accept the sun. She said a brief word of thanks to the universe for all of nature's glories, especially the ancient vine that they would be working with, so revered it was known simply as "the plant," a moniker Joline liked to think marked it as the originator of all other vegetation. Powerful, indeed. She was sure it would bring great healing to Ellie.

"I may have to meet with Bryce briefly this week," Joline said. "But otherwise, no work. This week is for us."

"At least you have the rest of your clients to fall back on if this goes sideways," Tess said. "As successful as Bryce is, I wouldn't ever want him holding my whole basket of eggs." Tess glanced at Ellie. "Or rubbing them on my body."

"Ha, ha," Joline said and jabbed Tess's arm.

FOUR

Tess

Tess had one hand on the wheel of the car while she rubbed her wool hat with the other. The tight alpaca weave had already made indents on her forehead, and the itch of it was driving her crazy. She wasn't sure how much longer she would last with it on.

What she needed was a good long run. The familiar ache in her shoulder was aggravated by inactivity, and her legs were itching for movement. Other than the hour or so they had spent in Don Emilio's basement and a quick stop for lunch, she had been sitting for almost fifteen hours.

"You haven't told me yet how the trial is going," Ellie said, leaning between the two front seats, her arms behind the front headrests.

"Nothing yet to tell," Tess said. She clenched the wheel.

"So no results yet, but give me the basics. How many patients? Any early indicators?" Ellie asked.

The last thing Ellie needed to worry about was how terrible this week was for her to be away. She wished she could just brush off the fact that the trial was running late as no big deal, but when they'd missed their deadline the first time, she had relayed in grim detail to Ellie how dangerous it was for her business.

If they got into the conversation, there would be no hiding the severity of the situation this time, and she knew herself to be a terrible liar.

"Are you sure we didn't miss a turn?" Tess asked. She swerved to avoid a ditch in the middle of the dirt road.

"There it is," Joline said, pointing to a sign hanging from a tree. The words "Casa Munay" were burnt into the wood next to crudely carved sunbeams. Tess pulled down a lane, along a wide field that stretched out on the left, filled with rows of corn, sunflowers, maybe sugar cane. One or two people hunched over each carefully tilled row, the brims of their hats shading their faces, perhaps thirty people in all. Not a small operation. A llama meandered beside the road, grazing. It raised its head, blinked at the car, then went back to gnawing on the grass.

They parked in front of a two-story building made of wood and white-painted stone. Windows stretched across the facade. The dark wood mullions framing each pane coupled with the reflections of the valley gave the glass a warm hue. Beyond the simple structure, fields dropped off out of sight, providing a clear view of hulking mountains. No snow like the ones she had seen from the plane—these mountains weren't nearly as majestic— but they would still offer a substantial hiking challenge, to be sure.

"It's lovely," Ellie said.

As Tess got out of the car, the smell of lilacs rushed at her, surprising her with their familiarity, a welcome respite from the cologne that still wafted off her skin. She helped Ellie drag her bag out of the trunk before rolling her own across the grass, following Joline to the entrance of the inn. A fluffy brown dog lounged by the door. Tess could barely see its eyes through all its fur.

The door was propped open to what looked like the den of a Spanish house. Several small rugs the colors of the mountains and the sky blanketed the red tile floor. A worn bench ran the length of a picture window, framing the mountain range beyond. Tess was about to tap the small bell on a desk strewn with papers when she heard a bass-tenor greeting from the front door.

"Ah, Joline! *Buenas tardes.*"

A tall Ecuadorian man gathered his hands in front of his

chest like a prayer and bowed slightly in the doorway. Not many men were taller than Tess, but he had at least two or three inches on her. About the same height as Parker. He embraced Joline and kissed her on both cheeks before turning to Tess and Ellie.

"*Mucho gusto*. I am Marco. Welcome to Casa Munay." He pronounced it moon-eye, making Tess picture the man on the moon with just one big eye. Marco shook each of their hands in turn. Tess felt the calluses inside his palm.

Marco's black hair was neatly pulled back, emphasizing his wide nose and bushy sideburns. He smiled without showing his teeth, his eyes carrying the warmth of his welcome. Tess reached up to smooth her hair, horrified when her fingers bumped against the dumb hat.

"Please let me help you with your luggage and show you your room."

Marco inserted her roller-bag under his right arm before picking up the other two bags. He backed through a door behind his desk and held it open. They climbed up a narrow staircase that opened into a living room, bound on two sides by enormous windows. Wide wood planks stretched toward an adobe fireplace in the far corner. Rugs in earthy hues were scattered around the room, and colorful cushions and pillows were propped everywhere, softening the hard angles. Tess had been in many ski resorts that had tried to mass-produce the feel of native furnishings, managing just a few repetitive fabrics stitched over cotton pillows. This was the real deal. Parker would have loved it.

Marco put their bags down in the far corner and opened a large chest that doubled as a window seat.

"Your sleeping mats and blankets are here," he said. "Please make yourself comfortable. Dinner will be served at seven." Marco turned toward the stairs.

"Can I say hello to Mama Rosita?" Joline asked.

"She has gone to the village to see a friend. She'll be back tomorrow." With that, he bowed again and disappeared down the staircase.

"Sleeping mats?" Tess said, looking around for a door that might lead to an actual bedroom. The one upholstered couch was definitely too short for her to fully stretch out. "Ellie doesn't have to sleep on the floor for a week, does she? In here?"

"No Four Seasons in Otavalo," Joline said.

"Bryce will need to change that," Tess said under her breath.

"Oh, I'll be fine." Ellie plopped onto the couch and propped her feet up on the coffee table. "What a beautiful view."

Tess followed Ellie's gaze to the sliding glass doors that led out to a deck. There, two rainbow-colored chair hammocks swung in the breeze, as if a conversation was already underway between them. Beyond, the mountains that stood guard over the valley were more impressive than she had originally realized, one peak taller than the next, surrounding them on all sides.

She took out her phone. Still no service. She dropped it back into her bag with a sigh.

"There's a router you can plug into downstairs," Joline said, sitting cross-legged on the couch beside Ellie. "And you can use the phone behind reception if you need to make a call."

This week would be a nightmare if she couldn't connect easily with the office. Who runs a hotel without Wi-Fi everywhere? She cursed herself for not making Jonathan check. Tess pulled off her hat.

"Tess—" Joline started.

"I know. Energy. I think I've got enough for one day." Tess unclipped her barrette and scratched her scalp. "God, that's a relief. Aren't you dying of heat?"

Tess thought Ellie looked a little pale, not that anyone in Minnesota had much color in May. But even the freckles across her nose carried little color.

"I'm going to keep mine on a little longer," Ellie said. "Can't hurt." She paused. "Except my hair might smell forever like cologne."

Tess laughed. "Maybe we should market a new body spray. Eau de Don Emilio."

"An unusual combination of Old Spice and saliva," Ellie said.

"We could call it Spit-Fire," Tess said.

Ellie's laugh rolled out of her throat. God, Tess loved that laugh, deep and reverberating.

"You guys are brutal." Joline bonked Ellie with a pillow, but she was laughing too, and fell into Ellie on the couch. Ellie buried her face in a pillow, and tried to stifle a cough.

"Before I do anything, I need to go for a run." Tess unzipped her bag on the floor. She considered showering first, but decided it would be more satisfying after she'd had a chance to do some serious sweating. There were no shades on any of the windows. "They're not really into privacy around here, are they?"

She changed into her running clothes and brought her toiletries into the bathroom. The sink was carved into an old dresser with a painted vine of flowers meandering across the drawers. A bag of potpourri stood on a small shelf with a note attached. "Welcome to Casa Munay. With gratitude and peace." Tess pushed it aside to make room for her hair clip bag. Parker marveled that she had a separate pouch for her prized collection of hair clips, headbands and ponytail holders. Some women had shoes. Tess had clips.

As soon as she opened the pouch, a quiver ran up her spine. Right on top of the bag was a tiny velvet box and a folded-up envelope with Parker's handwriting. She put the box aside and slipped a yellow, lined piece of paper out of the envelope.

Tess,

By now you are in the mountains of Ecuador, many miles away from me. I hope you won't be angry. I know this trip is about Ellie and what you are trying to do for her. I have no intention of interfering with that.

But I also know you run for the hills (literally) whenever you feel trapped, or when you think someone is trying to back you into a corner in some way. And that is the last thing I want to do. Maybe that's what happened last time.

I tried to tell you this morning, but maybe it is better for you to have the space to think about, not react, but really think about what I need to say. It is this.

I love you. Plain and simple. And I don't want to ever be without you.

I've had this ring for what feels like an eternity. Before I found a way to give it to you last time, you were gone.

Tess put the toilet seat cover down and sat. She tried to shake the tingle out of her hands.

> *From the moment I saw you again I knew that this wasn't all just in my head, that our love was still alive. Everything since convinced me not to make the same mistake twice. I can't let you escape because I never asked you to stay.*
>
> *Be my wife, Tess.*
>
> *What I am about to say will make this week the longest of my life, but please don't call or email while you are gone. Whatever your initial thoughts, don't react. Please use the week to think about it. In the end, if your answer is no, then I will respect that, and I will get out of your way and find a way to move on with my life. But if your answer is yes, you will make me the happiest man alive.*
>
> *I love you,*
>
> *Parker*

She stood up and looked into the mirror. She tried to smooth her hair, but her hands shook, a jumble of thoughts elbowing each other in her mind. He just proposed? In a letter? And if she wasn't ready to commit to that, they were done? And what was that supposed to mean, "don't react?" Like she was some rash child. She marched into the living room for her phone, and stood close to the window. Shit. Still no signal.

She went back into the bathroom, avoiding Ellie and Joline's looks, and picked up the small maroon box. She pictured it in his hands and opened it slowly, hesitant to look. A wide platinum band nestled inside. A string of amethysts ran through the center—her birthstone. They were surrounded on both sides by tiny round diamonds—his birthstone. It was gorgeous. But, is this what she wanted? Her pulse whooshed through her ears, the tiny bathroom suffocating.

She charged back into the living room. "Holy shit, you guys." She held out the box.

Joline and Ellie jumped in unison and turned toward her. No, she couldn't just show them the ring. They wouldn't understand. She hadn't had a chance to tell them any of this yet. She shut the box with a snap, and held out the letter instead.

"You won't believe this."

Joline and Ellie clutched opposite sides of the letter. Joline looked up at Tess with her hand over her mouth but kept reading. Ellie let out a yelp a few seconds later.

"Oh my God, Tess!" Ellie bounced off the couch and hugged her. "Why didn't you tell us you were back together? This is fantastic!"

"You don't seem overjoyed," Joline said.

"You mean about the fact that he proposed or the fact that he proposed by letter and told me to sit with it for a week? This week?"

"Oh, Tess," said Ellie. "He's terrified. You broke his heart once. Can you blame him? But you were crazy about him. You always have been—" She was talking faster than she had since they'd arrived. "This is so great! Where's the ring?"

Tess handed the box over to her. Ellie loved weddings, romance. Every guy Tess met was a new fairy tale in the making for her. But Ellie had taken a special liking to Parker. She said it was the way Tess talked about him. And the way he looked at her.

"This is stunning," Ellie said, still smiling. "Put it on."

Tess hesitated. "This is nuts. I need to think."

Before she had finished the sentence she was halfway down the stairs, leaving Ellie holding the box. She rushed past Marco's desk and out the front door. The dog flinched as she ran past, but made no move to follow her. Not knowing where she was headed, she turned right out of the gate.

Tess started out fast, trying to pound out her anxiety, and could feel the lack of oxygen at that altitude test her lungs. Her breath sped up with the pulse of her legs, pulverizing the road. About a quarter of a mile down that road she found two footpaths. One headed down toward the valley. The other went up. She headed up.

FIVE
Ellie

The next morning, Ellie woke to a wash of purple light flooding the walls of the room. Her right hand had dropped out of the covers into the layer of cool air that hovered along the floor. She curled back under the thick wool blanket, wishing she could sleep past dawn. Her eyes drifted over to the deck outside the room, and she suddenly wanted to be in the fresh air. Sitting up, she wrapped the sheet and blankets around her, trying to make as little noise as possible. She moved with each of Joline's exhales, stretching the tightness under her ribs as she rose to a standing position.

Tess's mat was on the other side of the couch and Ellie could see one foot poking out, callused from a lifetime of running, but it didn't move. She inched open the sliding glass door, pleased when she finally squeezed it closed that neither of her room-mates had stirred.

The morning air cooled her face and nipped her toes. She sat on her feet in one of the swinging chairs and adjusted her blankets around her. The mountains to the west were getting their first brush of color, their peaks covered in various shades of lush-green foliage and sunburnt thistle. A few airy clouds floating in the distance looked like they had colored light bulbs inside, the entire sky a rainbow of color. Standing out, like an iceberg floating in a Caribbean sea, was one mountain with fresh snow on its peak. Ellie rubbed her eyes to make sure it wasn't an optical illusion. It had been more than seventy degrees the day before, and the night sky had dazzled with legions of stars. How could it have snowed?

She watched the rolling landscape turn from purple to orange to pink. If her doctors were right, she didn't have that many dawns left. She had been gifted a second chance at life three years ago, and in the name of living in the moment or following her bliss or some such post-cancer delusion, she had wasted too many precious moments, like letting the thought of Gavin's hand on her back distract her during a board game, or barking at Connor for looking over her shoulder at her email, as if he could see the subfolder of hidden messages attached to a different address. And she had watched sunrises like this with David, her mind elsewhere. She wanted all those moments back.

The reality of her infidelity was bad enough, but she had thought when she ended it with Gavin that she would at least have time to move past it, to somehow turn that colossal betrayal into a shameful blip in a very long life. But now it loomed over everything. It was too destructive to bring out into the open, too huge to swallow and ignore. The possibility of dying with a lie in her heart broke some part of her from the inside.

She wanted to make a promise to someone, to some force out there that if she got well, she would be an even better mother, a much better wife. She wouldn't hesitate to help Lilly in her burgeoning chicken coop, and would be Hannah's best kitchen lab partner. She would ask Connor fewer questions, give him space to offer up whatever was on his mind. And she would treasure every moment with David during their sunrise cups of tea.

Their morning ritual had started that first Thanksgiving she had visited the Baker's house in Minneapolis, during her senior year of college. She had risen early on Friday morning and found the kitchen silent, the house still hushed under down comforters, the great lawn glistening with frost.

"Good morning, Dove," David said. Ellie startled. She hadn't noticed him sitting in the breakfast nook. And she thought for a moment he had said *love*.

"Dove?" she asked.

"You obviously keep the peace between my sister and Tess." David poured her a steaming cup of Earl Grey, as if he'd been expecting her. "Can't imagine they'd survive long as roommates without you."

"We're a magic trio," she said, and joined him at the table.

She was surprised when he asked about her senior thesis— she didn't take him for the poetry type. He offered that while he admired Rumi, he preferred the work of Rilke. He thought Rilke was more accessible, more philosophical, less flowery.

"Do you know that line of his?" he asked. "Something about how the young are 'bunglers of life, apprentices in love,' and must 'learn love like a profession.' Don't you think that's true?"

She must have appeared more surprised than she intended.

"What?" he said, looking a little hurt and laughing at the same time. "Did you take me for a backwoods Luddite like my brothers?"

"No. I just—"There was no easy way out of that question.

"I know," he said, letting her off the hook, "my father's more of a Robert Ludlum than a Robert Frost kind of guy. I never admitted to him half of what I studied in college. Let's keep it our secret, if that's all right with you?"

"But now I'm curious," she said, not wanting the morning sun to move too quickly. "Do you really believe that love takes work?"

"If it's lasting. I mean, there has to be a real connection." He looked directly across the table at her. "But then yes, I think both sides need to commit to doing whatever it takes. Real commitment to the relationship, it seems to me, is the difference between attraction and real love." David was only three years older, but he spoke like someone who knew enough of the world to be wise, settled. Ellie wished she wasn't wearing Joline's robe.

As the rest of the family woke up one by one and filled the kitchen, she had a hard time taking her eyes off of David. He made pancakes for everyone, in shapes of dogs and bunnies for the little ones, and regularly glanced her way, as if confirming that they were locked in a mutual understanding, an emotional alliance that had begun to take shape right there at the kitchen table. She and David had made a habit of watching sunrise together after that, the mugs changing from alumni association giveaways to registry china to the purple mug Connor had painted for her birthday when he was five.

They had no idea then what a toll cancer would take on their marriage, sapping it of its ease and flow. David barely hugged her anymore for fear of breaking her. Too many nights they did the dishes together without touching, David coming to bed after she had turned out the light, kissing her on the forehead, assuming she was asleep. She hadn't figured out how to get back to how they used to be. Now she might not have time.

The slider opened behind her. Joline dragged her blanket onto the other swing and climbed aboard.

"Stunning, isn't it?" Joline whispered.

"Look at that mountain," Ellie said, pointing. "Is that snow?"

"That's Cotacachi," Joline said. "There's a great story about it. See the mountain to its right? The one that's taller and really pointed? That mountain is called Imbabura. He is considered the protector of the area. Legend has it that he was deeply in love with the beautiful mountain to his west, the one you were looking at."

Cotacachi was broader, bigger by sheer mass than the other mountain.

"Imbabura competed for Cotacachi's love with many rivals, and was extremely jealous of all of them. Eventually, he won Cotacachi as his wife. But he was always worried that she would stray. So every night, regardless of the season, he dusts her peak with snow, which is meant to act as a veil to hide her beauty from other suitors."

"Did it work?" Ellie's throat caught.

"What do you mean?"

"Was she faithful?" Ellie asked.

"The legend only says that he never stopped loving her. There is a section of earth on his western slope that's in the perfect shape of a heart. Can you see it?"

Part of the slope was darker in color, but Ellie couldn't see a heart. She desperately wanted to see the heart.

"It is said that the ground there is enchanted. They say that no person or animal has ever been able to cross that section of the mountain. It's part of what makes this area sacred. The promise of everlasting love."

Everything had gotten too still. Ellie pushed off from the floor again to get the swing moving.

"I wish I could have slept longer. I'm going to be exhausted." Ellie rubbed her face, hoping to hide what was likely written there.

"We'll find plenty of time for you to rest. Don't worry."

They swung in silence as the yellow of the sky slowly turned blue. Ellie pictured her kids at home, about to start shuffling downstairs for breakfast. She loved the look of their rumpled faces, their hair askew as they said their quiet *mornings* to each other. It was her favorite time of day.

"I'm so grateful to be able to share this place with you, Ell," Joline said. "I hope you feel the healing energy. And if I haven't said it yet, I want to say thank you for coming all the way down here and putting your trust in me. It means the world to me."

Trust. There was a word that stung.

After breakfast, Joline suggested they make a quick stop in town for what she called "market day" in Otavalo on their way to their next shaman. About ten minutes down the long dirt road, they pulled around the perimeter of a huge square. It was so packed with vendor tables and pop-up stalls that Ellie couldn't see across to the other side. She had assumed there would be nothing more than a few roadside stands. She couldn't imagine where all these people had come from.

Joline directed Tess down a side street. On one storefront, a faded sign for Fanta hung next to a bright billboard advertising *fritatas* with photos of various dishes. Tess found a parking space beside two women sitting on the curb, selling enormous beans out of brightly colored bowls.

"How long do we have?" Tess pulled her bag onto her shoulder.

Joline looked at her watch. "Giuliana is expecting us at noon. So we should leave by eleven."

That gave them over an hour. Ellie was pleased to have some distraction before seeing their next shaman. She would love to find something to bring home to each of the kids.

"I'm going to start at the internet cafe. You said it was right off the square?" Tess asked.

"On the other side," Joline said. "I'll show you."

They walked together toward the square across a jigsaw puzzle of interlocking hexagonal concrete stones grouted with dirt. As soon as they stepped into the market, two women with babies strapped to their backs broke off their conversation and hurried to nearby stalls. A man squashed out his cigarette and held up one of the blankets he was selling. A girl Ellie estimated to be about five years old, dressed in an intricately embroidered dress, took a step toward them. She was cradling a baby goat in a sling. Lilly loved goats. When Ellie took out her phone to take a photo, the little girl held up her hand. Smudges of dirt were visible under the cuffs of her sleeve. A slightly older girl appeared at her side.

"*Dos dolares*," the older girl said, holding up two fingers.

"I'm going to show Tess where the internet shop is," Joline said. "I'll find you."

Ellie handed the older girl a five-dollar bill and took the photo before wandering down the first aisle. Hundreds of wool purses hung from hooks inside one stall, stacks of rugs overflowed in another, an army of carved animals filled the next. Lilly was her would-be farmer, a lover of all creatures in the animal kingdom. At eight years old, she already had talked her parents into housing six chickens and two bunnies. Ellie looked for a carved pig, Lilly's favorite, but didn't see one. When she touched a pile of hoodies on the next table, woven with every color imaginable, the man in the stall stood expectantly. She smiled at him and kept walking. She rubbed the side of her ribcage, trying to ease the feeling of constriction there.

At the end of the row, a shock of red hair caught her eye. The man was leaning over a table of wooden bowls. The way his hair was closely shorn in the back, the curve of his shoulder, his leather bag, all made him look just like Gavin. She turned away. *Stop it*, she thought. *How can you ever be forgiven if you can't even stop thinking about him?* A vendor approached her, holding out a series of scarves. She dutifully touched a green one, and then a rust-colored one, surprised by how soft they were.

A hand landed on her shoulder. She jerked around to grab her knapsack and gasped. She was looking right at Gavin.

"I found you," he said, that knowing smile lighting up his face. "I didn't know how long it might take me."

"Oh my God," she said, standing back. "What are you doing here? You can't be here." She looked over his shoulder and turned around to make sure Joline and Tess weren't wandering down the aisle.

"I had to see you, Babe. I had to."

"You can't be here. Joline is here. I can't be with you." She tried to turn away, but he pressed her arm to stop her from going.

"There's a little bakery around the corner, called *Harina*. That way," he said, pointing diagonally. "Meet me there. One cup of coffee."

The pull of him was still electric. Her body betrayed her and she nodded before she could stop herself. She watched him move through the stalls, his hands plunged into the pockets of his L.L. Bean barn coat. He dipped out of sight behind a huge tapestry of five musicians playing flutes under a navy sky. She leaned against a table full of jewelry to steady herself.

"See anything you like?"

Ellie spun around to see Joline examining the jewelry at her side. How long had she been there?

"There's some better jewelry over on this end." Joline patted the arm Gavin had released moments before. "Come see."

Joline headed in the opposite direction from where Gavin had disappeared. Ellie reluctantly followed, dizzy with adrenaline.

"Isn't this gorgeous?" Joline held up a choker studded with bright blue topazes. "Or do you like this one better?" She put on a chain that snaked through a chunk of malachite. Ellie waited for Joline to turn toward the small mirror on the table before attempting to say anything.

"I saw some rugs on the other side I'm going to go check out while you decide." Ellie took three slow steps before hurrying back down the aisle. She didn't have much time.

Turning a corner, she looked for the tapestry with the moon and the stars shining over the band of musicians. Wall hangings with mountain scenes covered one stall, paintings of women with baskets on their heads another. The piles of bags, shirts, and knick-knacks were endless. Which way had he gone? Panic began to gather somewhere around her ankles and climb up her bones. She forced herself to search more methodically, aisle by aisle, reminding herself that the place wasn't even that big. Finally spotting a dark weave with crude stitching for stars hanging above a shelf of sweaters, Ellie brushed past the vendor and onto the street. She found the bakery halfway down the block.

Gavin stood when she walked in.

"I was getting worried you weren't coming," he said. He led her to a table with two cups of coffee waiting. "How are you? How do you feel?"

She didn't know how to answer that question. She knew he was asking how well she was coping physically with the cancer, with the reality of dying, but as she stood in front of him, those issues seemed to belong to someone else. His presence filled her with a warm anticipation that made it difficult not to touch him, not to ask him to hold her. And yet, a trickle of anger ran not too far below the surface.

She had kept her promise to let him know if her cancer ever returned. The promise had been a mistake. Her email telling him about Joline's plan was meant to reassure him about the possibility of her recovery, not serve as some kind of invitation.

"What are you doing here?" she asked as she sat.

"You said Otavalo. I told you I would find you."

I'll find you. He had said that. But they used to end all their emails that way. It was a reference to what they told each other as teenagers, holding hands on a wool blanket down the steps from her grandfather's cottage, confident that no matter what happened in their futures, they would somehow find a way back to each other.

Gavin still looked in many ways like the young boy she had fallen in love with as a high-school senior, his strawberry-blond coloring, his lanky physique. But he looked tired, the spikes of his hair slightly trampled. Their history was so long and so short at the same time, hurried brushstrokes in a canvas filled with the meticulously rendered scenes of the rest of her life, scenes filled with other people. But she could still remember that magical summer vividly, how it had felt to have her t-shirt pulled over her head for the first time, how he caressed her breasts with his lips, the way he laid her down on the blanket and made love to her, his gentle movements only becoming urgent when she moaned for him not to stop. Sitting so close to him, Ellie couldn't resist touching his cheek for one moment and the stubble she knew would be soft. When he leaned his face against her hand, she pulled back.

"Gavin, I don't have much time—"

"I know, just a cup of coffee. I—"

"No, I mean I don't have time left. There's no space for anything but David and my kids."

"There's something I need to ask you," Gavin said. His eyes darkened, his pupils pushing across the deep blue of his eyes.

She suddenly felt tired, and wished they could just sit without talking. She worried she might let loose a cascade of words that would fill the divide between them, making it too easy to cross. Ellie reached for her coffee and looked beyond a couple sitting by the window. She nearly dropped her cup. The sign across the street said "Internet Aqui!" and Tess was sitting with her laptop in the window.

"Oh my God, I can't be here." She swung her bag onto her shoulder and turned toward the door in one motion. Gavin caught her arm, more fiercely this time.

"Wait, Ell. We have to talk."

Ellie put her back to the door. "I have to go," she said.

"I'll be here again tomorrow," he said. "Please come find me. It's important."

Ellie pushed out the door. She tried to keep her eyes on the pavement stones as she hurried back toward the square, but out of the corner of her eye she saw Tess stand up and look right at her. She rushed down the block and was walking past a slew of vendor stands when she heard Tess's voice.

"Ellie, wait," Tess called. "Who was that?"

Her feet slowed. She couldn't face Tess.

"What just happened?" Tess asked, her voice more urgent.

"Please," she whispered when Tess was almost beside her. "Joline can't know."

"Joline?" Tess asked. "What the hell is going on?"

Ellie saw Joline across the street, leaning on the car. Joline waved.

"Please," Ellie said again, and hurled herself forward.

SIX
Joline

Joline didn't know how she had lost track of Ellie in the market so completely. She'd hoped the chance to shop together would provide some level of normalcy, a fun way for them to balance the emotional intensity of the week. She finally spotted Ellie headed toward the car with Tess not far behind. Neither of them had any shopping bags.

"Didn't find anything you liked?" Joline asked. Ellie shook her head, keeping her eyes on the pavement as she crossed the street. Even when she got to the car, Ellie still wouldn't look directly at her.

"Ell, there's nothing to worry about. I promise seeing Giuliana will be a much more pleasant experience than Don Emilio," she said, rubbing Ellie's arm. "No need to be nervous."

Tess jerked open the car door and got into the driver's seat.

"Which way to get out of here?" Tess's tone was sharp, bordering on angry.

"Everything under control at the office?" Joline asked. She hoped Tess wouldn't let work invade the week. She needed to learn to let up once in a while.

"Fine," Tess said.

Joline felt the energy in the car shift immediately, as if Tess had locked herself inside a static bubble that took up all the space in the car and would shock you if you touched it. Ellie was usually the one to smooth over the crackles when Tess was in a snarl, but she made no such attempt during the drive. She stared out the window without saying a word. Joline was unwilling to let whatever was bothering Tess impact her, and decided to focus on creating a positive intention for today's ceremony, holding the idea of Ellie's recovery close, like a mantra.

"Anita will be here to translate for us today," Joline finally said, fingering the malachite stone at her neck. "She's the one I told you about who runs her own design business in Quito, but makes extra money translating. You'll love her. We've actually gotten to know each other pretty well over my last few trips. Her son is fifteen, too. We have shared some stories, that's for sure."

Still no response. She didn't try to break the silence again.

Instead she sent a quiet message from her heart to Dylan. It had been hard this past year to be away from him for the center. At least he liked staying with Joey. She wished for him a blissful week and deep knowing of how connected they still were, even when she wasn't there.

Giuliana's house was one of her favorite places in the area. The little bungalow was nestled amidst a spray of wildflowers with a grove of trees behind it. Stone walls that meandered across the property looked like they had grown out of the ground, a spontaneous collaboration of rocks held in place by vines and moss. As they drove down the long dirt road to the house, she recognized the hints of jasmine and elderberry that floated in the air, and she tried to summon inner calm through the pattern of her own breathing.

As they parked beside the chicken coop, Giuliana rose from the stone wall in front of the house to greet them, her long skirt billowing in the breeze. She wore an embroidered shirt that was more fitted than the Ecuadorian custom, making her look younger than her sixty-or-so years. Her dark sunglasses suggested a fashionista searching for her inner Jackie Kennedy, but the bulbous glasses were probably just a cheap knock-off that served the practical purpose of shielding the sun. Still, she instantly regretted that she hadn't found a way in the car to tell Ellie and Tess more about Giuliana's healing prowess. Skepticism never helped the healing process.

Giuliana held out her arms and Joline welcomed the embrace, hoping for some transference of positive energy. The medicine woman grasped her back tightly, the way one might offer support at the funeral of a close friend. Joline hoped Giuliana wasn't trying to tell her something. When she pulled back from the hug, she noticed Anita standing off to the side. Her linen pants were wrinkled from the drive, and a coffee stain on her shirt peeked out from beneath her multicolored scarf.

"You made it," Anita said, embracing her. "You look well. How's Dylan?"

"He's good. Emmanuel?"

Anita nodded, pulling her long black hair behind her ears, and then gave Ellie and Tess her complete attention as Joline introduced them. They followed Giuliana into the barn, where heaping platters of vegetables, potatoes, grains, and a terrine of stew awaited them. While the room appeared to be a converted stable, with wagon wheels and parts of old wooden plows hung on the walls and bits of straw hanging from the beams, there was no stench of long-ago manure or horsehair, just the faint odor of fresh paint and wafts of sage coming from the fireplace. Anita and Joline sat facing Tess and Ellie at a large wooden table, their stools made from sections of a tree trunk covered with square pillows. Giuliana didn't join them. Joline had rarely seen a shaman eat.

"Please enjoy the lunch," Anita said. "It is good to have nourishment before the ceremony."

"When you say ceremony," said Tess, ladling stew into her bowl, "can you elaborate? I'm finding omission of information to be a problem lately." Her voice was pointed and she flashed a look Ellie's way that was far different from the usual comrades-in-arms-putting-up-with-Joline's-crazy-ideas kind of expression that she was used to.

Anita looked stricken. "Has something gone wrong?"

"Nothing that will color our day." She glanced at Ellie, hoping she wasn't being swept up in Tess's black mood. "Tess just likes to have detail before stepping into things."

"Oh," Anita said, her face softening. "I think you will find Giuliana to be especially gentle in her touch. She works mostly with your pulse and your aura. And she is amazingly clear in terms of what she sees."

Ellie's fork clattered against her plate. She hadn't touched any food yet.

"Are you feeling all right?" Joline asked.

Ellie nodded. "Just not hungry."

Neither Ellie nor Tess seemed interested in small talk. She and Anita caught up on the lives of their boys as they ate. The challenges were similar, Emmanuel insisting that catching rides through Quito on the back of his buddy's scooter was essential to his social life, the same way Dylan whined that not being allowed to ride the train home through San Francisco late on a Saturday night would make him a social pariah. Joline had long imagined their sons becoming great friends.

"How's the retreat center coming?" Anita asked.

"I may have a lot of translating work this summer if you can fit it in," Joline said.

"Business has been slow lately. I will go wherever the work is."

"And hopefully Dylan will come down here with me this summer. He and Emmanuel can finally meet."

"That would be wonderful." Anita clasped her hands together.

"The whole summer?" Tess asked.

"I doubt it will be the entire summer."

"What about your other clients?" Tess asked.

She eventually had to tell Tess. Now was as good a time as any.

"I had to give up work with my other clients," she said. "This project really needs my full attention."

"Oh, Jo—"

"It's the right thing for me. But my next priority is to get Dylan to come with me. He thinks it sounds boring, but I'm trying to convince him he could write some great music down here," Joline said. "Anyway, it'll work out. Nature will support."

Joline filled her fork with rice while Ellie continued to move food around her plate. The tension in Ellie's shoulders was visible, and a level of exhaustion and sadness pervaded her eyes that Joline hadn't noticed since being in Ecuador. There was a depth to the sorrow she hadn't seen since the first time Ellie was sick. She told herself that Giuliana would help Ellie.

After lunch, they moved their stools into a semicircle in front of the fire, lit not for warmth, but for the sacred smoke. It would help protect their spirits and work as a key, of sorts, into their souls. Giuliana appeared and gracefully drifted onto a cushion directly in front of the hearth. Her skirt billowed around her legs as she patted the empty cushion beside her. Still wearing her sunglasses, she looked up at the group expectantly. She was ready to start.

Ellie's feet looked rooted to the floor.

"I might as well go," Tess said. Joline knew Tess didn't really believe in the idea of energy healings, but she was doing her best to be a good sport.

Tess folded her long legs onto the cushion, her bare knees grazing against the folds of Giuliana's skirt. Middle age hadn't seemed to kick in for Tess yet. Her hipbones still protruded from her abdomen, her legs as muscular as they were in the height of her volleyball years.

"She will start by listening to your pulse," Anita said.

Tess dutifully held out her arm and Giuliana took it in her lap, three fingers on the inside of Tess's wrist. She hummed slightly, not a melody, more of a thinking sound.

"You do a lot of physical exercise?" she asked, Anita translating.

"Yes," Tess said. "I try."

Giuliana nodded. "Your pulse is slow, strong. This is good." As she spoke she rose into a standing position with the grace of a gazelle and picked up several branches of lemon leaves from a pile next to the hearth. She held a bunch in each hand and began waving them.

"Go stand in front of her," Anita told Tess.

Giuliana worked the branches in a swirl around Tess's body, as if washing the air around her. Joline had seen Giuliana do this before, evaluating the flow of a person's energy, checking for anything that might be unbalanced. She moved the leaves up Tess's left arm, and then her right. When she got to her shoulder she stopped.

She looked at Anita and spoke.

"She wants to know if you have a problem in your shoulder?" Anita translated.

"Yes. I have separated it multiple times. I haven't had full rotation since college," Tess said. She looked over at Ellie and Joline with an expression that suggested she was half amazed and half already trying to figure out where the magician was hiding the rabbit.

"She says you have a circulation problem there," Anita said. "She will fix it with massage. You can sit."

Sensing Ellie still wasn't ready, Joline sat in front of Giuliana. Giuliana held her arm and made the same humming sound.

"She asks if you have an issue in your stomach," Anita said.

She shook her head. "No. Well, maybe some cramps this morning, but nothing unusual, I don't think."

Giuliana nodded and closed her eyes again.

"Do you have trouble sleeping?"

"Yes, I have been waking up through the night a lot." She had lately found herself dragged awake in the dark, feeling unmoored, like she had no firm grasp on the world around her. It was always the same awful dream, that she was groping in the dark, bumping along unfamiliar hallways, unable to find Dylan. Her deep breathing exercises didn't always work to get her back to sleep. Half the time she ended up getting out of bed and slowly prying open Dylan's door to watch his back rise and fall under his quilt.

"I will work on this with massage."

"Gracias," Joline said. As soon as she stood up, Ellie was beside her, ready to take a seat on the cushion.

Giuliana held Ellie's arm for no more than five seconds before she said, "You have trouble breathing?"

"Yes, I have a problem in my lungs," Ellie said.

Giuliana closed her hand over Ellie's arm and swayed side to side. She opened her eyes and looked at Anita. "*El cobayo para ella.*" Giuliana smiled at Ellie, patting her on the arm before floating up from her cushion and leaving the room.

Ellie looked stricken, and turned to Anita for translation. Anita helped Ellie up from the floor and spoke to them as a group.

"Giuliana is going to go set up for a massage for you two—"

"What did she say to Ellie?" Tess asked.

"Don't worry," Anita said. "Joline will explain. Giuliana has a room with a small bed on the other side of the house. You will go in there one by one and she will work on you there. Her massage is not like what you are used to at home. You will stay fully clothed."

"Well, at least there's that," Tess said. "But Ellie?"

"Joline can explain *el cobayo* to you to make sure you are comfortable with that while I help Giuliana set up," Anita said to Ellie. "Come over to the main sitting room when you are ready."

Joline put her hand on Ellie's arm. "This is wonderful, a powerful way for Giuliana to work on you. The guinea pig is considered a sacred animal here, and shamans have been using them for healings for centuries."

"Guinea pig?" Ellie asked.

"Yes. Did you see them in the chicken coop when we arrived? Let's go sit down on the other side of the house, and I can explain," she said.

Joline led them down a narrow hallway into the living part of the house. It would fit perfectly into an issue of *Architectural Digest* focused on making tiny spaces beautiful. Dark wood built-ins displayed ceramic bowls, baskets, sculptures, and talismans. Several tribal masks hung on the walls alongside bunches of pinecones and strings of beads. At one end of the room, a huge mirror sat above a table brimming over with green plants. At the other stood a small wooden altar, a colorful weaving draped over its edges. Tiled rays of sun dotted the mosaic floor. A series of stools like the ones in the barn had been placed in a row and covered with animal skins to make a bench.

"Guinea pigs serve several important purposes," she said, sitting next to Ellie on the bench. "First of all, the shamans believe they have the power to remove heavy energy from us, the kind that can cause imbalance and illness. They rub the guinea pig over your body, and it absorbs what is inside you, and takes it away." Ellie listened intently. "And don't worry, it will barely touch you. Remember, our energy is also on the outside of our physical body. The guinea pig just needs to get close enough to absorb it. But the thing you need to know," Joline said, "is that during this process the guinea pig will die."

Ellie sat up at that. "What do you mean?"

"It's part of their magic, and partly why they are so revered. They give their lives by taking the energy, even though they can't sustain it in themselves."

"Where do they come up with this stuff?" Tess muttered.

"Guinea pigs are diagnostic. Their anatomies are close to our own." She looked at Tess. "You must remember from biology—Western medicine used them for years for experiments before mice—it's where our expression of *being a guinea pig* comes from? Anyway, once the guinea pig has absorbed the illness, the shaman can look inside the guinea pig to see almost a mirror image of what is going on for you. This way they know what to work on."

"How do they look inside?" Ellie asked quietly.

"They cut it open," Joline said gently.

Ellie flinched and her hand went up to her forehead. Joline had also found the idea difficult to absorb when she first learned about it. But she had heard story after story of guinea pigs absorbing substantial illness, leaving the patient symptom-free. A true gift from nature.

"It's a wonderful ritual," Joline said. "I was hoping she would suggest it, but didn't want to get your hopes up."

Ellie's face was slightly gray.

"Why don't we give you a little time to adjust to the idea? Tess, do you want to go first?"

"I'd prefer to see you come out clothed and dry first. You go ahead."

Joline wanted to spend more time addressing any concerns Ellie might have about the guinea pig, but she could see that Tess wasn't going to budge. She had to trust that Tess wouldn't purposefully shower Ellie with any negative energy before her healing. Ellie would need to summon her most positive thoughts if this was going to work.

SEVEN

Tess

Tess waited for two beats after Joline clicked the door shut. "Who the hell was that?" She tried not to yell, but the question had been banging around her throat for more than two hours.

Ellie grabbed Tess's hand and dragged her out the front door of the house. She didn't say anything until they had found a patch of grass to sit on.

"It was Gavin," Ellie said.

"Gavin?" A memory flickered. "Nantucket Gavin?"

Ellie nodded. Tess hadn't heard that name in years. But it was hard to forget. Gavin was the handsome kid in the photo Ellie had perched on her dresser that first fall at Stanford. Tess remembered that photograph vividly. He wore a Cornell t-shirt and khaki shorts, his strawberry-blond hair spiked at odd angles, like he had just jumped out of the ocean and run his hands through his hair. His arm was thrown around Ellie's shoulder, her head turned toward him, her freckles scrunched by laughter—that distinctive cackle. Tess remembered wondering at the time if she would ever feel the way Ellie looked in that picture.

"What is he doing here?"

"I had no idea he would be here," Ellie said, looking at her hands as if she was searching for something. "I thought I was past all this. But Don Emilio saw it. He said I had an ache in my heart."

Ellie looked older in the harsh light of the sun. Her cheeks sagged at the jawline.

"I don't understand. What are you talking about?" Tess could hear the sharp edge in her own voice.

"It happened about three years ago. Not long after I went into remission. I bumped into him on Nantucket." Ellie pursed her lips to stop them from trembling. Her head dropped to her chest. She looked fragile, like a hollowed-out eggshell that would crumble if gripped too hard.

"Ell. It's me," she said as gently as she could. "Tell me."

Ellie winced and rubbed her left side before taking a tentative breath. Tess couldn't tell if she was debating what to say or if she simply couldn't find the oxygen. When she finally spoke, the words rushed out in one long exhale.

"I never meant for it to happen." Ellie's shoulders curled in on themselves. "But it was like nothing had changed between us. Remember how in love I was with him freshman year?"

"And how badly he broke your heart," Tess said. Ellie had desperately struggled with the long distance. They had no way to cross the country to see each other, and might not have another summer on Nantucket. The thought of it would sometimes drag sunny Ellie into the shadows and render her lifeless, unable to rally for days. Tess never did mind hunkering down with her and figuring out how to diffuse the darkness when it came. Whether ordering grilled cheese sandwiches and banana milkshakes from the Peninsula Creamery or convincing her to fill the crumpled prescription in her knapsack, Tess felt at her best when she could be useful.

Then one night in November Gavin called to say he was worried for her, for the toll the distance was taking on them both. If they were meant to be, he was sure they would find each other again later in life. Ellie's heartbreak had been devastating to watch.

"Seeing him again was surreal," Ellie said, pulling on a blade of grass. "We both admitted how desperately in love we had been, and how shattered we both were when we lost that. I finally got to yell at him for not sticking with me when I was hurting, for throwing it all away, for how much that hurt. And he told me how every day he didn't hear back after his letter was torture."

"What letter?"

"Remember? He wrote me that spring and told me he had made a terrible mistake, that distance didn't matter and we should be together?"

Tess had forgotten about that. Ellie had finally started to recover, and left the letter unanswered. She'd had to protect herself from getting hurt that deeply again, a decision she and Joline had fully supported.

Ellie put her head back down, kneading the edge of her sleeve.

"We had it out in a way David and I never do. Neither of us held back because we were worried about hurting the other person, or doing long-term damage. It was very freeing." When Ellie went on, her words sounded compressed as she struggled again to fill her throat with air. She looked toward the house and lowered her voice. "And then I slept with him, Tess. And I woke up the next morning, knowing that I had changed everything. And—" She couldn't get her next words out. She began to cry. "Sorry," she gasped.

"It's okay." Tess rubbed Ellie's back as she put her head into her hands. She sucked in a deep breath and swept her hair behind her ears.

"It's such a relief to tell you," Ellie said.

"You made a mistake." Tess tried to keep the shock out of her voice. Ellie was the last person she would ever have imagined would stray, make such a colossal error. But Tess could almost see the remorse seeping from her pores. "You let a moment go too far. And after what you'd been through—"

"No. It went beyond that weekend, Tess. I should have stopped it right then, but I didn't. I always had the excuse of opening or closing the cottage for the season or checking up on it after a storm. David didn't even think twice about it." Tess pulled her hand off Ellie's back. "It's hard to explain. It's like I was in a different world with him, like I was a different person. Nantucket has always felt like that to me. My place. My place with Gavin." Tess had been to Nantucket with Ellie many times. She had rarely mentioned him. "He came to Minneapolis once—"

"Minneapolis?" She didn't want to hear that Ellie had skulked out of some hotel parking garage in her SUV and headed for the pick-up line at school. She was trying to stay focused on what Ellie was saying, but couldn't stop thinking about Connor, Hannah, and Lilly.

"God, you must hate me."

"I could never hate you," she said quickly. But it did feel like Ellie was holding a precious photograph over a flame, allowing the glossy surface to bubble and crack, forever disfiguring the image.

"Does David know?" Tess thought of David like an older brother. For a long time she considered him too serious for Ellie, lacking in mischief and spontaneity. But she'd grown to love the counterweight he offered to Ellie's more impetuous side. When she visited, she and David would stay up late drinking Grey Goose and comparing business war stories. Parker said David reminded him of a sequoia, the real strength came from the root system that ran a mile deep.

Ellie hugged her knees, her body shrinking, her voice getting closer to a whisper with every word. "Things had changed with David. I think after the hell we went through with surgery and the chemo—I was so spent, I was so sick. David dealt with constant swings in my health, feeling great one day, horrible the next, wanting to go for a walk but then breaking down with exhaustion. It was hell for him, I know." She looked at Tess. "Gavin only ever saw me as the eighteen-year-old he had loved. Gavin saw me as vibrant and strong, and I adored him for that, you know?"

She nodded. Parker made her feel like that.

"And when I told him about the cancer, he didn't see me as a victim, but as a survivor." Ellie wiped her eyes.

"You are a survivor."

Ellie smiled with her mouth, but her eyes were flat, tired.

"I finally ended it, about three months ago." Three months ago? Ellie had gone into remission three *years* ago, and the affair had gone on that whole time? She tried to calculate how many conversations she had had with Ellie in that time. Hundreds?

"I went home and told David it was time to sell Nantucket. I told him it had been silly to hold on to the cottage for all these years."

"That must have been right before Sedona," Tess said. Ellie nodded. "I knew something was really wrong that weekend. Remember I saw your Lovan in the bathroom? You shrugged it off, but I could tell you were hurting."

"You have no idea how much I wanted to talk to you about it," Ellie said. "To both of you. But I knew I never could."

"You've been so alone in this," Tess said.

Ellie's lips began to shake. "I should have told David as soon as it was over. I wanted so badly to get the lie out of me, but it never felt like the right time. I was afraid. I thought with a little more time . . . but then the cancer came back. And now—" She looked at Tess with desperation. "How can I tell him now? I don't want to die with a lie between us. But there just isn't any time . . ."

Her words were lost in a flood of tears. Tess wrapped her arms around Ellie's compressed form, as if that would mend the fissures she had exposed.

"There you are." Joline's voice flowed down the lawn, snapping Tess back into the reality of what did, and didn't, need to be done. Joline tilted her head, taking in the scene, and began to walk faster. Tess put her head down on Ellie's back and whispered into her ear.

"Ell, we'll get through this. You did the right thing not telling David. And Joline can't ever know."

EIGHT
Ellie

*A*nita led Ellie to a small room with a twin bed and one chair. The honey-colored floors and the purple stripes on the alpaca bedspread were welcoming touches in the otherwise sparsely furnished room. The blinds drawn against the blazing sun reminded her of the hundreds of afternoon naps she had coaxed from her children when they were little. She missed those simple days.

Anita instructed her to lie down on the bed. As the pillow hollowed out below her head, she was tempted to ask Anita and Giuliana if they would just let her sleep. She wanted to fall away from the world for a while, to be free from her thoughts.

Ellie hadn't been able to hide her tears when Joline had arrived beside her on the lawn, but thankfully Joline didn't ask for an explanation. She simply added her arms to Tess's embrace, and unknowingly increased the weight of her betrayal. She didn't deserve Joline's comfort, and Joline certainly wouldn't offer it if she had any idea what she had done.

Ellie tried to push those thoughts from her mind and concentrate on her lung, on the idea of ridding herself of cancer. This is what she had come to Ecuador for, what she had pleaded with David to let her try. She couldn't stand to be around one more doctor who looked at her with pity and resignation. She wanted to dig into a place, if only for a week, where people lived by a different set of rules, a place where a person's spirit was considered stronger than any one disease. Joline had spent hours helping her understand that her own internal energy could create wellness. She needed to focus on that.

Giuliana placed the heel of her hand between Ellie's eyebrows and pressed down, making her head bounce off the bed a little. She chanted something that sounded like *em-poo-yay*. Then she walked back and forth along the side of the bed, clutching Ellie's ankles, calves, and forearms, calves, and ankles. Her grip was surprisingly strong, almost painful. Grabbing both of her feet, she heaved them up into the air, lifting her hips off the bed, up and down, up and down. *Empuyay, empuyay.* Giuliana was breathing hard. She wondered if Giuliana was trying to knock something out of her. Or maybe Giuliana was shaking her as punishment, the way Tess must have wanted to seize her shoulders and yell, "What were you thinking?" But there was no judgment in Giuliana's touch, as strong as it was. There was no blame in her gaze. Ellie caught a drop from her eye before it could roll into her ear.

"She's ready to use *el cobayo*," Anita said. "Are you ready?"

When Ellie nodded, having no idea what being ready truly meant, Giuliana disappeared behind a door she hadn't noticed before. She stared at the ceiling, trying to relax, following each grain of the wood until it pooled in a knot. When Giuliana came back into the room, her hands were cupped in front of her, cradling a mass of fur. Ellie could see brown and white tufts and closed her eyes to avoid seeing the animal's whiskers or eyes.

"Good. Keep your eyes closed and relax," Anita said.

Wafts of air brushed over her as Giuliana moved side to side along the bed from her head to her feet and back again. But nothing touched her. Giuliana began to move more slowly and Ellie could no longer be sure which part of her body she was nearest. A desire to sink as far as possible into the mattress washed over her and she began to feel the muscles of her legs and arms release.

She needed a carefree thought, and pictured her childhood summers on Nantucket with her grandfather, starting from the time she was ten. She adored being with him, learning about the tides, onshore winds, and the best time to find sand dollars. Of course, the joy of those summers was magnified by the relief of being away from her mother, a woman who could never see the positive in anyone, determined only to point out faults. Ellie decided even then, that when the time came she would craft the opposite life for her own children, bolster them with daily encouragements, and praise their unique gifts. Hers would be a happy home, one full of love and light.

She was pulled back into the room by a vibration that enveloped her, like she was lying beneath a huge magnet tugging at every cell in her body. Her muscles unwound another notch and the pull became more localized, starting at her feet and traveling up toward her knees, to her belly button, over her ribs. Her skin tingled with a thousand tiny threads moving up through each pore. It was a pleasant sensation, like finally getting the water out of her ear after a long swim. A stream of cool air whispered over her body, leaving her refreshed and calm. She took in a deep breath and opened her eyes.

"How do you feel?" Anita asked, dragging her chair over to the side of the bed. Giuliana was gone.

"Good, I think." She was surprised to hear that word coming out of her own mouth. "It's like I've been walking around with a heavy coat on, and now it's off." She wondered if the feeling had anything to do with finally telling Tess about Gavin, or if it was actually because of the guinea pig.

Anita smiled. "That's *sami*. Light energy is called *sami*. The heavy energy is called the *hoocha*. The shamans help us let go of the *hoocha* and let the *sami* fill our energy field."

When Giuliana came back into the room, Ellie was relieved that she didn't have the guinea pig with her. She sat up as Giuliana took a seat on the end of the bed.

Giuliana spoke directly to her, even though Anita still needed to translate from the side.

"She says you have only one lung that functions?"

A hitch of air caught in her chest. She nodded.

"We praise this sacred animal because it makes a great sacrifice. El cobayo took away much illness from you today, absorbed it, like the roots of a plant draining a puddle."

Ellie felt slightly dizzy and realized she had been holding her breath. She sucked in a gulp of air.

"But there is more work for you to do."

"How?" she asked, sitting up straighter. "What do I do?"

"Your energy is blocked here." Giuliana put her hand just on the bottom of Ellie's throat. "This is about truth."

Ellie felt the edges of her mouth begin to twitch.

"You must speak your truth," Giuliana said. "But first you must uncover what that is."

She wanted to lay her head down on Giuliana's lap. She had a profound feeling that this woman would understand, would even forgive her for loving one man and choosing another.

As they walked away from Giuliana's house, Tess slowly circled her right arm.

"Look at you," Joline said. "Full rotation. Isn't she amazing?"

"She barely touched me," Tess said. "Bizarre."

"How do you feel, Ell?" Joline asked, putting her arm around her. "What did Giuliana say after the guinea pig? What did you think?"

Ellie didn't have the energy to make up any answers that would satisfy Joline. She couldn't have this conversation right now.

"Actually," Joline said, her voice softer. "Maybe you should just stay in the healing zone Giuliana created for you. Better not to talk. Just rest on the way back."

Ellie sunk into the back seat, grateful for the silence. She felt a cramp sneaking up the left side of her ribs. She had to relax, and keep her focus on her health. She wanted to recreate the feeling of lightness she had experienced at Giuliana's, the sense of freedom from burden she hadn't felt in a long time. Closing her eyes, she imagined the guinea pig moving above her again, extracting anything menacing from her body. She pictured the creature pulling dark vapor straight from her skin, like the hood over her stove that immediately sucked the smoke from bubbling bacon right out of her kitchen. She filled the fumes with cancerous cells, with regret, with shame and guilt. She wanted none of it in her body anymore. At the same time, she felt the urge to picture an equally strong force beaming into her, a bright light full of her happiest thoughts—the sound of Lilly's infectious giggle, the flare of Hannah's stubborn streak, Connor's shoulders filling out in his teenage years.

She pictured an afternoon they had all spent together, not long after she had gone into remission. David had made them all go walk a trail in Cedar Park because, he said, it was too beautiful a day to pass up. They could count on their outdoor Lilly to be game, but Connor rolled his eyes, and Hannah tried to pretend it was too cold to be outside. But David talked them into the car anyway. She could still picture the sun skipping off the lake, Connor shoving his sisters into every leaf pile, Lilly begging them to let her bring home the fuzzy caterpillar she had put in her pocket, Hannah trying to catch the leaves that twirled through the air, marveling at how different each one she collected was from the last. Ellie knew on that day that she had been blessed with something as close to the divine as she could ever hope to get.

And then Hannah had jumped off a rock and split her shin open. Blood was everywhere. David calmly wrapped his scarf around her leg, made her laugh at her own clumsiness, and carried her on his shoulders the rest of the way, getting her even closer to the leaves she wanted to touch, distracting her from the throbbing below her knee. David told her that how a person deals with the bad stuff is a matter of choice, that the day was simply too perfect to be ruined. Hannah believed him, and even the stitches she had to get seemed more like a grand adventure than proof that the day had somehow been spoiled.

Ellie never questioned David's intent, but did sometimes wonder about the approach. Surviving cancer had made her less willing to tamp down any of her emotions. She would let herself cry openly at the end of a joyous movie, even welcome dark feelings as clues to something that deserved attention. Maybe Hannah should have been able to admit she was embarrassed by her clumsiness, Connor and Lilly allowed to bemoan going to the ER and missing the promised hot chocolate at the Green Street Diner. Had she and David sent the message that their feelings weren't valued unless they were happy ones? Maybe that's when things had shifted with David, when she began to feel the burden of selecting the emotion that would please him instead of the one she felt. Where did her desire to make David happy end and her responsibility to be honest with herself begin? At rational moments, she decided that any conflict between those two things was how life worked, the root of necessary compromise that kept relationships intact. But was that really true? David's determination to keep his emotions on an even keel was wonderful ballast for raising a family, but she sometimes missed the thrill that accompanied a more primal set of emotions. She wished he would yell at her, just once for something that bothered him, or weep with worry about her cancer.

Ellie opened her eyes as a cough escaped her throat, the reality of where she was rushing back. What was she going to do about Gavin? He would be waiting for her tomorrow. She couldn't just let him sit there. But how much strength would it take to walk away again, knowing he was alone in this faraway place? What would he do after the coffee had gone cold and he was sitting alone in that cafe, with nothing left to do but stare out an empty door? She sat up and pushed herself against the seat.

"Good nap?" Joline asked, turning around. "Ceremonies can be extremely draining. Probably not a bad idea to rest some more when we get back."

When they got to their room, Joline announced she needed a shower and headed straight for the bathroom. Ellie mouthed, "I have to talk to you," to Tess. Joline left the door of the bathroom open and sat on the toilet. She never had gotten used to Joline peeing in plain sight.

"Close the door, would you?" Tess called.

"Such prudes," Joline said, as she swung the door shut with her foot. As soon as Ellie heard the rings on the shower curtain scrape across the metal bar and water hum through the pipes, she slipped onto the couch next to Tess.

"I have to get back into town alone tomorrow morning."

"Are you crazy?" Tess said. "He needs to disappear."

"Not so loud. I can't just let him sit there."

"Why not? Nothing good will come out of seeing him again," Tess said.

Tess was right, but it seemed too cruel not to go back. She imagined stroking the back of his hand over the tiny scar above his wrist, letting him tuck a curl behind her ear and trace her eyebrow with his thumb before saying goodbye.

"I still don't get how he's here," Tess said.

"When I broke it off, he made me promise to tell him if I ever got sick again. I shouldn't have agreed, but I didn't think it would come back anyway, and definitely not so soon. I told him I was coming here with you two. He must have figured it was his only chance to see me away from David."

"Are you still in love with him?" Tess asked.

"Gavin?" This was the dreaded question, the one thing that had probably stopped her from telling David the truth more than anything else. She was afraid he would ask her the same thing.

"Look, I've got to go to him before he comes here," Ellie said. "All his years working in hotels, he's fluent in Spanish. It wouldn't be very hard to figure out where we are staying if he wanted to. He came all the way to Ecuador. What's to stop him from coming up here? I have to get to him first. But I need your help."

She watched Tess's eyes flick back and forth, trying to determine how this might play out, evaluating the options. The shower turned off.

"Here's what we'll do. In the morning you tell Joline you want to go back to the market," Tess said. "I'll suggest she and I go over the presentation for Bryce while you're gone. She wants me to take a look before Thursday anyway."

Ellie saw equal parts love and concern in the piercing green of Tess's eyes, and wanted to hug her for both.

Before she could, Joline walked into the room, a tiny white towel wrapped around her waist. Her small breasts jiggled freely as she brushed out her short sprigs of hair. The gray streaks around her temples stood out more when her hair was wet.

"I just had the biggest flashback," Joline said. "I was thinking about the first time you guys ever came out to Minneapolis and I caught you and David kissing in Graham's study after the Turkey Classic. And you guys tried to tell me you were just *celebrating* your winning touchdown." Joline used air quotes for emphasis. "Remember how shocked I was?"

Ellie nodded, trying not to look at Tess. Her David. Her husband. And yet here she was scheming to see her ex-lover. How had she become this person?

"God that feels like a century ago," Joline said and walked back into the bathroom.

Ellie didn't say anything as Joline dressed with purpose, shook the last drops of water out of her hair, and put on her sandals. "I'm going to visit with Mama Rosita before dinner. I'll see you down there."

She waited for Joline to reach the bottom of the stairs before she got up. She couldn't be sure her legs wouldn't be visibly wobbly.

"I'm going to go down, too," Ellie said. "I think I'll call home." She needed normalcy, some connection to the person she was supposed to be.

NINE
Joline

Joline found Mama Rosita sitting next to the adobe fire-place in a corner of the dining room that looked like it had been molded from one enormous piece of white clay. The cone-shaped hearth morphed into a pair of benches on either side, the same white color as the walls. Dark wood beams crossed the ceiling, mirroring the color of the floor and framing the room with warmth. Large paintings of ancient trees and blooming flowers adorned almost every wall and transformed the space into an anteroom to the gardens beyond, the late after-noon light just now dipping behind the mountains.

She breathed in a mix of cumin and cedar, her stomach wak-ing up to the suggestion of dinner. The table in front of Mama Rosita held two teacups with not much room for anything else. Several larger tables stood empty in front of French doors. Mama Rosita pushed herself up from the bench and stood with outstretched arms.

Joline had met Marco's grandmother only a year earlier, but was convinced they had shared a loving bond in a former life, per-haps as mother and daughter, or elephants from the same herd. She was sure she had never been Mama Rosita's equal, though, more like a lucky apprentice. Mama Rosita stood barely five feet tall, her stooped frame almost square. She shuffled toward Joline in cloth moccasins, thick ankles visible below a gray skirt, her waist lost inside the hang of bosom. Her broad nose and flat cheeks were softened by the brown folds of her skin. Joline thought she was the most beautiful woman she had ever met. She gripped Joline's shoulders and held her for a moment at arm's length before pulling her into an embrace.

"*Come esta, mi hija?*" Mama Rosita always called her *mi hija*, my child. Nothing made her want to improve her Spanish more than being with Mama Rosita. Despite her best efforts, she had never done well with foreign languages, and their verbal interactions never moved too far beyond pleasantries without Marco there to translate. But Joline sensed a level of communication with Mama Rosita that went beyond words, and enjoyed the silent connection.

"How was Giuliana's?" Marco came through the kitchen door with a fresh pot of tea and another cup. He held out a chair for Joline before sitting in the third spot at the table. Marco and Mama Rosita had been the ones to suggest most of the shamans she had met in the area. They had both been lovingly giving of their time and knowledge, eager to help the enthusiastic American discover the best traditional healers, the way she imagined hoteliers in Italy might share their favorite trattorias with connoisseurs of authentic food.

"It was wonderful to see her again." She hoped Giuliana had helped Ellie. She couldn't figure out how it was that Ellie had walked off the plane two days before with such resolve, visibly ready to surrender to the healing process, but now seemed reticent. A veil had dropped around Ellie in the last twelve hours that Joline couldn't get behind.

Marco towered above his grandmother, even while sitting. He lovingly cradled the ceramic teapot as he filled each cup, a level of grace not often found in the same hands that could split a log with one crunch of the axe. Mama Rosita held her palm out toward Joline, and she placed her hand there. Mama Rosita closed her eyes in a long blink before speaking.

"Mama says you feel strong," Marco translated. "It seems that you are well."

"*Si.* I'm glad to be back. Please tell your grandmother how grateful I am to be able to bring my friends here."

Joline wanted to ask Mama Rosita if she would be willing to see Ellie, to treat her, but Mama Rosita rarely conducted ceremonies any more. She said she was no longer strong enough to carry the spirits of too many people. She only performed ceremonies when she felt the calling, and only for those lucky few in close proximity. But it did happen. Mama Rosita had recently sent for a pregnant woman happily looking forward to the birth of her first baby. She'd been lurched awake one night by a vision that the woman was carrying twins and that the first baby was breach, a possible disaster during labor. Through a healing ceremony, Mama Rosita managed to turn the baby, and two weeks later the young woman delivered a pair of healthy girls. Mama Rosita's divine inspiration for healing was part of her gift, an internal alarm system that guided her. Joline's instinct was not to interfere with that kind of system, and she wouldn't even know how to ask exactly. But Ellie was only there for five more days.

"My grandmother wants to thank you for bringing Mr. Bryce to us," Marco said. "He reserved the room upstairs for the next six months."

"He did?" She tried to keep her face from jumping into an expression of complete surprise. Relationships with the local shamans were supposed to be her domain.

"He came two days ago. He paid us the money up front." Mama Rosita continued to pat her hand and giggled as Marco spoke. She reminded Joline of a demented old lady just then, laughing when nothing was particularly funny.

She resisted the urge to ask for the details of Bryce's visit. She didn't want to seem out of step with her colleague.

"Have you had any word from Mayu?" Joline asked. "He told me he might be able to come Thursday or Friday, but I haven't heard back." Mayu was a revered *ayahuascero*, trained by one of the last great masters, and she wanted Ellie to work with him almost as much as with Mama Rosita. Without either of them, this trip might prove fruitless.

"He didn't call you?" Marco asked. "I'm sure he will be coming. He said he would."

"I hope so," she said, reminding herself that shamans didn't exactly keep datebooks or electronic calendars. Nature would support.

Mama Rosita took her hand again and squeezed it, and then put her index finger on Joline's pulse point, her eyes drifting, like she was off in a distant place. Mama Rosita's fingernail was so short that a little pillow of skin rimmed the quick.

"How is your boy?" Mama Rosita asked.

"Dylan?" Joline hesitated. "He's a teenager."

Mama Rosita shook her head and looked confused. Marco strung several phrases together, perhaps looking for the right translation for all the hormones and rebellion wrapped up in that one word.

"He gives you trouble?" the old woman asked.

"He's a good kid," she said. But that didn't make it easy. "Raising a boy without a father at home gets harder as he grows up. He can push my limits sometimes."

Marco laughed before translating his grandmother's next words. "She says boys do this because we are simple in the brain. Pure in the heart, but we don't always know the consequence of our actions." Marco smiled. "It's true."

At least she had been able to more actively support his music lately, channel his energies there. The new apartment had given him space to invite friends over for jam sessions, and now she could get to know his band mates. She had even been able to surprise him with studio recording time before she left.

"He is an artist," Mama Rosita said.

"Yes, a musician."

Mama Rosita nodded. "He feels things deeply."

"Yes, I worry about that. The older he gets the more he wants to know about his father." His ex-rocker negligent father, Jax Tucker, who occasionally sent a postcard from some trailer park in Tennessee. "Dylan's gift for music comes from his father, and it is very hard for him to understand why his father wouldn't want to share that with him."

"Ah, but he shares it with you," Mama Rosita said.

It was true. Connecting through his songs was a wonderful way to communicate with him. She was thankful for that.

"One of the women upstairs," Mama Rosita said, Marco translating again, "she is your sister?"

People were often confused by the same last name. Or maybe

Mama Rosita felt it.

"Sister-in-law, actually. And a dear friend. But, yes, she's like a sister to me."

"We are all sisters in the eyes of Pachamama," Mama Rosita said. Then she added something that Marco didn't translate right away. Joline looked at Marco expectantly.

"My grandmother says that your sister is quite ill. Her system is weak."

Joline was both grateful and devastated that Mama Rosita had sensed it that quickly. She nodded. Surely she would help Ellie now.

"I will see her if I think I can help," Mama Rosita said. "But it's too early for me to tell."

Her throat constricted. "I'm not sure I understand."

Mama Rosita's dark eyes softened, her words coming from Marco. "Pachamama will tell me if I can help her."

By the time Ellie and Tess came down to the dining room, four place settings had been laid out on the largest table. Tess was freshly showered, her long hair pulled back even though it was still wet. Ellie still looked tired, her eyes distant and foggy. Joline introduced them both to Mama Rosita, who touched their shoulders lightly before sitting back down on the bench next to the tea table, a faded cushion disappearing beneath her.

"Did you find the router?" Joline asked Tess.

"More like a modem. It won't be much use for downloading anything big," Tess said.

Ellie sat forward in her chair. "Shouldn't you be getting results soon?"

"Not soon enough," Tess said. She looked a little sheepish.

"Seems slow this time. I thought the first month was critical for feedback about side effects," Ellie said.

Tess sighed. "The truth is, we missed our deadline. We haven't actually submitted for phase two yet."

"You missed it?" Ellie asked.

"I'm sure the guys in the lab will find a solution this week,"

Tess quickly added.

"This week? Oh Tess, shouldn't you be there?" Ellie looked stricken.

"I'm no use in the lab anyway." Tess shrugged. "They'll work it out."

Tess was trying to keep her tone light, but Joline saw the stress locked in her jaw. Now she understood Tess's uneven energy from earlier in the day. Tess was a lone draft horse, pulling the weight of her whole company. But she had come to Ecuador anyway.

"You have a great team," Joline said. "And it's a perfect opportunity for them to step up and show they can solve this while you're away."

"May I join you, ladies?" Marco pulled out his chair as he asked the question. This was one of the things Joline adored about Casa Munay, no artificial line drawn between guests and owners. It made everyone feel as if they were staying at the home of a friend.

"And your grandmother?" asked Ellie. "Would she like to join us?"

"No, she will have a small bit of soup and then go. She gets too tired sitting at a table with a lot of conversation not in her language. Please don't worry."

Two women came out of the kitchen carrying steaming bowls. They were Mariana and Arabella, sisters from the village. Joline knew they slept on the floor of the kitchen, and yet their aprons always looked bleached and pressed. The soup was bright orange with a hint of nutmeg drifting up in the steam.

"Can I offer a glass of wine?" Marco gestured to two carafes sitting on a side table.

"I have never found healing ceremonies to mix well with alcohol," Joline said.

"I assume that's more of a guideline than a rule?" Tess asked, winking at Ellie. "I would love one, thank you."

"How are you enjoying your time in Ecuador so far?" Marco asked, pouring the wine for Tess. Ellie declined. "I hear you went to see Don Emilio yesterday. Did you learn anything interesting?"

"Have you done it?" Tess asked.

"With Don Emilio," Marco said. "Yes, of course."

"And what did you learn?" Tess asked.

Marco looked right at Tess as he spoke. "I learned that I am at my best when I find a way to sit quietly with nature."

Tess reached up to smooth her hair and ran her hand down the back of her ponytail.

"He used similar words, with you, Tess," Joline said. "Definitely something about needing to be quiet." Joline chuckled, crunching on the ice in her water.

"Ha, ha," Tess said.

"I can't imagine he would ever suggest quieting your voice," Marco said sincerely, still looking at Tess.

"What he said was that I need to quiet my mind. That I was too busy in my mind," Tess said.

Joline had forgotten that Don Emilio had said that. He had been right about something.

"Then you have come to the perfect place," Marco said, leaning forward on his elbows. "Casa Munay is designed to help you move out of your mind and into your heart." Marco was focused solely on Tess. "Stilling the mind is not an easy task for a woman with a strong intellect, but one I'm sure you will find extremely powerful."

Joline suppressed a laugh. He had no idea who he was dealing with.

"My reading was interesting," Joline said. "He told me that something was holding me back in my life, like a hand clasped over the wings of a bird. He said not to spend energy looking for the hand, rather to find the strength in the wings."

"What do you think that meant?" Ellie asked.

"I don't know," Joline said. "I've always considered myself to be a rather free bird."

"I have found," said Marco, "that it's best not to judge what we think we hear. These shamans see much deeper than we can. Wait for a few days and its meaning will reveal itself to you, like an onion that needs several layers peeled back before you can get to the core." His voice had a musical quality and reverberated after he stopped talking.

"Excuse me for a moment, ladies, I need to check something in the kitchen."

After he left the room, Ellie spoke in a low voice. "What a charmer."

"I hadn't noticed," Tess said, laughing, and blew on her soup.

"Tess!" Ellie said, letting her spoon clink into the bowl. "Don Emilio said you were at a crossroads, didn't he? That you had a big choice to make. He knew about Parker before you did!"

"Lucky guess," Tess said. "I still can't believe he proposed like that."

"He did give you a whole week," Ellie said. "Gotta give him credit for that."

"I don't know," Tess said. "I can't decide if that was bold or cowardly."

"I think it was smart," said Joline. "He doesn't want your first answer, he wants your real answer."

"But this is essentially an ultimatum, right? Which is totally unreasonable." Tess fiddled with her spoon. "We were really enjoying being together again. It's been great. But does that mean I should be forced to commit for life? It's so sudden."

"You were together for three years," said Ellie. Joline was relieved to see her fully engaged. She was a pushover for a dramatic love story.

"I thought he knew me better than this. I don't see why he has to try to force some major decision."

"Tess," said Ellie. She moved the spoon out of Tess's reach. "Listen to yourself. You just said that you love being with him. That your life is better now than when you weren't together."

"Exactly," Tess said. "Why not just continue to be together? Why marriage? Wouldn't it be better to decide to stay together every day because we want to be, not because of some unrealistic contract?"

"It's not just a contract. And it's not unrealistic." Ellie sounded unusually defensive. Joline was used to Ellie being the lone proponent of marriage. She and David were blessed with the kind of relationship everyone aspired to, but few ever experienced.

"I'm surprised you're even considering it," Joline said. "This is when you usually jump ship."

"No, I don't," Tess said.

"Remember Robert?" Joline asked.

"Robert broke up with me," Tess said.

"Seriously?" She marveled at how easily people managed to reframe their past. "You knew he was about to ask you to move in with him, and you went out and bought your bungalow."

"Who's to say that I had to move into his place? Why couldn't he move in with me?"

"Tess, the guy was an architect. A modern architect, and you buy an old shingled bungalow? What was he supposed to think?"

"He was too clingy anyway," Tess said.

"Then how about the screenwriter guy? What was his name?" Joline asked.

"Oh yeah, Jeremy," Ellie said. "I forgot all about him. He was gorgeous."

"As long as he stayed in L.A. it was great," Joline said. "You popped down there whenever it suited you, but every time he tried to come to you, you made an elaborate excuse." How did she not see this?

"Look, the Hollywood thing was fun for a while," Tess said. "But he would have found Palo Alto extremely boring. Trust me."

"Maybe he could have used a little boring," Joline said.

"Thanks." Tess chuckled.

"You know what I mean. My point is that you wave your need for independence around like a battle flag."

"This is my point. You're the one who always says to 'find your truth.' What's wrong with being a lone wolf? That's who I am. Plus I have lots of commitments to think about, people who count on me, like my sisters, and my business. There's not a lot of room on the list. Just the idea of someone waiting for me to get home for dinner makes me queasy. I thought he got that. No pressure. Can't say that anymore."

"Maybe he just wants you to know how much he loves you. And have you love him back." Ellie's voice was quiet. "Something to be said for that."

The sadness was back in Ellie's eyes.

Marco reappeared and lowered a large platter of vegetables onto the table as the sisters cleared away the soup bowls. Before he sat, he helped his grandmother up from her seat, and walked her to the edge of the room. She gave a girly wave before disappearing through the curtain. The smell of saffron encircled the table.

"I hope you enjoy the meal. Every vegetable was picked from our property this afternoon," Marco said.

"I noticed all the people in the field." Tess sat up straight again. "That's quite a large staff."

"They are not employees. They don't work for us, they work *with* us."

"What do you mean?" Tess asked.

"They live on the hillside around Casa Munay, and we work together as a community." Marco wiped his mouth and carefully placed the napkin back on his lap. "The people who work in the fields, they harvest the food that we serve here at the Casa. The extra food they sell in the market. Or they use it in trade. Everyone in the community has a role. Some families provide the milk. A group of women makes blankets for everyone from the alpaca. Rafael teaches the little ones two days a week." Marco spoke directly to Tess, as if no one else was in the room.

"Two days a week?" Ellie asked.

"Yes. We are lucky to have him. He teaches on days when the market is closed."

"What about things you can't make yourselves?" Tess asked. "Like shoes?"

"Jorge and Antonio make moccasins," Marco said. "But you are right, there are things we must buy. That is why the Casa is so important. When there is not enough money from the market, the money from guests like you pays for things like pencils and books. And soon we hope to have a dentist visit our village."

"How many families are you talking about?" Ellie asked.

"On the hillside? Twenty-five? Maybe more."

"Like a commune," Tess said.

"A community, yes," Marco said. "It's a concept we call *Ayni*. It is an idea that runs deep in my culture. Do you know the word?" Joline knew it well, one of the many things she loved about this part of the world. "*Ayni* means reciprocity that stems from unconditional love. It means giving whenever you can and getting in return when you need. Like Signora Tornida. She is too old to tend to her chickens anymore, so Eduardo goes to collect the eggs. And we all make sure she has the food she needs and firewood to stay warm."

"How did you learn such beautiful English?" Tess rested her chin on her hand.

"I spent two years in your country. Studying medicine."

"I never knew that, Marco," Joline said, wondering what Mama Rosita had thought of that.

"I didn't finish my studies. I realized that it was the relationships with the patient that I enjoyed much more than the science."

"Too bad," Ellie said. "We could use more doctors who are interested in good relationships with their patients, believe me."

"Yes, I sensed that also. Has this been difficult for you?" Marco asked Ellie.

Ellie nodded. The pause in the conversation lengthened.

"What did you think of the U.S.?" Tess asked.

"I enjoyed it. But I missed home," he said gently. "I felt too far from nature there. In nature all things are connected. I feel sad for cultures that have forgotten this truth. Our feet stand together on the same mother earth."

"That's well said." Tess sat back and ran her hand over her ponytail.

Joline was sure Tess would have rolled her eyes if she had said such a thing. What was it about being muscular and male that made Tess finally listen? The group fell into companionable silence as they finished their meal, Ellie scooping the last of the risotto off the platter. Joline was relieved that she finally seemed to have an appetite.

As the dishes were cleared, Marco excused himself. "I apologize but I have some paperwork I must attend to before morning." He put his hand on Tess's shoulder before going. "I truly enjoyed dining with you."

Arabella and Mariana brought three large mugs to the table, stuffed with fresh sprigs of mint steeping in hot water. No tea bags, no string to pull the mint out. Joline admired, not for the first time, the elegance of it, the simplicity. She imagined the wasted resources that go into a cup of tea at home—drying the spices, grinding them, layers of packaging—when all you had to do was pull a sprig of mint from the garden and add water.

"What in the world is this?" Tess asked. "I feel like I'm drinking a tree."

TEN
Ellie

E llie slumped onto the couch in their room after dinner. The furniture was surprisingly comfortable, even though most of it was made of wood and wool. The chill of the evening had pushed most of the day's warmth out of the room. She reached for a throw.

"Let's make a fire," Tess said, already grabbing small sticks out of the basket beside the hearth. She crumpled up some paper and stuck it under the logs, then put a match to the bundle. Keeping her eye on the growing flames, Tess stood up and circled her right arm three times.

"Amazing," Tess said quietly.

Ellie realized she hadn't coughed once at dinner. Could that be because of the guinea pig? Was she ridiculous to think she might see an improvement that fast, as if she had gone to a masseuse to work out a kink in her back?

Tess pulled the elastic band out of her hair, and Ellie couldn't help but envy her long gorgeous locks. Hers had lost its deep chestnut luster and no longer had enough body to grow past her shoulders.

"God, I'd give anything for that hair," Ellie said.

"Thanks, honey," Tess said, redoing her ponytail.

"Chemo just wrecked mine. It's never been the same. My curls are more like frizz."

"Not so," Joline said, stroking Ellie's hair. "You're as beautiful as ever."

"And you, my dear, are starting to look like Jamie Lee Curtis, with your short, short hair," Tess said. "Very hot."

"Ha!" Joline said. "I wish."

"Hey, is that the belt you got in Memphis, Tess? You still have that?" Ellie asked.

"So tacky it's back in style." Tess rubbed the studs on the leather.

"Got? You mean stole," Joline said, laughing. "That bartender's probably still looking for his jeans. You always were a sucker for a guy who could make a good martini."

"And you? Put a guy behind a drum set and you swoon," Tess said.

"As a matter of fact, I think I got some beautiful Zildjian wood out of that weekend," Joline said.

"You didn't just say that," Tess said.

"I meant drumsticks," Joline said, with a mischievous smile. "God, what were we, like twenty-five?"

"Twenty-six," Ellie said. "David and I had just gotten engaged."

"That's right," Tess said. "Remember the bridal shop we went to, and you tried on every awful frilly thing they had?"

"I think I shot champagne out my nose we were laughing so hard," Joline said.

"I had to talk the lady out of charging us for that champagne," Tess said. "That was hilarious."

The flames in the fireplace changed from orange to gray, and smoke puffed into the room. Ellie fanned the air in front of her. Poking the logs to no effect, Tess let out a resigned sigh as Marco's voice spilled into the room from the top of the stairs.

"Please," he said. "Allow me."

He opened the glass slider an inch and took the poker from her hand. His motions were gentle, but he wasted no time. He lit a rolled-up tube of paper and held it high inside the chimney for a few moments before dropping it on the fire. Then he got down on his knees, and blew over and over again into the few embers below the fire. On the sixth or seventh breath, a rush of air and sparks ignited, lighting the logs and sucking the smoke back up into the chimney. He leaned back on his heels and clapped the ash from his hands.

"These chimneys are very narrow and need to be warmed before you light a fire. And letting in a bit of the air from the downslope of the hill is the best way to make a draft. You can close the door again once the fire is bright."

"I'm sorry you had to come all the way up here," Tess said.

"Please. It is my pleasure. *Ayni.*" He stood up and brushed off his pants. "And now you know the secret." He winked and headed back down the stairs.

"That must be why Bryce rented the room," Joline said, her voice so low she may have been talking to herself.

"What?" Ellie asked.

"Marco told me Bryce rented this room for six months, and I couldn't understand why. But it makes sense based on what Marco told us about the community here. Rather than give some sort of donation to help the community, he rented the room."

"Doesn't sound like Bryce," Tess said. "He always wants value in exchange for his dollar."

"You don't know him like I do. He's looking for more meaning from his life now, for things that his millions can't buy him."

"But his whole career has been about fulfilling pent-up demand," said Tess. "If he has a need, he figures lots of other people do too. Like his first business, right? He wanted to be able to transact online but there was no secure way to do it. He figured out how to encrypt credit cards, and then sold it to every bank on the planet. The need was already there. He saw it before anyone else and jumped on it."

"He has great vision," Joline said.

"Yeah, but there's no leverage in a retreat center. No real scale."

"There can be real value without huge scale, you know," Joline said.

Ellie hoped this didn't turn into a full-blown debate. When Joline and Tess got going, they sometimes stayed up for hours trying to prove the other one wrong. She would invariably give up trying to follow either of their arguments and head off to bed, but here she had nowhere else to go.

"Come on," Tess said. "Bryce has played in the big leagues for a long time based on some pretty clear operating principles. And the most critical is going after an enormous market. No one ditches that criteria without a specific reason."

Joline pushed her bracelets up and down her arm and said nothing.

"Ah, hah!" Tess pointed her finger at Joline, her blue eyes bright with anticipation. "There is something else, and you know what it is. Spill it."

Joline hesitated. "Look, you know him professionally. It's not right for me to break his confidence."

"But you've asked me to advise you on this business plan. I can't do that without knowing the whole story," Tess said.

Ellie could picture Tess in her own boardroom, confident and persuasive, her running shoes traded in for three-inch heels, arguments at the ready to counter any investor concern. But she sat now, the better approach with Joline.

"If you say anything to anyone—" Joline started. Tess gave Joline a *give-me-a-break* glare. "Bryce had a minor heart attack two years ago." Tess's mouth fell open. "He didn't want anyone to know. He hid it by claiming he had a last minute invitation to climb Kilimanjaro with an old friend."

"Oh my God. That's the year he missed TechWorld. It actually gave a bunch of the investment bankers hard-ons that Gardner could be cocky enough to skip the conference and go climb a mountain. Holy shit. That's when he hired you."

Joline nodded. "No male in Bryce's family has ever made it past sixty-five. Which is why he's always been such an exercise freak. But then at fifty-eight—heart attack. He saw me quoted in that article about how health is about more than nutrition and exercise, that it's also spiritual. He's been trying to lead a different life ever since."

"But why not just work on his own lifestyle? Why create a whole retreat center?" Ellie asked. She hated talking about her health, and couldn't imagine building a business around the topic.

"Because he's an entrepreneur," Tess answered, nodding. "And if he can create a new trend around this stuff, then he not only gets credit for it, but everything he is doing also becomes socially acceptable. Kind of like how Richard Branson tapped into the midlife crisis. Turned it into an itch for adventure."

Joline was shaking her head. "This is different. This is about soul-searching for Bryce. His kids cut off ties with him right before his heart attack. That's no coincidence."

"How awful," Ellie said.

"The whole thing's a bit crazy. He's always been a bit at odds with his son, Peter. Big pot smoker in college. Bryce was worried he'd never make anything of himself. So he decided to set up his estate plan as an incentive scheme. Instead of splitting his money equally between his kids, he told them he would match whatever financial success they had on their own, dollar for dollar. The rest would go to charity."

"Interesting," Tess said. "The guy *is* creative."

"Problem was, his daughter—brilliant, joint JD, MBA— decided not to pursue a career as a patent attorney. She passed up partnership at Wilson Sonsini and opened up a small design store in Sonoma instead."

"Wow," Ellie said. "No one passes up partner at Wilson Sonsini." Ellie hadn't ever gotten that far. After several years as an associate, she had figured out that the partnership track didn't mix with kids. As soon as Connor came along, she gave it up. She was better at motherhood anyway.

"Peter, as it turned out, is a crazy successful hedge fund guy, made money hand over fist," Joline continued. "And when Mallory stepped out of the law, Bryce decided his estate plan wasn't fair after all, that Mallory shouldn't be punished. He changed his estate plan back to splitting his money between them."

"Ballsy," Tess said.

Ellie couldn't imagine playing her kids off each other like that.

"Stupid is what it was. Peter was devastated, not that he needed the money. But it was always pretty obvious to him that Mallory was the favorite, and this was too blatant for him to ignore." Joline's mouth curved down into an expression close to sadness. She knew all too well what it was like not to be the favorite. "Peter told his father he was done with him. And Mallory stopped talking to him too, because she knows how hurt Peter is. And Mallory is everything to Bryce. I've been helping him try to work this out. I've been mediating this whole thing with his kids, believe it or not. And the thing I've tried to help him understand are the underlying emotions and energy that got him into this mess in the first place. And not just that one situation, but his whole approach to working with people, his leadership style, his relationship with power. It's been huge for him. He wants to share some of what he has learned with other people like him. Anyway, it's not the same as putting bars on planes," Joline said.

"Call it what you will, but as soon as it's a business, it's all the same," Tess said. "And why the hell did you give up the rest of your clients, Jo? I thought we talked about that."

"Bryce required it." Joline moved closer to Ellie and tucked under the other side of the throw. "He's investing a lot in the center. It's understandable that he wants my full attention."

"But you worked so hard building your own business," Tess said. "And you're really talented. You get people like I get numbers. The rest of the Valley shouldn't be deprived of your expertise."

Ellie nestled deeper into the couch. She couldn't stop thinking about her phone call home before dinner. She'd loved hearing the kids' voices, but the conversation with David had been stilted. She was back to worrying that every word she spoke might reveal her storehouse of lies. She had cut the conversation short by saying that there was too much to relay over the phone, that she would give him a full report of everything when she got home. Another lie.

Joline stroked her hair again. "You're awfully quiet," she said. "How're you doing?" Joline's voice was soft, comforting. It made Ellie want to cry.

"I think I'm just tired," she said.

"Ellie B, I've been wanting to say something to you. You're going through the worst thing imaginable. I know you try so hard to put on a brave face, but at some point, you need to let yourself break down. It's such an important part of healing," Joline said. "Weep, yell, whatever it is. Let yourself go. It's what we're here for."

"I'm scared," Ellie said, in a whisper. She put her head on Joline's shoulder and swallowed back her tears. Tess sat on the arm of the couch and held her hand. "This week just has to work."

"I believe in my soul that it will," Joline said.

She closed her eyes, with her friends in close. *Please let Joline be right.*

ELEVEN
Tess

The next morning, Tess snuck out early for a run. It would have to be quick; Ellie would be anxious to get into town. She decided to take the route she had found the first day, relatively short and steep. As she ran down the driveway of the Casa, a man was already at work in the field, bumping a hand plow down one of the lanes. She thought he must enjoy the early morning solitude before the rest of his co-workers arrived.

She still couldn't quite get over the fact that Ellie had cheated on David, and kept at it for such a long time. Ellie, the one who could be counted on to do the right thing, the one who prioritized relationships above all else.

In college, Ellie had decided that the three of them were going to be best friends before they had even met. The way she saw it, roommates should stick together by day, and review everything during bunk bed chatter by night. While Tess knew her life would never be that simple—her little sisters still frequently needed her at home—she had often wondered what having a friend like that might be like.

Ever since, Ellie had put enough effort into their trio for all three of them. Even though she was the one who lived far away, it was Ellie who somehow made sure that Tess and Joline didn't get too far out of touch. It went beyond their girls' weekends, which Ellie was usually the one to plan—except, of course, for Ellie's "remission victory tour," which Tess had organized: four days of spa appointments and chardonnay lunches in Napa, plus shopping for Ellie's wine cellar with an eye toward vintages that would age well. Ellie held a deeply rooted conviction that the three of them should and would always be equally close. She expected that Tess and Joline would see each other whenever they could, no matter how busy either of them were. Just like Tess stayed with Ellie when she was on business in Minneapolis, so should Tess and Joline get together for dinner if Joline had afternoon meetings in Palo Alto. If Dylan had a big part in the school musical, of course Tess would go see a performance. It wasn't that Tess didn't want to do those things, but if she didn't have Ellie asking about it on the other end of the phone, it would have been easy to let them slide. And Tess was grateful for it. Joline was one of the few people who had an inside view of the huge egos she had to put up with in Silicon Valley. And Joline never hesitated to be on her side.

Tess had to make sure Joline never found out about Gavin. If there was one person she was more loyal to than her friends, it was David. Given that Joline had such a strained relationship with her father, and practically no interaction with her mother or her other brothers outside of holiday nonsense, David was her only true familial connection. He was her safe harbor.

Tess tried to pick up her pace. She missed her usual shot of espresso before her morning run. Her brain felt fuzzy from a night of broken sleep. She was usually a solid sleeper, but last night she had dolphined between wakefulness and deep dream-space for hours. It had been a long time since memories of her mother had woven through all her dreams. She figured it was her worry about Ellie that had brought thoughts of her mother to the surface, but they had been such vivid images, full of sensation—her mother caressing her temples with her soft fingertips to help her fall asleep; the smell of her mother's cinnamon French toast with extra melted butter dripped on top the way Tess liked it; her mother laughing uproariously at her imitation of the Chiquita Banana lady, bowl of fruit on her head and maracas rattling. And then there were a slew of imagined interactions as an adult, those

KATHERINE A. SHERBROOKE

things she had never had a chance to experience, but they felt no less real. In one, she and her mother fell into each other laughing after they had given each other the same Stephen Hawking book for Christmas. In another, Tess introduced her mother to the BioZang research team, proudly listing the breakthroughs each scientist had spearheaded. The images were so arresting that she had had to quickly remind herself when she woke that they hadn't actually happened. An imaginary world, a whole part of her life ripped from her grasp thanks to a drunken driver.

Her sneaker snagged on a rock. Tess caught herself as her body jolted off-kilter, and she admonished herself for wasting time on pointless musings. She needed to focus on Parker and make a decision. But she was wholly unclear what to do. It wasn't that she didn't want to be with him. She did. But why did he have to demand lifelong commitment?

She should just be honest with Parker. Tell him that she wanted to continue to be with him, but she didn't believe in putting the level of constraints on their relationship that marriage implied. Why not keep their own places, their own bank accounts? That's who she was, and if he truly loved her, that was a part of the package. He wouldn't actually go through with his ultimatum and walk away. Would he?

The only other time he had forced such a choice, it had been solved for him. After several months of dating, Parker announced that if she didn't introduce him to Ellie and Joline during Ellie's next visit, he would take it as a sign that she wasn't serious about their relationship, and he should move on. Even after she explained that there was a strict rule about their girls' weekends—no boys, no kids—Parker shrugged and said it was her choice. As it turned out, Ellie and Joline schemed to get to Palo Alto a night early to surprise Tess for her birthday, and even put together a mini surprise party. They had managed to get Parker's contact information to make sure he was there. Parker, of course, charmed Ellie and Joline with self-deprecating stories about his inability to keep up with Tess when they ran together, and had them laughing hard at his descriptions of her failed attempts to cook him something as simple as an omelet, eggs everywhere, cheese melting onto the stove. They were all pals before she even got to the party, which was hard not to adore

82

him for. It ended up being a great night. But it didn't answer her question about what would have happened if things hadn't gone his way.

Tess looked at her watch. Time to turn around. She needed to get back before breakfast to spring Ellie for her trip into town. She still wasn't convinced Ellie should see Gavin again, but she had promised to occupy Joline. She had barely been able to stop Joline from pulling out her whole retreat analysis last night. But Tess had effectively feigned exhaustion and convinced her to wait until morning.

When Tess got back to the room, she was surprised to find the sleeping mats already put away. Ellie and Joline were showered and dressed, relaxing on the couch and talking with a young man she hadn't seen on the property before. He wore jeans and a Coca-Cola t-shirt, his black hair as shiny as Marco's, but cut at an angle, framing his face from his forehead down to his angular jowl. She guessed he was in his twenties.

"Tess," said Joline. "Come meet Mayu. He's the shaman I mentioned that I really hoped we could see this week. He just arrived."

She found it hard to believe he was a shaman. Too young. No lines of wisdom cut across his face. She wondered if any of these people had credentials of any kind, something Joline could have checked. No, of course not, that would require actual training. Joline hadn't mentioned scheduling a ritual today. This would make getting Ellie into town a challenge.

"Mayu was explaining a bit about the plant to us, so you got here just in time."

Tess had no idea what plant Joline was referring to, but walked over to shake Mayu's hand. Before she could offer her hand, Mayu hugged her.

"*Mucho gusto*," he said, gripping her forearms when he stepped back, his dark eyes appealing to her for a response. His smile emphasized the point of his chin, giving his face the shape of a diamond.

"*Mucho gusto*," she said, having no idea if that was an appropriate reply.

She sat on the rug in front of Ellie and stretched.

"I say to your friends," Mayu said, "my English is not so good. I understand mostly, but sometimes talking is not as good. Apology if anything I say you no understand."

"No problem," she said, and bent her head over an outstretched leg.

"So," he went on, "Ayahuasca. She take care of you. She knows what you need."

Ah, maybe Ayahuasca was the real shaman and Mayu was her assistant.

"The brew has two plants truly. Ayahuasca and chacruna. I boil in the jungle for six days. Some call it, ah, your word is... hall-uce-ogen, yes?"

Tess looked up at him. He had taken time with the word, as if he had practiced it many times yet still couldn't quite get all the syllables.

"But no. Ayahuasca makes strong your own consciousness. Everything you see is real. The plant shows you what is already in you. It is you with you."

"I'm sorry," Tess said. "Is he talking about some kind of drug?"

Mayu smiled. He had perfect teeth.

"Not a drug. Not like you think of it. Ayahuasca is sacred plant, a vine that is on this earth for thousands of years."

Now he was stepping into her territory. All drugs were derivatives of something that originally came from nature, and that certainly didn't mean that nature's original formulation was safe to ingest.

"After you drink the brew that I give you, you may start to see things in your head. The room is black. No light. Light too distracting. But in your mind you might first see colors, shapes. Then pictures. But what you see is from your own life. It is you with you. Nothing else. And it is no scary. Maybe hard, but no scary." Ellie nodded. She had always been the studious one, and Tess could tell she was taking notes in her head. "The plant know what it is you need to see. Things that maybe cause you trouble. Things that make block in you. When you feel sick, it okay if you"—he made a gesture with his hands thrusting out of his mouth—"if you vomit, yes? It is not like when sick. It is not from stomach. It is bad emotions you need to get rid of. This is normal. This is good. This is the plant helping you."

Throwing up? Was he kidding? Ingesting some fucking jungle brew that would make Ellie's system weak was a terrible idea. Tess looked at Joline. She was actually smiling.

"Once you are through with those moments," Mayu went on, "you will start to—"

"You're not really going to do this," Tess said.

"I've wanted to work with the plant for a very long time," Joline said.

"To purposely make yourself sick?" Tess could not imagine the point of that.

"It's not for the whole time. It's usually only in the beginning, right, Mayu? And like Mayu is saying, it's really a gift from the plant. She helps to release emotions and areas where your energy is stuck to get it out of your system."

Joline's reference to this "plant" as a "she" made Tess want to strangle her.

"Ellie, this can't be a good idea for you," Tess said. "You shouldn't overtax your system."

"I want to try it," Ellie said.

"The plant knows what each person can handle. She will never give you more than you can take," Joline said.

As far as Joline knew. But she had never even tried it. And now she wanted Ellie to try this liquid-acid bullshit. Her head was going to explode.

"Is no scary," Mayu said again. "The plant, she will take care of you. She knows what you need. And if it feels bad, no worry. It no last forever. Five or six hours and then it is done."

"Five or six hours?" Tess moved up to sit on the arm of the couch. "I think you better back up and explain this in a bit more detail."

"Here's how I think about it." Joline shifted to face Tess. "Whenever our bodies are attacked by something external, we have no issue banishing it from our system. Like food poisoning. We eat something toxic, and our bodies know how to expel it, and it's over. No one questions that process. We are grateful for it, right? But deeply ingrained diseases, like cancer, are something that has essentially grown from within. In a way, we have without realizing it, set up a welcoming atmosphere for the disease to grow, usually in areas where our energy is blocked, where we have some emotional trauma, or stressor, or a place where were are struggling. Western medicine is set up to eliminate the symptom, cut it out, like the tumor, or open up the block in the arteries. But it doesn't give us a way to find the true source of the issue, the emotional and spiritual reason our energy is blocked, and release that. If we can do that, it takes the tumor or the pain away with it. This is what the plant does."

"That's a simplistic view of medicine—"

"And by the way, we all have energetic blockages, and they reveal themselves in hugely different ways. Anger, depression, exhaustion, they all come from the same place. And if you don't deal with them, I think it's hard to be truly healthy or spiritually content. The plant works for everyone. But no one is required to do this, Tess. If you don't feel comfortable taking part in this journey, there is no pressure. Please know that."

Pressure? Joline couldn't pressure her into taking some jungle juice in a million years. But she made it sound like this was a done deal for Ellie. She needed to understand the facts.

"When is this supposed to happen?" Tess asked.

"The ceremony is scheduled for tonight." Tonight? "I asked Mayu to discuss it with us so that everyone would know what to expect. If you plan to participate, we will eat breakfast but then fast for the rest of the day. No solid foods. The ceremony will start at about seven o'clock tonight, and it will last until two or three in the morning."

Tess looked down at Ellie. "You really intend to do this?"

She nodded. "It's one of the main reasons I came. I think it can really help me."

"But getting sick like that?"

"I've dealt with much worse, trust me." Her eyes were pleading. "Remember I told you about those stories of people being completely cured of cancer? It was this plant."

Tess wanted to tell her that anyone with a computer could spew outrageous stories on the internet. Scientists had never bothered to read them.

"I completely understand if you don't want to do it with

us," Ellie said, "but you should at least hear about it before you decide."

Tess saw her island of sanity depopulate before her eyes. Ellie had already made up her mind.

"Mayu," Joline said, "maybe it would help if you told us a little bit about yourself. I know Mama Rosita thinks highly of you and brings you here when her guests are in need of the plant. Tell us a bit about your background and how you came to this."

"About me?" he asked with surprise, pointing to himself. When Joline nodded, he cleared this throat and swept his hair off his face. "My name, Mayu, it means river in Quechua. Is not my real name. My grandmother give me this name. She said I was part of nature, winding through it." He gestured with his hands like the movement of a snake. "She call me Mayu. She lived in the mountains. But I grow up in the city. I had normal life. My name was Richard." He laughed at that, like he had told a silly joke. "Richard, you know, like Nixon? My father, he like Richard Nixon. And Richard Burton."

The relevance of this escaped Tess.

"My parents they think I am crazy. I have good job. I have money in bank. I have good life. But I meet the plant and I know I have a life that is different. The plant she talk to me. I understand things I understand no other way. And I want to help people. So this is what I do. My master, he talk to me through the plant. I learn to make the brew, not because he write down, or he show me. The plant, she showed me in a journey."

In other words, Tess realized, he had learned the recipe for his jungle drug while he was tripping. This just kept getting worse.

"Now I work with the plant for *dies y ocho anos*, eighteen, yes? Eighteen years. And I still learning things new about myself every day."

"Eighteen years?" said Tess. "Can I ask how old you are?"

"Me?" Apparently he wasn't used to getting too many questions about himself. "Me. I am *cuarenta y dos*." He looked at Joline. "Forty-two?"

Joline nodded. Tess was shocked. He was almost their age.

"And can you tell us about the healing power of ayahuasca? People sometimes come to you with illness, people who are sick. And you can help them?"

"Not me," said Mayu, "but the plant, she can help, yes. My own mother. She live in city, very, very sick. Many big doctors told her, they say they can do nothing. I help her to work with the plant. She is happy. Healthy now. She not think her son is crazy anymore."

"See, Tess?" Ellie said, sitting up straighter.

Great. Now she had a personal story to grab onto, in the flesh.

"It is not like take a pill and everything fine," Mayu went on. "It is much work from the person. The person has to let go of what is making them sick. Emotions, blocks in energy. There are things that make them have sickness, and the plant, she tries to help get those things out. Some persons are not ready to look inside and see those things. But person who can release the bad feelings can let go of the sickness. Yes, it is possible."

Ellie looked like she was listening to instructions for jumping out of an airplane, terrified but determined to keep fear at bay so she wouldn't forget any life-saving steps. She even seemed a little excited, as if she thought she might learn to fly.

"And where is this going to happen?" Tess asked.

"You haven't seen the roundhouse yet, have you?" asked Joline, standing. "I'll show you this afternoon. Meanwhile, we need to go eat breakfast. Last meal for the day."

"You all go ahead. I need to take a shower," Tess said. *And get my thoughts together before I explode.* "I'll be down there soon."

She closed the bathroom door to get undressed. As she put her ponytail holder away, her hand grazed the ring box. She wondered what Parker would say about all this now, about the importance of fully supporting Ellie's choices? Being spat on by a man wearing feathers was one thing. Ingesting an unregulated substance was entirely another.

By the time she got to the breakfast table, Mayu was gone. She wanted to lay into Joline for tempting Ellie with something so depleting, maybe even dangerous, but she would save that for when they were alone together. She hadn't forgotten her promise to Ellie. She sat facing a large painting of an old tree. Its limbs were gnarled, as if it were crippled with arthritis, yet there was something regal and strong about the tree, despite its contorted posture. She was usually more of a photography person, but found the canvas surprisingly compelling.

One of the sisters brought her eggs and coffee. She had barely picked up her mug when Joline pushed her chair out.

"This is a drag, but I have to run back into town this morning. Bryce has moved our meeting up yet again and he wants to see me today."

Ellie's fork hung in the air, mid-bite.

"Today? How can he do that?" Tess said, her question sounding more naive than she intended. She had to figure out the next move.

"He's got some property not too far out of town. He flies his private jet in whenever he likes and pops up a tent, if you can believe it. His way of getting back to nature. Fortunately, he doesn't make me meet him in his tent."

"There were a few things I was thinking about picking up at the market for the kids that I didn't manage to buy yesterday," Ellie said, meekly. "I'll come with you."

Tess was horrified. Ellie clearly wasn't thinking straight.

"I'll go down too," Tess said. "I could use some connection time with the office."

"Great. I'm meeting Bryce at a bakery right across the street from the internet cafe, so we can meet there when we're done."

Ellie jerked her head toward Tess. Her eyes were wild with desperation.

"I don't think you should go into town, Ell," Tess said slowly, running through the options in her head as she spoke. Ellie narrowed her eyes at Tess. "You need to conserve your energy today. The idea of this plant drug is crazy enough. The last thing you should do is go into it feeling weak. Fasting saps your energy, and it's even worse at a high altitude." She put her hand on Ellie's arm and looked her squarely in the eyes. "I think you should stay here and rest. What you need in town can be dealt with later."

"Tess does make a good point, Ell. Resting before the ceremony is the better idea. I would be doing that if it weren't for Bryce."

Ellie's face dropped into an expression of total defeat.

"But I gotta get going," Joline said, standing. "Don't look so left out, Ell. We won't be gone long. And then we'll do a soothing meditation this afternoon to prepare."

Tess parked the car about a block from the bakery. Slinging her computer bag over her shoulder, she contemplated what to do. She didn't know if Gavin had any idea what she or Joline looked like. When you're in the throes of an affair, do you spend time looking at snapshots of friends and family? She might not recognize him either, unless he was the lone American in the place. She only had the memory of one photograph to go on. Granted, it was a photograph that was the centerpiece of their room for a few months, but a photograph nonetheless.

"Mind if I come in to say hello to Bryce?" she asked. "I haven't seen him since the investor showcase."

"Of course," Joline said. "I'm sure he'd love to see you."

As they opened the door of Harina, Tess scanned the room. There were twelve tables with mismatched chairs, about half of them occupied. She immediately spotted Bryce sitting to the left of the door. Joline headed his way. An older couple shared a bowl of fruit at the table next to him. A man sat alone two tables away, but he was way too young to be Gavin. She surveyed the other side of the room and immediately saw the strawberry-blond hair, shorter and more groomed than she remembered, but unmistakable. He was sitting alone close to the counter. If he had looked to the door when they first walked in, he had already returned to the paper he was reading. She digested the setup and created a mental plan. Step one was to dispatch with seeing Bryce. She approached his table.

"Well if it isn't Tess Whitford," Bryce said. "You're the last one I would have guessed would follow Joline down here."

Tess thought she saw Gavin's head pop up at the mention of her name, and turned more fully toward Bryce. Silicon Valley was a casual place, but seeing Bryce Gardner in shorts and a t-shirt, looking like he hadn't showered in three days, was off-putting. He smelled of sweat and dirt, a mixture of scents she might find alluring after Parker's mountain bike rides, but not something she associated with business. The only familiar thing about him was the thin leather portfolio that sat on the table. He took that with him everywhere.

"Always ready to support my friends," she said, shaking his hand. "Congratulations on the sale of Guardian, by the way. That was a great valuation."

Bryce tipped his head in acknowledgment. "And your GLUT 1 drug? Charlie says you may be knocking on the door of something viable?"

Tess bristled. Bryce was tennis buddies with her biggest investor and probably knew they were burning through thirty-two thousand dollars every day that they were late for trials, like a slow but alarming leak in a high-performance tire.

"We're working on it," she said. "I don't want to hold up your meeting. Just thought I'd stop in and grab a breakfast roll."

"You already ate breakfast," Joline said.

"Not really. You forced me out the door too fast." Tess faked a smile.

As she walked over to the counter, she felt Gavin's eyes on her. Maybe he had seen a recent photo of her after all. She pointed through the glass display to a cone-shaped pastry with powdered sugar on top, and rummaged through her bag for a pen. Grabbing a napkin off the counter, she quickly scribbled her message. The woman behind the counter placed her pastry in a bag and rang up her purchase. As she brushed past Gavin's table, she dropped the note onto his paper and hurried toward the door.

"See you later, Joline," she called from the door, the cliché of the loud American, but she didn't want Gavin to do something stupid like jump up and introduce himself. "Good to see you, Bryce."

Clutching her paper bag, she headed across the street to the internet cafe.

TWELVE
Joline

"You didn't tell me Tess would be down here with you," Bryce said, blowing on his coffee. "Do you want something to eat?"

Joline shook her head. "She's the third in the college trio I mentioned."

"Ah," he said. "That explains it. She's sharp. I wish Charlie could get her to stop working on such insignificant diseases and do something that might actually have some market scale."

"They're called orphan diseases, and for the people who have them, her work is hugely significant."

"Fair enough," he said. "It just may never pay the bills."

She didn't know what he meant by that. Tess's company was well funded, and she had always done fine.

"Any news from Mallory?" she asked.

"No."

Bryce glanced out the side window. He had done everything Joline had suggested to repair the relationship, including writing Mallory a heartfelt letter of apology that revealed a vulnerable side she was quite certain his children had never seen before. Waiting to hear back from her directly was killing him.

"My sense is that she's almost ready to see you, but she's still holding out for Peter. She won't do it without him."

He closed his eyes and shook his head. "I don't know what else I can do."

"Peter has agreed to meet with me in person when I get back," she said. "It's a good sign."

"Good. That's good. He may have a harder time forgiving me, but tell him not to stand in his sister's way. We've got to get her down here to see the work we're doing. She'd love it. She might actually be proud of her old man." Bryce pulled his lips into a smile that didn't register across the rest of his face. "Anyway, thank you." He covered the top of his cup with his hand, as if he didn't know where else to put it. "I miss her. I miss them both."

"I know." Joline could feel the compression of his loneliness, like a dried-out plant that has become too small for the pot. She had never intended to become this kind of mediator, almost a family therapist, but he had come to her a desperate man. She couldn't resist trying to help. And he trusted her.

Guilt washed through her. She never should have told Tess and Ellie about his health and family issues. He had come to her in good faith, and she had no right to break his confidence.

"You said there were things to discuss about the center?" she asked.

"Yes, some exciting developments I need to fill you in on." He sat up and sipped his coffee. "But before we jump into that— I'm sorry, I should have asked right from the start—how is your friend? Have the shamans been helping her?"

"Thank you for asking, and thanks again for this week," she said. He had suggested that Joline expense the week as part of her research. She didn't like the idea of Ellie's quest being associated with a business objective, but she appreciated the relief from the expense. "It's early yet, but we'll see."

"I hope you don't mind me saying, a teacher I worked with in Nepal recently told me that death is not something to be feared. It isn't the end. It is simply our souls shedding our bodies so we are free to move on to the next phase."

Joline had heard this many times. She even believed it, logically. But it felt different when the person in question was your best friend, your brother's wife, and the mother of your beloved nieces and nephew. It is those left behind that bear the hard burden of death, something she had learned from Tess.

"I'm sorry. I didn't mean to upset you. I personally find the thought comforting," he said.

"No, it's okay." She forced herself to focus. "Marco tells me you reserved the room at Casa Munay for six months? That's kind of you."

"Not kind. Just a logical move. You told me Mama Rosita is one of the most revered shamans around, right? And that she no longer sees people who aren't staying on her property—"

"Unless they are part of her community," she added.

"Right," he said, waving his hand as if brushing that idea aside. "But if we have control of who stays there, then no one can get access to her while we build unless they are a guest of ours. And you said it yourself. Casa Munay is a great story. Generations of shamans living and healing on that property. It makes it quite special. Authentic. You've always said we need authenticity."

"I've explained that you can't just make an appointment with her, right?" She was sure she had made this clear to him. "She has to feel the need to serve someone. It's not at all a guarantee of staying there."

"I know. That's okay. Builds the mystique," he said.

She was confused. One sparsely furnished room didn't fit with their vision for the retreat center, or the requirements of their future clientele. She decided to play back his own words to him to make sure they still registered.

"But we've said that the kinds of people we're targeting would demand totally different accommodations than something as simple as Casa Munay," she said. "By building a separate facility, we can take guests out into the world of the shamans, but they know they have three-hundred-thread-count sheets to come back to."

"That's the best part." Bryce sat back and smiled. "The real-estate engineers have been doing some research, and the land at Casa Munay is fully buildable. It's the perfect site for the retreat center."

"What land at Casa Munay?"

"Those huge fields that run along the road on your way in? They're flat, which is hard to find around here, and fully build-able."

And the site of the community farm, she thought. "But not for sale," she said.

"Are you kidding?" he said. "Mama Rosita practically kissed me when I gave her the cash for the room rental. She was actually giggling. She would swoon over what I would pay her for her share of that land."

This is why they made a strong team. He was known for his business savvy, but he needed her to help sculpt the right energy for the center. There was no way Mama Rosita and Marco would sell that land out from under the community, but it was essential that Bryce understand the underlying issue.

"Even if you could buy it, it's not the move we want to make," she said. "There are a huge group of families that rely on that land. And there are no other jobs for them. If that farmland goes away, they would be devastated. That would be bad karma for the center, not to mention get you on the wrong side of the locals. We'll find somewhere else."

"Joline, you think I haven't learned anything from you? Give me some credit." He shifted to the edge of his chair and leaned halfway across the table. "I know about those families, and this will be great for them. A win-win. It's turns out that by old tribal law, that property is actually jointly owned by everyone on the hillside. Tradition has been that the shaman—and in this case it has always been someone in Mama Rosita's family—runs the show, so the land has been used as a homestead for that family and joint farmland for everyone else. Half these people probably don't even know that they actually own a section themselves. Heck, Mama Rosita probably doesn't even know the rule. But my guys estimate we could buy out those families for an average of ten to fifteen thousand dollars apiece."

Oh my God. He's trying to put a price on sacred ground.

"Short money to us," he said. "But do you realize how much money that would be to them? They have been deprived for generations of their proper share of that asset. We can fix that. They all walk away with serious cash, and we get to control the land that surrounds us." He took a sip of his coffee. "Not to mention cleaning up the hillside of those shanty houses. You couldn't invent a better deal for all sides."

The smell of sweat mixed with stale coffee drifted across the table, making Joline feel slightly ill. She could already envision families piling their pots and pans onto the family goat, their brightly woven blankets tied across the kids' shoulders, a clutch of cash stuffed in the pocket of the eldest as they wander away. Divine connections, lost.

Bryce was still talking. "Now, I recognize that it's human nature to be resistant to change, so I'm going to make the decision even easier for them. Anyone who agrees within a week gets a ten percent bonus on the price. My guys think it's overly generous, but I want to be fair, more than fair. The paperwork is just about ready to go. I asked the team to get it done in a hurry so you can get this in motion next week. I know you want to get back home for Dylan. But it shouldn't be hard. Once we get a majority of the families to agree, the rest will see how great this is for them." She knew if he could, he would have reached around and patted his own back for what he considered to be a magnanimous deal.

"Mama Rosita won't support this," she said.

"She'll get ten times as much as anyone else. She'll be delighted. She can go live like a queen in Quito."

"But this is their life. These people rely on each other. They don't have anywhere else to go."

"Don't be condescending, Joline. People are resourceful. I'm talking about giving them a huge financial boost. They'll be praising us for it. And think about all the people the center will help."

She could see the excitement in his eyes. He honestly thought he would be doing something generous for Mama Rosita's clan, the strong helping the weak evolve to a more modern life, a life he was convinced was better. But something precious would be forever lost. She could almost hear the backhoes and bulldozers clawing at the sacred land that had stood witness to the mountains and moon for centuries, all in the name of bringing spiritual healing to a cadre of American executives. He couldn't actually want to make that trade-off, not if he fully understood the consequences. She had to make him understand.

"I'm telling you, Bryce. It would be a massive mistake. You need to trust me—"

"With all due respect, Joline, I didn't hire you for your

real-estate expertise. You found us Otavalo, all the shamans. It's the perfect place. But my job is to deal with the money and the logistics of building. You focus on creating the best experience for our clients when they get here."

"You hired me to be more than an activities counselor on a cruise ship." Her face was hot. "The energy matters, Bryce."

"No need to get feisty," he said. "This is why we have a team. Different skills, different roles. Real estate is not in your job description."

She wasn't getting through to him. She needed some space to get centered. Then she could help him see.

"I've got to run to the restroom," she said. "I'll be right back."

THIRTEEN

Tess

Tess found a table at the back of the internet cafe and sat facing the door. She would see Gavin, assuming he came, and would easily spot Joline if she headed over sooner than expected. Her note had told him not to follow her right away, but hopefully he wouldn't wait too long, either.

Seeing Bryce wrangled her. On Sand Hill Road, the address of all the biggest venture capitalists in Silicon Valley, success was easily measured—the more money an entrepreneur made for his investors, the higher up on the pecking order they lived—and everyone knew exactly where they stood on the list. Bryce resided in the upper tier, a place where politeness toward those on the lower rungs was strategic, a hedge against some upstart leapfrogging to the top. Tess had made her investors decent money on her first company, but hadn't made them a dime yet on BioZang. She would probably always be looking up at the bottom of Bryce's dangling shoes, and they both knew it. His comments to her felt false, encouragement in the most patronizing way, like he was patting her on the head and sending her back to the kids' table.

Tess logged onto her email and waited while eighty-six new emails uploaded. She scanned the sender names to find the latest report from Rafferty, her chief scientist. As soon as she saw the subject line, her pulse banged on the side of her neck. *Urgent: Expenditure Approval Needed*. He was requesting to triple the number of cultures they were testing to ensure an appropriate volume of positive samples to meet the new deadline for the FDA. She opened her latest balance sheet. She had exactly eighty-seven days of cash left. Rafferty's request would inhale nearly half of that cash. If his suggestion worked, and the drug was successfully placed into trials, raising a bridge round to get them through to approval would be no problem—it was the only way her investors could protect the millions they had already poured into the company. But if this last series of tests failed, she would be in the worst possible position to raise money, and her company would be dangerously close to that grim moniker known as "the walking dead," not officially deceased, but not likely to survive. The word would get passed around the Sand Hill Road gang between tee shots, and partners and junior associates alike would claim they always knew BioZang wasn't ever going to be successful. It wouldn't be long before her investors would agree and move on to the next entrepreneur panting at their door.

She wrote an email back to the lab approving the increased testing. She tried to give them encouragement while emphasizing the importance of getting it right. It was critical for them to understand that the stakes were high without cramming the entire future of the company into their petri dishes. Success would be credited to them. The possibility of failure was her burden to bear.

She shouldn't be doing this from a distance.

Tess was so engrossed in word-smithing her email that she didn't see Gavin until he was standing at her table.

"You're Tess," he said.

She nodded. "Please, sit down."

"Where's Ellie?"

Tess took the time to really look at him. He was certainly handsome, his boyish look weathered slightly by a few gray streaks and deep laugh lines beside his eyes. He looked to be in decent shape. She guessed he was a runner, lean and strong. His eyes were what gave her pause. They were navy blue and filled with oceans of sorrow.

"She planned to come, but then Joline—do you know who Joline is?" Gavin nodded. "Joline had a meeting at the cafe, so Ellie couldn't come."

He stared at his hands. They were freckled and slightly tan. He wore a Seiko watch with a leather band. No ring. Not like Ellie.

"How is she? How is she feeling?" he asked.

Tess wasn't interested in any substantial conversation. Her role was clear.

"Look. Here's what I know. Ellie ended things with you several months ago. She needs to focus on her family. You need to go away. You need to leave her alone."

Gavin looked her straight in the eyes.

"Did Ellie tell you to say that?"

"Why did you even come down here? What gives you that right?"

"I—listen, when I let Ellie go, I never intended it to be forever. I mean, I left it up to her. I always thought she would come back to me in time. Maybe in a few years, maybe it would take until her kids went off to college, but I didn't care. I was sure she would. I was willing to wait. But now—I had to see her."

She sat back in her chair. This was college all over again. Ellie thought it had been over, but Gavin had never been ready to let go. Tess pictured David, oblivious to this whole situation, waiting desperately at home for his wife to get back, ready to shepherd her through the end of her life. She didn't want to be at this table with him anymore.

"You don't get to make that decision," she said. Her voice was shaking. "Ellie is too sick for this. Go home and let her be."

He put his hand on her arm.

"Can I ask you to do one thing for me? For Ellie? Tell Ellie that I will be here for the next two days. I'm at the Santa Maria Hotel right in town. She can come find me anytime. If she doesn't, then I will go. But it needs to be her choice, not yours. Will you tell her?"

Tess hesitated. She should just tell Ellie that he had to leave town, end it for good, take the burden off her. But she needed Gavin to leave before Joline walked in, and suspected that the best way to shut him down was to say what he wanted to hear.

"I'll tell her," she said.

She watched him evaluate her expression. The indigo of his irises shimmered when he spoke.

"I can see why Ellie loves you like a sister. Thank you."

He lifted his bag onto his shoulder and left Tess with her own reflection, flat against the gray of her computer screen.

Tess stared at the email she had written to the office for a full two minutes after Gavin left without reading a word, her mind flitting between the various scenarios that might unfold based on what she decided to tell Ellie. She could control how this played out. But the look in Gavin's eyes was hard to ignore. She wished she had never met him, never seen firsthand how deeply he loved Ellie.

She finally sent her email. Timeliness was more valuable than perfection. Everything was in the hands of the lab. She knew she should update her board on the situation, but she had limited time, and there was something more important she needed to do.

She logged in to a clinical pharmacology database. The connection wasn't as fast as home, but it wasn't bad. She made several attempts to spell the name she thought Joline had used for the plant. It sounded like eye-a-wha-ska, but nothing came up as a possible match. She knew that the young man at the cashier's desk spoke at least some English. She had no idea how complicated it might be to explain what she was looking for, but figured it was worth a shot.

"Hi," she started, standing in front of his desk, a simple wood table with pieces of tile stuck to the top. "My friend is doing a, ah, ceremony? With a plant of some sort. I'm trying to remember its name. It's something like eye-a-wha—"

"Ayahuasca?" he asked.

"Yes." She was surprised at his quick response. "Could you write that down for me?" She felt like an idiot in front of this kid, like she was standing in a library in Berkeley trying to figure out what marijuana was.

He ripped a sheet of paper off a pad on the desk and wrote the word down for her.

"Are you looking for a ceremony to join?" he asked. Did people hock this stuff on the streets?

"No," she said, taking the paper. "Just needed the name. Thanks."

Back at her laptop, she carefully typed in the correct spelling. The search came up empty. Of course. Ayahuasca wouldn't be its clinical name. After a quick Google search she found the technical term: Banisteriopsis caapi. The pharmacology site finally clicked to a blue results page, but there was a frustratingly limited amount of information. It was listed as a "primary source" of Dimethyltryptamine. DMT. No surprise. DMT was key to many hallucinogenics. Classified as a Schedule I drug in the U.S., meaning illegal.

But wait.

"That doesn't make sense," she said out loud. Mayu had said they would drink it. DMT wouldn't affect the consciousness unless it was inhaled or injected into the bloodstream directly. If they drank it, the enzymes of the digestive system would break it down before it ever reached the brain. There had to be something else.

Tess switched to a botany site she used on occasion and found what she was looking for. Ayahuasca had two active elements. DMT and MAO inhibitors. Of course. MAO inhibitors allowed the DMT to cross the blood–brain barriers and ensure a good long trip.

MAO inhibitors.

No way.

The instincts that had been trickling through her mind all morning exploded like gas touching fire. Ellie had gone back on antidepressants a few months ago. Her system was teeming with MAO inhibitors already. Taking ayahuasca would be like overdosing. Ayahuasca could kill her.

FOURTEEN

Joline

Joline shut the door of the cafe bathroom and could touch all four walls from where she stood. The encasement of the overhead light doubled as a tray for dead bugs, and the white of the ceramic sink had faded to gray, scrubbed so often with disinfectant that the glaze was gone. She never imagined she would long for the ladies' lounge at Bryce's club in San Francisco—the upholstered sitting area with the long row of mirrors and full-time staff member holding out towels seemed ridiculous—but at least there she would have enough space to breathe.

Disappointment weighed on her. She thought she had finally found her place in the world, the contribution she could offer to the universe that would feed her passions and make a positive difference. She had seen the opportunity to partner with Bryce as a divine gift. It was perfect. She had been the one to stretch his thinking beyond the P&L, to challenge him to take emotional risks, not just business risks, to do the hard work of examining his life and his relationships. The retreat center was meant to be a larger incarnation of those same ideas, a carefully balanced venture. And a key part of that would be integrating with, not pushing aside, the local people. But he just couldn't see that money was no replacement for real community.

She looked at her face in the mirror, the lines getting deeper on her forehead. How had following a path guided by her inner truth brought her here? Of course, she couldn't deny that the financial upside of working with Bryce had entranced her. She would soon be able to pay off her loans from David. And she had finally bought an apartment for herself and Dylan, a place he would always be able to call home. It had been a stretch, even with her new salary, but the bonuses that would be coming her way would fill in the gaps. But she didn't want to do it like this.

What Bryce wanted to do was a mistake, whether he saw it or not. The question was what to do about it, how to convince him his plan was deeply flawed. She was well practiced in telling him tough truths when it came to relationships, but challenging his business decisions was virgin territory.

She ran through her options, not liking any of them. If she marched out there and threatened to leave the project if he insisted on building at Casa Munay, he would call her bluff, she was sure of it. She would be out of a job, and he would go ahead with his plan anyway. She couldn't afford to be out of work. No, she couldn't just disassociate herself with him, she had to stop him. But he wouldn't be dissuaded easily. The problem with someone as smart as Bryce was that he had thought through all the angles already, and had an answer for every objection she could throw his way.

No, she had to work the other side of the equation. She would have to gather the families together and advise them to act as a group and agree not to sell. There was no guarantee they would all agree, but at least it would give control back to the community as a whole. Yes, that made sense. She had to let Bryce think she was happy to go along with his plan, and then do what she had to do in the background, after he left town, after Tess and Ellie were gone. She would be doing him a favor. They would eventually find a different location, and the center would be more successful for it.

She stared at herself, disbelieving her own toxic thinking. Did conviction in her own beliefs loosen with age, like taut skin? How pathetic. If there was one thing she hated more than greed, it was dishonesty. She couldn't look Bryce in the eye and lie, and she couldn't keep taking his money and work under false pretenses. She had to be nothing but honest with him.

But maybe she was being too dramatic about all of this. He had paid her to analyze various options, find the pluses and minuses of various locations. Otavalo wasn't all pluses, and she hadn't even shared that with him yet. She had to hope it would be enough.

She sucked in long breaths of cinnamon-spiced air through her nose on her way back to Bryce. She sat squarely on her chair, and pressed her palms on the table.

"Can we back up for a minute?" she said. "There are a few things about Otavalo that your real-estate guys may not know, the first being about the internet."

"What about it?"

"The technical infrastructure in Otavalo is almost nonexistent. Very few internet connections, all hard-wired off really old cable. Our clients will demand high-speed connections. We'd have to lay down fiber-optic cables for hundreds of miles for that. It'd be too expensive."

"We wouldn't lay cable. We'll put up a tower," he said.

"The shamans won't allow it. They believe that interferes with their communications with the Apu, their mountain gods."

"That's ridiculous."

"I'm serious. They won't go for it. And no infrastructure gets approved without agreement from all the local medicine people. And that wouldn't be the only infrastructure approval you'd need."

"Every project has obstacles to be overcome, Joline. We'll figure out a way around that. I just know that land is the right place for the center."

"I vehemently disagree," she said.

"I'm not asking for your approval, Joline. This is a done deal. I don't get why you're against it. It's good for everyone."

"Bryce, stop for a minute and reflect on what you are doing here. This is exactly what we've been working on—redirecting a plan without consulting the rest of your team, the team you've hired to figure this out for you. It's demoralizing, and not good for business."

"It's good for business when it's the right decision."

"But you'll destroy a whole community if you take away that land. It's not right, and it's not what the center is meant to be about," she said, unable to stop the emotion from sneaking into her voice.

"Ah, this has become personal for you now," he said. "I appreciate the relationships you are creating here, Joline. That's very important. But you can't let them stand in the way of our vision."

"But disrespecting those relationships is not what I brought you down here for."

"Not what you brought me—are you kidding me? Who do you think has paid for every single trip you have made down here?" There was an edge in his voice she had never heard before.

"Okay, but coming down here in the first place was my idea."

"Ideas are cheap," Bryce said. "And what did you expect exactly, Joline? That you would open this world up to business and no tree would be put out of place? That the money that would flow down here wouldn't create any change?"

"No, but it doesn't have to be like this." Her own voice sounded childish in her head. She cursed him.

"Tell me then, how should it be?"

A deep dread settled into Joline. She felt the seesaw tipping back to Bryce's old way of thinking, all their work together losing its weight. She thought they had made meaningful progress together, covering intense personal ground, like the night they worked with the soul cards. He pulled a card with a picture of what looked to her like a hawk building a nest. But as soon as he saw the card, his hands began to shake. He said all he could see was a vulture. He'd had a major breakthrough that night, admitting how hard he had been on the people in his life. How much he wished he could apologize for. But that was a different person than the one sitting in front of her now.

"That's what I thought," he said. "You have no alternate plan."

"No, but I can't let you go through with this one," she said, trying to summon the divine power of the truth through her words.

"Excuse me?" he said. His whole body went eerily still, the way a leopard stops moving just before a strike.

"Let me make myself perfectly clear." His voice was quiet, but she felt his anger. "You're under contract with me. If you do anything to sabotage this, not only will you destroy the opportunity for a new start for these people, you will find yourself in court. And don't forget. You have a non-compete with me. You walk away and you can't go anywhere near your old business for two years."

She had tripped an invisible wire. He was actually threatening her, legally. She realized that all her work hadn't begun to diminish his predatory instincts. There is no compromise in the food chain, only winning or losing. Bryce didn't lose.

"Bryce, I know you're hurting about Mallory—"

"This is business, Joline. Don't confuse the two."

She clenched her fists and kept as still as possible, sensing that anything else she might say would provoke him further. She couldn't afford that. She had Dylan to consider. Everything could unravel overnight if she wasn't careful.

"Now, assuming you would still like to be part of this retreat center," he said, popping back into the congenial tone she had associated with his voice until now, "which will be wonderful, you'll see, I'd love to keep you as part of my team."

She tried to lick her lips, but her tongue felt like a dried-out sponge.

"Good. Before I forget," he said, "I'd like a ceremony organized for Saturday. At the roundhouse with Mama Rosita."

Mama Rosita? Ellie needed Mama Rosita, not Bryce. And there was no way she could force any of it to happen, especially now that she knew his plans.

"But—" she started. Bryce put up his hand.

"I'm sure you'll figure out how to make that happen considering what a strong relationship you're building there. Consider it a show of good faith. See you then."

He leaned on the table as he stood, knocking it off kilter, his coffee cup tipping into the saucer. Not the sturdy mahogany he was used to in his California boardrooms. Ignoring the slosh of coffee on the table, he snatched up his portfolio and slid it under his arm, then banged through the bakery's screen door.

Joline walked across the street in a daze. She remembered Don Emilio's comment, that she was like a bird restricted from flight.

She felt more like a feather, thrown up one minute on a fortuitous gust, kicked sideways by a fierce gale the next, with no weight of her own to control her destiny. She was grateful Tess was here with her. Tess would help her figure out what to do. She needed to steady herself, to find some measure of calm. It was critical for helping Ellie heal. Dammit, she loathed Bryce for interfering with that.

As soon as she was within ten feet of Tess's table, she slammed her laptop shut and stood up.

"Are you out of your mind giving Ellie this stuff?" A small group, huddled behind one computer, looked up with distaste. Tess didn't seem to notice. "Do you have any idea how dangerous it is?"

"Whoa. Slow down." Joline tried to emphasize her hushed tone. "What are you talking about?"

"Ayahuasca. Do you have any idea that if it is used in combination with antidepressants it could cause a coma, even kill her?"

Christ. Another storm. She took a deep breath and tried to tap into an inner calm.

"Come outside and we can talk," she said. "Sorry," she whispered to the threesome still staring at them. With each step toward the door, she tried to banish Bryce from her mind. She would have to be logical and measured with Tess.

"Ellie stopped taking Lovan as soon as we planned this trip," Joline said, "so we could have a plant ceremony."

"What was that, like two weeks ago? It can take three or four weeks for the drugs to get completely out of your system."

"She was on a low dosage. She'll be fine."

"How can you be so casual about this?" Tess had stopped on the sidewalk. They were still half a block from the car.

Joline walked back to where Tess stood rooted. "Tess, you have to trust me. People here have been using the plant for centuries."

"And have people around here been on antidepressants for centuries?"

"She stopped two and a half weeks ago. Please don't worry."

Tess threw her hands into the air. "I swear everyone has completely lost their minds this week. This is so fucked."

"Tell me about it," Joline said, pulling open the door of the car. "I just got completely railroaded."

"Don't try to change the subject. I was already worried about Ellie throwing up all night, but this is completely insane." Tess put the car in drive and pulled out onto the road. "I knew this trip was a bad idea."

"No one made you get on that plane, Tess."

"And if I didn't? Someone has to be here to protect Ellie."

"Protect her? From who, me?" Joline tried to keep her voice at a reasonable pitch, but felt the anger rising inside her gut.

"You have to admit that this is a little out of control, Jo. It's not like we're trying to fix someone's fertility issues and want to see if a voodoo doll does the trick. Ellie doesn't have any time," Tess said. "And somehow you think it's okay to give her a completely unregulated drug, and make her sick. And risk a coma? Or worse? I knew I should have talked her out of this trip."

"I don't believe this." Joline hated being stuck inside the car. She rolled down her window. "And tell me how it is that you and everyone else in Ellie's life are so convinced it makes sense to hook her up to a constant drip of toxic chemicals that will do nothing but, oh let's see—make her throw up, even though they've told her it will only give her a few more months. A few more months of what? Looking like a skeleton about to snap in half? Is that what you want for her? I'm trying to help her find life again. Find a way back to life." Her voice cracked. She couldn't let Tess get to her. Tess had never believed in any of this.

"I'm not pushing her to do chemo, Jo—"

"Okay, but what then? If one of your biotech buddies had a new drug, even something totally untested, you'd get it for Ellie in a heartbeat. How is that any different? You have this blind faith in labs and PhDs and spreadsheets."

"Blind faith? Jesus. It's my business, my life's work," Tess said.

"But it's not the only answer. I wish you could see that," she said. She was baffled by the confidence Americans had in big pharma, which had been around for a nanosecond compared to ancestral medicine.

"We're both grasping for something that's not there," Tess said. "When is it time to face reality?"

"Reality is what we envision it to be," Joline said. She couldn't let Tess's doubt get to her.

"I wish that were true, Jo. I just don't see it."

"You *choose* not to see it," Joline said.

"What's that supposed to mean?"

"Like when we were in college. Remember how we were all on the same cycle? After about four months of living together you could've placed bets on us getting our periods within twenty-four hours of each other, remember? That was our energy aligning."

"Oh, here we go again," Tess said.

"I'm serious. You know it happens to women all the time. But medicine doesn't explain it, does it? Does that make it untrue?"

"Science would call that a phenomenon. It happens, but it's not predictable, or necessarily replicable."

"Dammit! You needed to take that left," Joline said. Tess hit the brakes, but couldn't make the turn. "Just make a right up here and we can go around the block. God, you're maddening sometimes."

"Look," Tess said, circling the block. "I have to talk to Ellie about this to make sure she completely understands the situation. Make sure she is making an informed decision."

"Informed decision? You seriously think I haven't talked this all through with her already?"

"I need to hear myself that she understands the risks."

"Fine. Have it your way. But please don't fill her head with a lot of worry. The plant has a way of magnifying what we bring into the ceremony."

"She certainly doesn't need more to worry about, that's for sure."

When they got back to the left-hand turn, Joline saw in her side-view mirror what looked like the same silver Nissan behind them. Was she imagining that? Who would want to follow them?

"What did you mean, by the way, when you said you got railroaded?" Tess asked, her tone friendlier.

She wasn't in the mood to tell Tess she had been right about Bryce, but she couldn't exactly ignore the situation. She replayed the conversation to Tess.

"I knew it," Tess said. "What a bastard."

"The thing is, he really thinks he's doing something positive. He just can't see the other side," Joline said.

"You actually buy that?"

"I don't know anymore." Had she been that wrong about him? "And Mama Rosita isn't getting any younger. Once she's gone, the community will have a harder time staying on its feet. I'm sure he will use that to his advantage."

"But what about Marco? Can't he take over?"

"Marco wasn't born to be a shaman—they can tell from the time you're like four years old. It's not something you learn. The gift isn't always passed down directly."

"Does Bryce even know that?" Tess asked.

"Everyone knows it. Marco's father was the last in the line. After he died, and since Marco has no children, it's quite sad. A long line of shamans will come to an end."

They drove past a small house that clung to the hill beside the road. Overlapping slabs of ruffled tin made up a roof, which didn't look completely attached to the cement blocks beneath. A laundry line the length of the house stretched out to one side, with two little gray t-shirts, a yellow bra, and a white sheet flapping in the dusty breeze. Inside, a small television flickered with the scenes of a cartoon. These people relied on Casa Munay.

"Is there any upside for the community?" Tess asked. "I assume the center will create jobs."

"Mama Rosita could live another twenty years. Shamans often live well past one hundred. I can't ruin the rest of her life," Joline said.

"Bryce threatened you?"

"He's right. I'm under contract." A ridiculously detailed contract she had known she couldn't negotiate any more than she could change the liability waiver at the paintball park Dylan liked. Sign or don't participate.

"Well, I'm not under contract," Tess said.

"Don't be a hero. He could make your life difficult too if he wanted to."

"He'd probably nail you for involving me anyway. I hate to say I told you so."

"Then don't." The same silver car was still behind them. "Have you noticed that that car has been behind us since town?" Joline asked.

Tess shot up in her seat and stared at the rear-view mirror.

"Are you sure?"

"Pretty sure. Why would anyone want to follow us?"

"Shit." Tess's grip seemed to tighten on the wheel.

"I'm sure it's nothing," Joline said. She heard the waver in her own voice.

As they pulled into the driveway at Casa Munay, she watched the silver car slow, and then continue on, the glare off the windows making it impossible to see inside.

FIFTEEN
Ellie

*E*llie pushed off the railing with her right foot to keep her hammock chair swinging. Brightly lit clouds dragged a patchwork of green shadows across the lush mountains in the distance. She had been swinging in rhythm with the wind for what seemed like hours. On each backswing, her hand grazed the fur of the fluffy dog—Chi-Chi, she now knew its name—that had followed her upstairs after breakfast, as if knowing she needed the company.

All morning she had imagined multiple versions of what might have happened in town, what Joline might have seen walking into that bakery, what Gavin had said to Tess, if they'd even had a chance to talk. Exhausting all possibilities, she had eventually forced herself to focus on simpler things, the sway of the chair, Chi-Chi's deep breaths, the smell of the freshly tilled dirt that surrounded the Casa.

Two dragonflies darted across her line of vision, silvery wings sparkling in the sun. The flickering reminded her of the fireflies back home, and life before. One perfect July evening, David had brought home a picnic to take out on their boat. The five of them pushed off the dock as the sun began to wash the lake in an orange glow, the heat of the day folded into a soft summer breeze. They splashed into the reflections of the watercolor sky, Lilly still bundled in a life preserver and Ellie's arms, Hannah and Connor practicing dives and flips until the sun went down. By the time they pulled back into the dock, it was deep into dusk. And as they walked the short path back to their house, Lilly draped over David's shoulder, they all saw at once that their lawn was lit with fireflies.

"Look, Lilly, the angels are here," David said into her hair.

"Connor, run inside and grab the Mason jars," Ellie said. She loved this time of year, when night fell as a gentle shade against the heat, the kids drawn back toward the steady glow of home.

Connor handed out the jars, one this year for Lilly too, and they hopped around the lawn until they had each captured a firefly inside. Ellie showed Lilly how to hold the jar upside down and then screw the top into place.

"Now," Ellie said, kneeling in front of Lilly, "you have to name your firefly, make a wish, and then let it go. Once it is set free it will protect you all year, your own personal angel."

She clearly remembered every firefly's name from that night. Lilly's was Blinky. David picked Winky because he knew the rhyme would make Lilly giggle. Connor's was Draco, and Hannah chose Ariel. Ellie named hers July, the best way she knew to keep that perfect night with her all year. After the lids were unscrewed, and the fireflies set free, the last part of the ritual was to say in unison, "Thank you Blinky, Winky, Draco, Ariel, and July for keeping us safe all year long." Little Lilly got so tongue-tied that they never got through it without dissolving in laughter.

She was diagnosed with lung cancer two weeks later. They hadn't collected fireflies since.

Ellie heard the crackle of gravel in the driveway and steadied her swing. A murmur of voices rose as car doors opened and then faded at the entrance of the inn. The sliding door opened behind her.

"Well, that was interesting," Tess said casually. Ellie searched her voice for warnings.

"You mean revealing in the worst possible way?" Joline's words were pointed. Chi-Chi popped up as Tess and Joline leaned their backs against the railings on either side of her feet.

"How was your morning?" Joline asked, changing her tone, peering into Ellie's woven cave.

Ellie put her feet down and looked at Tess for guidance. The pause threatened to mushroom into something requiring an explanation if she didn't compose herself.

"Quiet," she said. "Yours?"

"Highly disappointing," Joline said. Tess gave a tiny shake of her head. "Turns out that Tess may have been right about my business partner."

"Bryce?" Ellie worried the relief in her voice sounded off. "What happened?"

As Joline recounted her conversation with him, Ellie tried to translate Tess's body language for clues about Gavin. Other than the small shake of her head, she was sending no signals. Did the shake mean that she hadn't seen Gavin at all?

"You know what, Ell?" Joline said. "I don't want to fill your day with negative energy. Enough about Bryce. I think we should meditate together. I have a soothing journey in mind that would be a great way to prepare for tonight."

She couldn't think of anything that sounded less relaxing. She needed to know what had happened and if there was a plan.

"Let's not put the cart in front of the horse. We agreed that I could have a talk with Ellie first," Tess said. "I learned some things in town about ayahuasca, Ell, that I want to go through with you to make sure you really want to do this tonight."

"Here we go," Joline said, frustration creeping back into her voice. "Fine. Talk."

"Without you playing counterpoint to everything I say, Jo. We're adults here. Let me have a little time with Ellie. Then if she's still game, you can have all afternoon to do your thing."

Ellie felt like a child, when she used to watch her parents argue and they forgot she was still in the room.

"I'm going to get the roundhouse ready. I'll come get you in a bit." Joline squeezed Ellie's shoulder before walking off the deck.

"Let's go for a walk," Ellie said. "I could use a change of scenery."

"I found a great path yesterday," Tess said. "Not too steep, great views."

She followed Tess around the side of the Casa with Chi-Chi

wagging happily behind them. Outside the back door of the kitchen, Marco split a log with a huge axe. A white dog with black spots snoozed at his feet, apparently accustomed to the bang and splinter of the job. Marco waved to them before balancing another piece of wood on the tree-stump workbench. Smoke billowed from a grill next to the kitchen door, reminding Ellie that she was fasting. Her stomach grumbled, already hollow.

"I see you found a friend," he said, wiping his hands on his pants.

She looked back at Chi-Chi. "She found me, actually."

"One of the pleasures of the Casa. An extra connection to Pachamama."

Ellie tilted her head.

"Four paws on the ground are better than two," he said. Ellie had never thought of it that way. "If you're going for a walk, there is a great waterfall not too far away. She loves it." At the mention of the word *waterfall*, Chi-Chi started to bounce up and down. Marco laughed. "See what I mean? It's a winding trail, but she can show you the turns if you'd like to go. It's a perfect day for it."

"Winding means steep. Not great while you're fasting," Tess said as an aside. "Thanks, Marco. Maybe another time."

When she and Tess kept walking, Chi-Chi started to whine, apparently alerting them that they were going the wrong way.

"It's okay, Chi-Chi. They're fine," Marco said behind them.

As they walked, she waited for Tess to say something. Tess snapped a branch off a bush and slowly shed it of its leaves, pulling the sinew of each one as far down the stem as it would go. Competing emotions somersaulted inside Ellie, like rocks on the edge of a wave, banging into each other with the push and pull of the tide. She wasn't at all clear what she wanted. In her logical mind, there was no reason to see Gavin again. The relationship was over. She should have had Tess make that clear. But just knowing he might be waiting for her made staying away feel impossible. It wasn't something she could have explained to Tess. As painful as seeing him would be, as horrible as it would be to say goodbye again, the pain was real, true. With Gavin, she wouldn't have to lie about that.

"Did you see him?" Ellie finally asked.

"He's come to get you back," Tess said.

"Get me back? Is that what he said?"

"He said he was sure you would come back to him eventually. So he's pressing the issue."

"But that's not what I told him," Ellie said.

She had replayed that last conversation over in her mind many times, internally speaking the words that had surprised even her that winter day. A freak ice storm had hit Nantucket, and she had told David she had to go check on the cottage. Gavin had shut off the water at his inn to be safe, and they ended up staying at the Jared Coffin House, risky because the innkeepers all knew each other. Walking through the lobby with him, she could no longer ignore how reckless she was being, how foolish it was to pretend she could live two lives.

"I told him it was over," she said.

"And that was it?"

"He didn't want to accept it. That's when he made me promise to tell him if I ever got sick again. I knew that saying yes was the only way he would let me leave."

She remembered the bitter wind on her face as she walked the cobblestone streets to the ferry. The cold stung her throat when she breathed, her tears robbed of their warmth as soon as she blinked them off her lashes. She had buried her face in the loom of her scarf and left the island for the last time. She didn't think she'd ever see him again.

"Why didn't you tell me about Gavin before?" Tess asked.

The path opened onto a clearing with a one hundred and eighty degree view of the valley and the noble mountains beyond. Ellie caught sight of a bird floating on an updraft, wings outstretched, perfectly poised in the air. It wasn't trying to fight the wind, nor was it being swept up in its force. The bird looked almost stationary, only flapping its wings occasionally to maintain equilibrium. She wished she had that level of stability in her own heart. She was too easily swayed by Gavin.

"Part of me wanted so badly to talk to you about it, but I was ashamed. I am ashamed. You love David." The bird found a gust to play with, angling to one side for a sweep around an invisible curve, then tilted the opposite way to correct. "And it would have put you in an impossible position with Joline. I couldn't ask you to keep a secret like that. Or expect you to sit at our dinner table without feeling awkward. Without revulsion written all over your face."

"Revulsion? I would never judge you."

"I wouldn't blame you if you did."

"I hope you know that I will stand by you. No matter what," Tess said. "I just can't lose you."

Tess enfolded her in a hug. She held on tight. Tess's sorrow went deeper than most, even though she never talked about it. Ellie knew Tess was worried about the black hole that might engulf Connor, Hannah, and Lilly, an abyss Tess understood all too well. Ellie was comforted that Tess would know just how to rescue each of them.

"My kids are so lucky to have you in their lives," she said, and then pulled back from Tess.

They turned around to walk the path in reverse. Sunshine speckled the ground from openings in the canopy above.

"Ellie, we have to talk about the ayahuasca," Tess finally said.

"But how did you leave it with Gavin?" She needed to know. Had Tess told him to leave? It wouldn't have surprised her, and the tired part of her hoped Tess had done just that, taken it out of her hands, ended the drama. Which would be better for him, to think she didn't want to see him, or to know with certainty how deeply ingrained he was in her heart? Which would be better for her?

Tess sighed. "He's here for two more days. If you want to see him, I know where he's staying. If you don't go, he'll leave."

It was up to her to decide.

SIXTEEN

Tess

The rest of the afternoon evaporated with nothing to show for it, and by the time Tess walked into the dining room for dinner, anxiety ripped at her like barbed wire. She'd utterly failed in convincing Ellie not to try ayahuasca. Ellie had read too many stories about people vanquishing a terminal illness by using it, and Tess had been caught between refuting every outrageous claim Ellie had heard, and Parker's theory that belief in a positive outcome was critical. In the end, she knew she had to let Ellie make her own choice.

But sitting and waiting for impending doom weren't in her make-up, so she decided to call the office and then go to dinner. Before leaving the room, she gave Ellie a long hug punctuated with words of encouragement—fear would not serve Ellie well, Joline was at least right about that. Her call to the office did nothing to lift her spirits. It only uncovered more issues that she couldn't solve from Ecuador. Tripling the size of their sample set created a layer of logistical issues that boggled the mind. What she needed was a stiff martini and slab of rare sirloin, two things she was quite sure were never on the menu at Casa Munay.

She walked through reception and down the long white hall to the dining room, the click of her clogs on the tiled floor mocking the quiet of the night that lay ahead. Halfway down the hall, multiple voices filtered toward her from the dining room. When she pulled the tapestry aside, she saw that her usual table was full of men mixing laughter and rapid Spanish. Their dirt-smeared jeans tucked into tall rubber boots suggested that they worked on the farm. Tess was about to go into the kitchen to ask where she should sit when Marco touched the back of her arm.

"You are not partaking in the ceremony?" he asked. "Then you must eat. Please, come with me."

Nodding at one of the women serving the large group, Marco led Tess to the edge of the room and held out a chair for her at a small square table, washed with a rust-colored paint. Before she had even settled in her seat, there was a full place setting laid down in front of her and another set across from hers, with a wine glass at each. Marco put his hand on the back of the other chair.

"Perhaps you'd like some company," he said.

She met Marco's eyes. She had planned on an evening of solitude. "That would be lovely. Thank you."

"I hope everything is all right? Since you're not in ceremony?"

"Not for me. And I'm more than a little worried about Ellie." She explained her concerns about the MAO inhibitors and antidepressants. Marco listened quietly but didn't say anything.

"Have you done it before?" she asked.

"The plant ceremony? Once." His expression remained neutral.

"And?"

"It's a deeply personal experience. But powerful. Mayu will take care of your friends," he said.

He poured wine from a carafe into two goblets. The thick blue glass with its lines of tiny bubbles trapped inside turned the wine a deep shade of purple. Her senses rallied when a whole half of a chicken appeared at her place, smelling like it had been rolled in rosemary and grilled on cedar planks. It wasn't steak, but it did look delicious. As she picked up her fork, her eye caught the sparkle of Parker's ring on her finger. She had assumed she would be alone and had wanted to see how it felt. Marco didn't seem to notice.

"Did you grow up on this property?" she asked.

"From the time my parents died." He wiped his mouth with his napkin and took a sip of wine. "They lived right near here, though, so yes, this has always been home."

"Do you mind if I ask how they died?"

"Mudslide," Marco said. "They were out collecting plants— my father was a great medicine man—and they were caught in a horrible rainstorm. Swept off the mountain."

"My God, how old were you?"

"Eight," Marco said. Tess recognized the residue of pain in his eyes. "A thousand-year-old Lucuma tree that stood on this property was lost that day. My grandmother always said that as soon as she saw that tree fall, she knew my father was gone."

"A burden no child should have to carry," she said. "I'm so sorry."

"You understand loss," he said, refusing to let her drop her gaze. One thing hadn't changed from the other night: Marco wasn't afraid to broach uncomfortable topics. She twirled her ring under the table with her thumb.

"My mother died when I was twelve. It's not something many people understand."

Marco put his fork down and placed his hands on the table.

"My father was pretty destroyed. He couldn't really function for a while. I mean, he was there, but it was like living with a ghost."

"Who took care of you? Did you have grandparents nearby?"

"No family nearby. I was okay. The bigger problem was my little sisters. They were only nine and seven. They still needed so much. I couldn't bear to watch them grow up in a broken house-hold, so I did what I could to make things normal."

"I doubt life felt very normal to any of you."

"I just tried to do whatever was needed. Simple things. Like groceries. After we had gone back to school, and people stopped delivering food, I realized that my father still hadn't gone to the grocery store. So I grabbed my mother's credit card and went on my bike." She shook her head and smiled, remembering countless afternoons peddling along with her basket full of gro-ceries. "And then when I couldn't get a dial tone on our phone one night, I realized that my father hadn't paid any of the bills. When I went into his study to ask him about it, I saw him sitting at his desk, staring at nothing. I think he did that for hours every night. I was afraid to break that silence."

"Silence is scary for a child," Marco said.

"Yeah, so instead of asking him about it, I just got very good at forging his signature." Tess laughed.

Marco nodded his head but kept looking right at her, waiting for her to say more. His eyes seemed to be searching her well of memories. She swallowed.

"My mother always read to us before bed, so I did that too." She was too old by then, but her sisters had still loved to huddle in their mother's bed to hear *The Velveteen Rabbit* or a chapter from *James and the Giant Peach*. The three of them crammed into Tess's small bed every night, one on each side, their little heads leaning against her shoulders. "And if either of them had a nightmare, back into my bed they would come."

"You survived by taking care of them," Marco said.

"I'm still kind of amazed that they are adults now, with kids of their own," she said, taking a sip of wine. "I think I understand how mothers must feel watching their children grow up and form their own families, that empty nest feeling."

"Lonely, I would think."

"I hate when people ask me why I never had kids. They don't get that I have in a way. I mean, it's not like I get to be Grandma or anything—I'm too young for that anyway, right?—but I have more responsibility to them than just being their sister. It's different." She caught herself. "I'm sorry. I don't usually dive into it like that."

"As you said. Not many people understand." He kept his eyes on her while he sipped his wine. "It explains the responsibility you feel to protect your friends."

"And here I sit eating dinner while God-knows-what is going on in that hut," Tess said, the worry coming back. She had gotten through her whole meal without thinking about them once.

"Mayu is a master," he said, and placed his hand on hers, over her ring. "Don't worry."

"There's no way I'll be able to sleep until this is over." She sat back in her chair and tapped her fingers on her thighs. Her pulse kicked into her ears.

"I know what you must do," he said. "I'll be right back."

Tess glanced around the room while he was gone, abruptly aware that they hadn't actually been alone that whole time. She was surprised at how easily she had told Marco about her childhood. Maybe it was because she had been dreaming about her mother every night since arriving in Ecuador. The images from the night before came rushing back to her, exact playbacks of moments from the year before her mother died. Eleven-year-old Tess lying on her stomach on the back lawn doing her homework while her sisters played on the swing set, her mother grading biology tests, telling her that she would be a shoo-in at MIT if that's what she wanted. The day Maggie, who was supposed to be her best friend, told her she wasn't good enough to play volleyball with the other girls at recess—Tess hadn't hit her growth spurt yet—and her mother going straight to Kimball's, buying a volleyball, and practicing with her every day after school until the recess gang named Tess captain. And her favorite memory— sitting with her mother on the porch one night after her sisters were in bed. Tess had strep throat and was chilly with fever even though it was balmy outside. Her mother had wrapped her in a down comforter and snuggled her into one of the rocking chairs on the porch. She sipped melting sorbet to sooth her throat, and listened to her mother read out loud until she drifted off. Whenever she reconstructed that memory, she immediately heard her mother's chimes tinkling overhead. Her mother loved those chimes. She said they sounded like a nymph running across the strings of a harp.

Tess reached for her wine. One glass later, Marco returned.

"Please follow me."

He led her outside, showing her with his flashlight where to step when the shadows of the moon obscured a gnarled root in the path. They walked down the hill in the opposite direction of where she understood the roundhouse to be. There was a tall fence outlined against the dark purple sky. On the other side, he stopped in front of an enormous barrel with the top cut off. Three wooden steps led up one side. Steam swirled around the edges.

"Our Japanese soaking bath," he said. "It will help you relax so you can sleep."

"But I don't have anything," Tess said, gesturing to the obvious fact that she was fully clothed.

"That's no problem," he said. "Once you get in, I will come back with a towel and a robe." He said this without moving, looking right at her. Was he expecting her to undress in front of him, out there against the dark landscape? The idea of it seemed rather erotic to her, baring her body to him while he watched, and then slipping under the water.

"The temperature should be perfect, but if you need it a little colder, there is a faucet in the back over there," he said, pointing to a handle next to the steps. "Take your time. I'll be back before it is time to get out."

Marco bowed his head and left. So the fantasy was in her head. Marco was playing the part of hotel manager again. But she hadn't even agreed that she wanted to get into the tub. She wasn't sure she wanted to get wet. She walked around the edge of the fence to follow him back, but he had already disappeared into the shadows of the trees. Tess knew she could call out to him, but the stillness of the place kept her quiet. She would wait for him to get back. It would kill some time, anyway.

A cloud of steam wandered across her face, tempting her. She rolled up her sleeve and touched the water. Scalding. Perhaps it was the contrast with the cool night air, but it was too hot to get in. She looked out beyond the bath. It was situated in the perfect spot, poised in front of an expansive view, the quarter moon blanketing the whole area with a faint golden glow. Tess had never seen such a tall tub, perfect for someone her size. Usually, the water only came up to her waist, or breastbone, if she was lucky. This one was clearly designed to have the water above the shoulders. The idea of it made her relax a little. She turned on the faucet and listened to the cold water whir through the nozzle.

When the water was easier to touch, she stirred it with her hand. The temperature was approaching that ideal state of muscle melt. When else would she have the chance? She stepped out of her clothes and hung them on a hook in the wall, conscious that Marco could come back around the corner at any moment. She climbed the ladder, the night air pocking her normally smooth skin. The water was still a bit hot to the touch of her foot, so she splashed it carefully over her arms and legs before fully submerging.

As the steam billowed up to her face, Tess re-clipped her hair to keep her ponytail dry. She submerged to her chin and looked at the stars. She could hear the faint hoo of an owl in the distance, and the rustling of a tree behind her. It was an extraordinary spot. Parker would have loved it. The pull of nature while being sprawled out in his birthday suit. She chuckled. That man did love being naked.

The bubbles in the water fizzed around her legs. She slipped a little lower, softening her shoulders. A waft of steam poured over the edge of the tub. She realized with some measure of surprise that she missed Parker. Now that he was back in her life, she would have liked to be able to talk to him about the craziness going on with Ellie. He always had good perspective.

David had given Parker the thumbs-up the first time he had come out with her for Thanksgiving weekend in Minneapolis. She had brought a few other men to that house before, and Ellie was always hopeful that the new guy would be the final guy, but Parker was the only one that got David's full approval. It might have been the night that she and Parker volunteered to cook, and after she scorched the tenderloin, he saved dinner by picking up a pizza and some very nice wine. Or maybe it was the flat on the rental car, which, despite the fact they could have missed their plane, he used as an opportunity to teach Connor how to change a tire.

In bed that night, Parker told her for the first time that he loved her. She remembered feeling lucky to be loved by someone confident and self-reliant, someone who needed little from her. And now he wanted it all.

She fiddled with her ring. She wasn't used to jewelry, and the ring was tight on her swollen hand. She re-read Parker's letter in her mind. It hadn't really left room for her to talk him out of his ultimatum, call his bluff. She knew in her heart that there was no bluff. It was all or nothing. Her choice.

Marco came around the corner with a fluffy white robe and a towel. "How is the temperature?" he asked, walking toward her. While she hoped the deep tub and the reflection of the moon would give her cover, she wondered what he could see. She crossed her arms over her chest.

"Perfect," she said.

He hung the bathrobe on a hook and put the towel on one of the steps.

"I hope you are relaxed." He bent toward her, his shoulders headed in the direction of hers. Was he going to kiss her? Tess pulled her head back toward the edge of the tub. He leaned past her and turned off the cold water. She let out her breath.

"Don't stay in much longer," he said. "You don't want to become faint." He was right. She had probably been in long enough. "I will wait for you up the path to make sure you get back all right."

She listened to his boots on the path as he walked away. When she couldn't hear him anymore, she stepped out of the barrel. She steadied herself. The wine and heat had made her a little lightheaded. The water evaporated off her in tufts of mist, as the cool air caressed her skin. She put on the robe Marco had left her and stepped into her clogs.

She found Marco on the path, not too far away, looking at the stars. He quietly turned up the hill and walked ahead, letting the beam of the flashlight trail behind him. He turned to her inside the entrance of the Casa, presumably to say goodnight. How many hours did she still have in front of her to worry about Ellie and Joline?

"Would you be willing to light the fire in my room?" she asked.

Marco smiled. "Of course."

SEVENTEEN
Ellie

As soon as Tess had left for dinner, Ellie took a hot shower to calm her nerves. What if Tess had been right, and this was all a bad idea? The antidepressants should be out of her system by now, but Tess's level of concern had left a residue of fear in her. She needed to think about something else.

She wondered if Tess had gotten any closer to a decision about Parker. She hadn't even asked about that today. Some friend she was at the moment. She hoped Tess wouldn't sabotage her relationship, like Joline assumed she would. Tess was at her happiest with Parker. She'd never forget the first night she met him, at the surprise party. She and Joline had used the time before Tess arrived to suitably grill him. He didn't seem to mind; in fact, he seemed to rather enjoy it. Joline warned him that Tess had managed to find something about every guy she was determined to change, and asked him what his might be. He smiled and said, "I'm not sure, but if you find out before I do, will you let me know?"

When Tess arrived, she let out a whoop of happiness at seeing her and Joline a day early, and then became completely flustered when she realized that Parker was there, that she and Joline had met him without her, had already had a drink' with him without being there to orchestrate any of it. Tess tried to hide her discomfort by making the rounds, greeting work friends, and laughing too loudly at someone's joke, but Ellie could tell she kept him in her sights. It wasn't long before Tess gave up, and spent the rest of the evening right beside him, their hands effortlessly entwined.

Ellie dried off and put on a pair of loose pants and a light cotton sweater for the ceremony. She felt a bit woozy, probably from the fasting.

"We should get down to the roundhouse," Joline said. "Ready?"

"Maybe I should call the kids really quickly."

"If you want," Joline said. "But my advice is to stay present. Stay in the energy here at Casa Munay. I know you're feeling nervous. But everything's going to be fine."

"Tell me what I should be focusing on through this. I want to make sure I'm doing this right. If I have a chance of this helping me, I don't want to blow it."

Joline pulled her over to the couch and held her hands. "You are not going to do it wrong, Ellie B. Not possible. The plant is there to guide you and help you. All you have to do is try to be welcoming of what she wants to show you. Try not to resist any color or vision or words she brings forth. If you are open to hearing and seeing what the plant wants you to see—and again, like Mayu said, they're things that are already inside you—then you will heal in the places you need it most."

"Do you really think it can work?"

"You know I do." Joline pulled her into a long hug. "This may sound impossible, but try not to put pressure on yourself. You got yourself here, you are about to go accept the plant, you've done everything you can to make this possible. Just try to stay open, and the plant will guide you."

"Stay open," she repeated. She needed to get this right.

"Stay open."

It was a bit like being told to relax with a scorpion crawling up your arm. But she trusted Joline. She had to do her best to trust the plant, too. Even though she didn't know exactly what that meant.

"All right," Ellie said, "let's go."

They walked around the right side of the Casa in a direction they hadn't gone before. A tiered garden stepped down the hill-side, full of herbs, many of them in full bloom. Down the slope another twenty yards, a stone cylinder with a messy head of straw hair for a roof squatted in the grass. As they walked far-ther down the hill, it seemed to grow, as if standing up for their arrival. They walked three-quarters of the way around the perim-eter before coming to a large woolen tapestry that covered an opening in the wall. It was heavy and stiff, more like a rug than a blanket. Inside was one big, circular room. The walls stood ten or twelve feet high, gray stones locked together with mud. A pile of large, smooth rocks hunkered in the middle of the room, some of them molten red with heat. The light in the round house was dim. Dusk was settling into night, the sky visible through four small rectangles that had been cut into the wall near the roof. The rocks gave off a faint glow, but two candles on the floor were the strongest source of light.

Large straw rugs loosely covered the dirt floor. Four long spongy mats, each covered with a thick woolen blanket, were set up like makeshift beds, a square pillow at the end of each, and an extra blanket folded on top. The butterflies in her stomach flapped into a frenzy when she noticed that beside each mattress was a large plastic bucket.

Mayu was already there. As soon as she and Joline walked in, he stood up from his mat, smiling shyly and looking relieved, as if he had been unsure that his guests were actually going to attend the party. He gave both of them a silent hug. He led Ellie to the mat on his left, and Joline to the one on his right.

"Where is the other friend?"

"She won't be joining the ceremony tonight," Joline said.

Mayu nodded, sitting on his mat. Joline unfolded her blanket and put it over her lap. Ellie did the same.

Mayu asked if there were any questions. When she and Joline said nothing, he explained that he would give each of them a small cup of the brew. She was almost disappointed not to see a cauldron hanging from a stick. Instead, Mayu put his hand on a plastic water bottle full of a brown sludgy liquid. Once they had each drunk the plant, he said, he would blow out the candles so it would be dark.

"Light is too much when in our journey. Too confusing. Best

to keep your eyes closed. Go inside."

Then he restated that it is perfectly normal to feel sick at first. He picked up the bucket next to him. Why he had his own bucket, Ellie didn't know, but he cradled it on his lap as he spoke.

"It is possible that you no get sick." She tried to release the tight shrug of her shoulders. "But it is fine, if you vomit. Is no problem. It is good. A release. It is the plant helping you get rid of things that are bad for you. Emotions that are problems for you. This why you are here." Ellie tried to get hold of a deep breath. She knew she wasn't likely to escape the gruesome part of the experience. She tended to get sick on the early end of the spectrum during her chemo treatments. And then a weakness would overcome her that she worried might never leave her system.

"But there are many other kind of release. You may cry." He pulled his fingers down his face, miming. "This fine too. It is release. You may laugh. You may aah, aah, aah—moan. This is good. This is all release." A new anxiety fluttered into her chest. She imagined a night full of strange sounds, some of them coming, uncontrollably, from her.

"It is important that you not go to your friend. You may hear her cry or she may sound like she having a hard time. This is my job. This is what I do. It is important that each person be able to stay in their own journey."

She looked over at Joline. Joline mouthed, "It's okay."

"I say this morning," Mayu went on, "that the journey should last five or six hours. I will know when you are done. But please don't leave until I am able to do a healing with each persons. Then you may stay here for long as you like, or you may go back to your room."

Ellie shifted on her mat. Her ankle bones were already getting sore. The mats weren't that thick after all.

"How are you?" Mayu asked. She looked up, not sure who he had asked. "All persons. How are you? Good?"

Ellie was feeling anything but good. Terrified was more like it. She reminded herself that Tess would only be a holler away. That was an idea she could hold onto.

Mayu said it was time to start. He lit a hand-rolled cigarette and took a long pull. Cupping his hands in front of his face, he puffed the smoke into them and wafted it over the top of his head. He started to mutter in Quechua. It sounded like he was reciting some incantation he had repeated hundreds of times. Strange words, in a repetitive pattern. Something like *Wayra-tira soon-a-rye, soon-a-rye-a-tee* and *Chu-chu washa soon-a-rye, soon-a-rye-a-tee*. He repeated the same thing with the smoke two more times, and looked skyward with his last words. Anita had said that tobacco helped protect against the bad spirits, washing away any that have been released. She wondered if there was anything within her awful enough to warrant protection.

Mayu picked up his plastic bottle and filled a small cup, twice the size of a shot glass. Ellie was grateful that she wouldn't have to drink more than that. He nodded to Joline and waved her over. As Joline knelt down in front of him, he stood and put his hands on her head and then on her shoulders. He blew smoke onto her head, pulled on the neck of her shirt, and puffed down her spine. He was protecting her, too. Her eyes were closed and her face looked calm. He stood for some time with his hands back on Joline's shoulders, chanting in a whisper, as if it was meant solely for her. Then he knelt back down and handed her the cup. Joline took it in one gulp, but grimaced and had to swallow twice to get it down. Then she stood and returned to her seat.

Mayu nodded at Ellie. As she knelt in front of him, she became acutely aware that she was moments away from the point of no return. Once she swallowed his offering, she would have no ability to go back. When he put his hands on her head and on her shoulders her whole body began to vibrate, as if he was passing an electric current through to her with his touch. She hadn't seen Joline shaking, but she was sure that her trembling had to be visible. When he removed his hands, only an echo of the tremor remained. He surrounded her with smoke and then placed his hands once more on her head, making her quiver again. He was more than a man at that moment, he was connected to some mystical force. A sense of trust and confidence spread through her.

He handed Ellie the cup. She took a deep breath to avoid the smell of it as she gulped, but she could not avoid the taste: pungent, sweet, and bitter at the same time, like swallowing chewing tobacco. She almost gagged but managed to get it down.

Turning to go back to her seat, she forced one more swallow to get the dregs off her tongue.

She pulled the blanket back over her knees and tried to calm a rising sense of panic. She had no control over anything that was about to happen. She had taken the drug and could only wait. She tried to relax. She had to stay open. Be open, that's what Joline had said. She focused on her breathing and began reciting two things in her head. "The plant will take care of you," and "be open." And Mayu was there. He would know what to do.

After she sat down, Mayu filled the cup for the third time. Ellie didn't think she could stomach a second round and hoped it was simply an offering for his version of an altar or something. But then Mayu drank the cup himself, and her relief turned to horror. How could he possibly take care of them if he was going to be in the same state? Her logical mind was demanding she make sense of it, but just then she started to feel a liquid glow cascade through her limbs.

Mayu blew out the candles and then poured water on the glowing rocks. Smoke sprung toward the ceiling, darkness blanketing the room with a hiss. After her eyes adjusted, she could see just a hint of purple through the cut-out windows at the top of the wall. The rocks held barely any light anymore. She closed her eyes. Be open.

Mayu began to sing, and Ellie was pleasantly surprised by the fluid beauty of his voice. He sang words she could not understand in a rhythm or melody unlike any music she had ever heard. She wanted to be inside that music. Her chin drooped to her chest as she listened. The room was swirling with his music, with his words. She tried to pick her head up, but her neck had the strength of a thread, unable to hold any weight.

Blue triangles whirred through her mind. They spun and receded. Like a kaleidoscope, the same shapes kept repeating, large to small, large to small. She tried to hold one in her sights and follow it, but that made her dizzy. She went back to his voice. His voice was where she wanted to be. Just as Mayu's melody bent around the curve of the roundhouse walls, a jittery rush from her limbs attacked her gut. Her face burned and yet she had started to shiver. The whirlpool inside grew urgent. She reached out for her bucket and pulled it onto her lap, under her dangling head. She didn't want to be sick, but she wanted the sickness out of her.

Darkness clutched her and she thought she might pass out. She gasped for air two or three times and then began to retch. Bile erupted from every cell in her body. Flashes of red and black pulsed in her eyes. The spinning shapes began to morph into scenes that she could barely catch on the periphery of her mind. A blue rectangle became a sloshing pool where Hannah was swimming. She walked toward her but found her feet walking down her driveway. Connor was shooting baskets and tossed the ball at her. When the ball bounced, it became Lilly, jumping on the trampoline, trying to turn a flip.

A toxic river pushed through her veins and she vomited again, hanging onto her bucket, praying to make it through. She had read that people called ayahuasca the vine of death. It had the power to drag a person to the verge of death, dangle them over the void. But what if the vine didn't release her? What if it pulled her under? What if she couldn't get back to her kids? She vomited again.

An image came into focus for her. She was somewhere she recognized. It was her kitchen, but everything was too bright, like a Technicolor movie that had been enhanced with too many unnatural colors. Connor was sitting at the kitchen table, his head in his hands. Ellie put her hand on his shoulder and he pushed it off forcefully. She thought she heard him say, "Don't touch me," before standing and walking away. Then Lilly was teetering on the edge of the counter by the sink, reaching up to grab an ice-cream bowl from the top shelf. Ellie covered the distance in an instant and caught Lilly just as her foot slipped off the edge. Lilly screamed as if she had just been doused with boiling water, or had just been grabbed by a monster. Ellie let go and caught a bit of her own visage in the refrigerator. Unlike the electric blue walls and Lilly's neon green dress, her own reflection was too gray, too dark to be her. She ran to the small mirror in the hall bathroom. She saw with horror that she was a charred version of herself. Her face was graphite black around the edges, her skin a crackling charcoal gray. The only color was where her eyes should be, orange cinders smoldering in the sockets. Ellie screamed, an echo of Lilly's scream. Then Hannah was in the door of the bathroom. She didn't seem afraid. But when she reached out to touch Ellie, her hand turned black and began to burn.

"No!" Ellie heard herself yell, but the sound was muffled as if she were under water. She reached for the bucket and heaved several times. Weakness grabbed at her limbs and the darkness behind her eyelids swirled in circles. She felt like she was going to pass out. She needed out. She needed help. Where was Tess? She tried to yell for Tess, but couldn't tell if anything more than a garbled moan came out. It took too much energy.

She hugged her knees and began to rock back and forth involuntarily. The room became very quiet and she heard a voice speaking to her. It was the plant speaking to her, from where she didn't know, but she was sure that's what it was. It was a language she couldn't understand, and yet she understood exactly what it was saying. As she listened, a deluge erupted out of her that overcame her. She put her head down as sobs wracked her body. The voice circulated through her, repeating the same thing until it had wrapped itself around every vein in her body, every organ, searching out her wounds and cauterizing them. She rocked and cried, her sleeves drenched from covering her eyes. And then the vine began to comfort her, injecting her with a cool mist that soothed the scorched sections of her soul.

Eventually her sobs subsided, and the voice receded until there was no sound inside the room accept the low hiss of the steam still coming from the rocks. She almost fell asleep, but was jolted by hands on her shoulders, arms reaching under her to scoop her off the mat. She was being lifted, carried. Tess must have heard her calling. Tess had come for her. She was so weak it was difficult to open her eyes. She let her head fall to the side and rest against a strong chest. It wasn't Tess. She breathed in and knew before she opened her eyes, by the sweet saline smell, that it was Gavin. He was cradling her in his arms and was taking her out of the roundhouse. Mayu was dancing in a circle, on his own trip, and didn't notice what was happening. She scanned the darkness for Joline, but couldn't place her before they were through the door.

Gavin spoke gently in her ear. "You were calling for help. I'm here."

She tried to tell him that he wasn't who she had been calling for, but still couldn't manage to get the sounds right.

"Shh. Don't try to talk. I'm here. You're safe."

She dozed against his chest as he walked. The cool air rushed against her cheek. She put her hand up to it to feel the chill, but couldn't locate her own cheek. She drifted off. When she came to again, Gavin was gently laying her back down on the ground, onto a beautiful thick blanket, like the ones made at the Nantucket Loom, lamb's wool and cashmere. The grass below was spongy, cushioning her. Gavin lay down beside her on the blanket and held her hand. She opened her eyes to a dazzling night sky, thousands of stars, some of them diving into the atmosphere at the speed of a slingshot. A tree branch swayed above them, the one visible anchor to the earth. Gavin rolled onto his side and stroked her hair. He ran his thumb across her eyebrow.

"I've missed you, Ell." He kissed her. Her mouth filled with mint and the cooling touch of his tongue. She instinctively wrapped her arms across his back and lifted toward him. He rolled on top of her and their mouths stayed entwined for a long time before she sunk her face into the side of his neck.

"I know you feel trapped," Gavin said. "But I know you still love me. You are my soul mate."

An awful feeling rose inside her, and Ellie thought she might be sick again. She swallowed, steeling herself.

"No! Don't say that. You don't get to say that," she shouted, and before she knew what she was doing, she started to pound Gavin on the chest, her fists working in the small space between their two bodies, hitting up at him.

"Whoa, Ell," Gavin said, trying to hold her wrists. "I'm not the one you're mad at. You're mad at David. He has no idea what you are giving up for him."

"No!" she yelled. "No, no, no! Stop it. I'm not giving up anything anymore." She freed her hands and put both palms on Gavin's chest and pushed at him hard, as if she could catapult him into the air. Somehow, his body lifted off hers, the weight of him leaving her legs, her belly, her chest, and all at once, he was gone. And then she was running through Nantucket in her mind, down familiar lanes, up staircases she knew well, and Gavin was nowhere to be found.

Ellie turned her head toward the comfort of the blanket. It was scratchy against her face. She felt for the grass to the side. There was just a thin mat and dirt. She looked up and saw criss-crossed pieces of straw in the ceiling. Mayu's singing weaved its way across her consciousness. She was still on the floor of the roundhouse. She had never left.

She sat up and grabbed the bucket. It sloshed as she jerked it toward her. The retching came more violently this time. How could she have anything left? Trying to catch her breath, she heaved again. Finally shoving the container away, she curled onto her side. She was interminably tired. Her head swirled, and every part of her body felt weak. She blinked at a holograph of Connor and Hannah and Lilly, waving at her. David might have been standing behind them but she couldn't be sure. She wanted to reach out for them, but couldn't raise her arms. She was too weak.

And then everything went black.

EIGHTEEN

Tess

Tess quickly changed back into her jeans and sweater in the bathroom and joined Marco in the living room. He was blowing on the fire he had built, coaxing the flames to ignite. She sat down on the couch behind him.

"Do you ever miss medicine?" she asked.

"Not really." He blew another long stream of air at the logs. "I found modern medicine less equipped to care for people than I had hoped."

She refrained from telling him what business she was in.

"And do you miss the U.S. at all?"

He sat back and watched his fire take hold before answering. "Only because of what I left behind there." He turned around and sat on the edge of the hearth. "The woman I went there with, Anna. She wanted to stay. She said we could build a better life in the U.S. We had different opinions of what was better. And I realized I went there for the wrong reasons. I could never have done what I really wanted there. And so I left."

"What you really wanted?"

"To paint."

"You're a painter?" She looked at his hands. She remembered the calluses on his palms. He was a painter?

"When I was a little boy I was always drawing. Using a piece of burnt wood on a stone, or the juice from berries, whatever I could find. I drew everything I saw. Trees, birds, flowers. Anything outside."

"How in the world did you go from painting to medicine?"

"When my parents died, I stopped drawing. I don't know what happened, but I stopped. I was lost. I had nothing. The only way I could think of to survive was to try to become who my father was supposed to be. My grandmother had been so proud of him. He was to be the next great healer." He paused and shook his head, still pained by the loss. "When Mama Rosita explained to me that I was not a chosen one, not intended to be a shaman, it was like losing him all over again." She wanted to ask Marco to move off the stone hearth and sit on the couch, somewhere less harsh and cold, but didn't want to interrupt. "I was very angry for a while. Very angry." Marco stood up and prodded the fire with a poker. The flames were bright. "I decided I could prove everyone wrong by becoming a real doctor." The word *real* was thick with sarcasm. "Stupid, really."

Marco's shirt moved with his muscles as he stabbed at the logs.

"So what happened?" Tess pulled a blanket onto her lap. The hair at the base of her skull was still damp.

"I went to see Don Emilio."

"Don Emilio?"

"He helped me understand that my place is in nature. That I see it differently than most people, and that my real gift is to translate that for others. To listen to nature and speak for her." Marco sat in the chair next to her side of the couch. He was close enough to touch. "As soon as he said it I knew I needed to go back to my painting."

Every time she saw him he was cutting wood, or fetching something from the kitchen. Did he actually paint, or was this a childhood fantasy living in the mind of an innkeeper?

"I'd love to see your work sometime."

"You already have. All the large paintings in the dining room are mine." He grinned.

She immediately remembered the painting of the tree, its wizened limbs fighting time.

"They're wonderful. Do you sell your work?"

"At the market sometimes. A gallery in Quito has a few of my pieces. But my real hope is to eventually make Casa Munay a haven for artists."

"How do you mean?" She had forgotten about Bryce and his plans.

"Mama Rosita and I have been saving to build a few small casitas on the property. They will be designed for artists who need a quiet place, who desire being in nature, a way to be in these sacred mountains and connect with their art. It is a different kind of healing. Painting saved my life, I think. I want to do that for other people."

"So this is a business, of sorts?" He was an entrepreneur, too.

"Yes. And a way to continue to help the community. It is important that I show them I can take care of them after Mama Rosita is gone."

"Are people worried about that?" She could almost sense Bryce hovering.

"They see her slowing. They know she doesn't perform many healings anymore. But the money from Joline's friend will help us build the first casita. I am really grateful to her for that, and the friends she has brought here." He looked at her intently.

He shouldn't take that money.

"Marco, there's something you should know."

Marco dropped his gaze to his hands and bobbed his head. "Yes, I can see it. You have someone in your life."

What were they talking about? She twirled her ring. "Yes, but—"

"But?" His eyes were so warm.

"I don't know if I can sign up for the long term. If that's what I want."

Marco nodded his head. "Too much risk."

Marco still didn't know anything about her.

"That's not it. I'm an entrepreneur. I'm all about taking risks."

"That's business. Those are risks you can analyze. Just like medicine. We are taught to use the protocol, weigh the odds. I'm talking about love. Love is a pure leap of faith."

"And leaps like that are dangerous."

"Yes. When we are intimate we are at our most vulnerable."

He hadn't blinked. She shifted in her seat and repositioned the blanket over her knees.

"We have a saying in my country. 'Only a flat heart breaks.' Flat, you know? Like empty. A heart without love is—what's the right word?—brittle, like a plate. If you drop it, it shatters. But a full heart." He grinned again. Tess noticed how perfectly straight his teeth were, how his eyes turned down slightly on the edges when he smiled. "A full heart is like a ripe piece of fruit. It will bruise, but it won't break. It does not mean you are not vulnerable. Any fruit that isn't tended to, that is left to wither and decay can be easily crushed. But a full heart? No."

"You think I'm afraid of getting my heart broken?" Was that what Joline had been saying? That she sabotaged her relationships to avoid ending up with a broken heart?

"No, no, I can tell that you are not. Remember when I told you about *ayni*? Giving what you can with unconditional love? I can see you have been practicing *ayni* with your friends for a very long time. Your heart is full of love for your friend. And you might lose her. But you would never back away because you are afraid."

How did he know all this? He seemed to understand her completely, and without judgment. She was so fixated on what Marco's next words might be, so aware of the air crackling between them, that when she first heard the rumble in her ears, she couldn't compute the source of the sound. In the seconds it took her to recognize the noise as thunder, a deluge let loose on the Casa. It started to pour, buckets of water gushing against the roof and the windows.

"How is that possible?" She asked, looking up, as if she could see the clouds above. "It was a beautiful, starry night."

Marco walked over to the sliding doors. "A very good sign," he said. "For your friends."

She tossed the blanket aside and joined him at the door. Rivulets of water snaked down the glass.

"Nothing in nature exists without water. It is in every creature. It is the source of life. And the source of all emotion. And for water to have the power to cleanse us and change us it must be in motion, always moving. Tears are one proof of that." He leaned on the glass door and turned to her. "Rain is particularly powerful. Tradition says that before the rain, the apus, the mountain spirits, fill the sky with their powers so they can gift them to us through the rain. It means that something is shifting. It is good."

Tess didn't know what to make of that. She had never heard a man talk like that before. She wanted to tell him he was being dramatic, it was raining over the heads of lots of people as far as she could tell, but she also wanted him to be right. They stood next to each other, watching the rain pelt the door. Their reflections were close.

"You have a full heart, Tess. You understand that you don't need to ask for everything from one person, from one source. You have your friends, your sisters. They have filled you with love."

Her face blurred against the dark sky, her body wavering in the glass. The current pulsing through her body was growing hard to ignore. And then Marco touched her, grazing his hand down her arm.

"I realize now," Marco said, his voice quiet, "I left Anna, not because I was afraid she might break my heart. People like you and me, we have already suffered so much loss, we know we can survive." He put his hand on her cheek. She inched toward him. "We're just not sure about everyone else."

Marco brushed his lips against hers, a caress that made her tremble. She wrapped her hands behind his neck, surprised by the softness of his skin. He was right. Hadn't she broken off with Parker in the first place because too much of his own happiness depended on her? And now he was asking for a lifetime guarantee. That was impossible.

She pulled Marco's face closer and opened her mouth to his. Marco's hands moved across her shoulder blades, down her spine, to the small of her back, pressing their bodies together. She ran her hands up the inside of his shirt as he explored her neck with his lips. She tilted her head back and felt him rising at her abdomen. She kissed him again, more urgently, craving that deeper connection. He picked her up effortlessly and carried her to the couch. He gently laid her down, his hand on the flat of her belly. She arched under his touch. His hand slipped under the top of her jeans as the door at the bottom of the stairs slammed open.

"Marco, *donde estas*, Marco!" a woman's voice yelled from below.

Tess met Marco's eyes. She questioned for a split second whether he would let the interruption happen. Would he admit he was there? Or could they hide in the cocoon the rain had created for them and keep the rest of the world out? But the panic in the voice below registered. Something was wrong. She sat up at the same moment that Marco jumped to his feet.

"*Estoy aquí!*" Marco called back. "*Qué pasa?*"

Tess straightened her shirt as Arabella rushed up the stairs. She was soaking wet. "*Ven. Mayu te necesita. Alrededor de la casa.*"

"What is it?" Tess asked, following Marco as he bounded toward the stairs.

"Mayu needs me in the roundhouse. Something must be wrong."

Her body went cold. "No," she said.

Marco took the stairs in threes in front of her. They both rushed past Arabella and ran out into the rain. Tess couldn't keep up with Marco in her clogs. She hit a patch of mud and slipped, slamming into the ground hard. Marco turned and she waved him away. "Go!" she yelled, pulling herself up, and limping the rest of the way. When she got to the outside of what had to be the roundhouse, she couldn't see Marco. The light from the Casa was too far up the hill to help. She held on to the stone wall and followed it around until she heard Marco's voice. He and Mayu were speaking rapidly to each other. She saw the doorway and tried to enter. Marco stopped her.

"Wait," he said, the rain banging off his shoulders. "One of your friends is still in her journey, so we must move quietly."

Tess couldn't see his face clearly. Was he joking? She swung the tapestry out of the way and stepped inside the cold dark room. The smell of vomit mixed with something like fertilizer assaulted her. She scanned the dim space for Ellie. Relief swept over her when she saw Ellie sitting up, hugging her knees. She was swaying and muttering. Clearly not with it, but physically she looked fine. What was the emergency? Then she saw Joline, lying on a makeshift mattress across from Ellie. She was shivering uncontrollably, convulsing on the floor.

Marco got to Joline before her. Wasting no time, he picked Joline up, cradling her like a child, and headed out the door. When Tess got back out into the rain, Mayu was standing there, his hands up in front of her as if to say *stop* or *slow down*.

"What the fuck is wrong with her?" Why did she let them do this?

"I stay here. Go help Marco."

She wanted to shove him against the wall but instead rushed back to the Casa, ten steps behind Marco the whole way. Upstairs, Marco laid Joline down on the couch. Her convulsions came in rapid waves.

"Bring me blankets from the chest," Marco said. "I think she has hypothermia."

"Are you sure? It's like sixty degrees out."

What if Marco was wrong and Joline needed some kind of antidote? What if she was having an allergic reaction to the plant? Tess grabbed four or five wool blankets and brought them to Marco. He already had Joline half undressed. Tess tried to put the image of herself on that same couch out of her mind. She touched Joline's cheek. It was freezing.

"Can you hear me, Joline?" Tess asked quietly. "How're you doing?"

Joline continued to shiver, rapid convulsions that shook her whole body. She still hadn't opened her eyes.

"I'll get some towels," Marco said. "Take off the rest of her clothes, she can't be in anything wet. Then you can dry her."

Marco waited to the side until Tess could get Joline dry and covered, and then they wrapped her in a deep bed of blankets. Tess sat on the edge of the couch and stroked Joline's forehead.

After about half an hour, Joline's temperature seemed to come up to normal. She had stopped shaking and her skin looked less ashen. She opened her eyes and asked Tess what had happened.

"You're back. Thank God."

Joline mumbled a few words, but Tess calmed her and told her to rest.

"Thank you," Tess whispered.

"I think she'll be fine," he said.

She nodded, avoiding Marco's eyes. What had she started? And did she want to finish it? Footsteps on the stairwell broke the silence. She stood up gently, careful not to disturb Joline, and met Ellie at the top of the stairs. Mayu was behind her. Ellie looked remarkably dry. She hadn't noticed that the rain had stopped.

"How are you?" Tess asked.

"Fine. Tired." She looked over at the couch. "What's wrong with Joline? What happened?"

"She'll be fine, thanks to Marco," Tess said, glaring at Mayu. "You should get some rest."

Ellie headed straight for the mat she had set up before the ceremony. To Tess's surprise, she gave Mayu a long hug before climbing under her blankets, fully clothed. Mayu turned and left without saying a word.

Marco took her hand. An invitation?

"I should stay with them," she said.

Marco nodded, rubbed her arm, and left the room, his hair merging into the darkness at the bottom of the stairs.

NINETEEN
Joline

Bright light diluted Joline's sleep. Boring deeper into her mound of blankets didn't help. Her body seemed vaguely distant, as if the connections between her brain and extremities had gone overnight from fiber optic to soup can and string. A wave of nausea surged. She had to have water. She peeked over the pillow and saw a glass of water miraculously set on the side table. Sitting up gingerly, she untacked her tongue from the roof of her mouth and took a tentative sip. The liquid sparked her senses, and an inkling of strength returned. She tried to remember what had happened.

"Hey." Tess tipped up from the chair next to the couch—had she spent the night there?—and crawled onto the cushions beside her. "How are you? You gave us quite a scare."

"What happened?"

Tess did her best to replay the scene after she and Marco had found her in the roundhouse.

"What a disaster." Joline rubbed her face. "How is Ellie? Is she okay?"

"I think so. Still sleeping. How do you feel?"

"Like hell." She rested the glass of water in her lap. "Like I got run over by a truck ten times. I was so sick. I could hear Ellie getting sick too. It was awful." She had heard such remarkable stories about people working with the plant, having divine revelations that changed their lives, or being cured of terrible things. She had also heard that the experience was hardest on those not willing to embrace the plant, people afraid to look deep inside. She put her head on Tess's shoulder. "Ellie must be ready to kill me."

"Actually, I had an amazing experience." She and Tess both looked over the edge of the couch. Ellie was still on her back, talking to the ceiling.

"You did?"

"I was really sick too. Really sick. In fact, I think I may have passed out at one point. But I had these visions." Ellie sat up slowly, wrapping her blanket around her. She tucked her hair behind her ears. "And I think the plant might have spoken to me."

"What did it say?" Joline was amazed.

Ellie had withdrawn into a thought. Something significant had happened. Joline waited for her to say more.

"I, wow. . . . It's a lot to process. I remember at one point feeling a deep sadness, and then water started rushing down everywhere, all around me. Like the sky was crying. Like it was washing me clean, healing me." Ellie's mouth quivered.

"It poured last night," Tess said, fixated on Ellie, "out of the blue."

"Really?" Ellie asked, wiping her face with her hands.

"I hope you let yourself cry with the sky," Joline said. "It's such an important release."

"I learned a lot last night," Ellie said, her eyes searching her blanket as if trying to remember it all. "I saw some things in a new way, that's for sure."

Joline was supremely grateful. She had come in with high hopes for the gifts the plant might bestow on Ellie.

"Anything you want to talk through?" she asked.

"I think what I need right now is food," Ellie said.

Tess looked at her watch. "Wow. It's almost eleven."

"I hope we can still get breakfast," Ellie said.

The idea of food brought the green bucket back into Joline's mind.

"You guys go," she said. "I'm wiped out. I need to lay back down."

She didn't move as Tess and Ellie got changed and put away their sleeping mats. She thought about lying down, but decided that repositioning the blankets would take too much energy. It was easier to sit where she was, feet up on the coffee table. She pulled a pillow onto her lap and felt for the knots and bumps in the woven cover. The rough wool made her feel grounded, a connection to an object with texture and weight.

Her phone trilled with a text from the table across the room. "Tess, chuck me my phone, would you?"

Tess handed it to her before leaving to go downstairs. She had a string of unopened texts, all of them from Bryce. The last one said: "Where r u? My RE guys are done with paperwork. We need to move on property ASAP. Call me."

She wasn't moving anywhere. She tossed the phone to the side of the couch, put her head back, and closed her eyes. She was enormously relieved that things had gone well for Ellie. But she couldn't also help feeling a bit embarrassed. Why hadn't she been able to embrace the ayahuasca? Wasn't she supposed to be the one open to revelation?

She heard a brush of feet on the stairs behind her. Ellie or Tess must have forgotten something and were trying to sneak into the room without disturbing her. She put up her hand.

"It's okay, I'm awake."

No response. She twisted to look over the back of the couch. Mama Rosita pulled herself up the last step and paused at the top of the stairs.

"*Buenas Dias*," Joline said.

Mama Rosita was breathing hard, and raised her hand in greeting before grabbing the railing again. She shuffled over to the couch and sat next to Joline. Her cheeks were red. She took a Kleenex out of her pocket and dabbed her forehead. After heaving under a big gulp of air, she put both her hands on Joline's head and closed her eyes. She moved her hands to Joline's cheeks, cupping them. Warmth radiated from her hands. Taking Joline's right hand in both of hers, she settled into the couch without a word, bringing to her mind the image of an elderly couple on a porch swing, watching traffic go by. In August. Mama Rosita's hand was actually hot. Joline relaxed, welcoming the wordless visit. Just sitting next to Mama Rosita made her feel better. She glanced at her phone, which was teetering on the edge of the couch.

"You fine?" Mama Rosita asked, finally.

"*Sí*," she said, wishing for the umpteenth time that she could have a complete conversation with Mama Rosita.

"Your journey. You were in water. *Achachay.* Cold, cold water. I could feel it," Mama Rosita said.

"Yes." Joline was stunned. She had forgotten about the water.

"Tell me, *mi hija*," Mama Rosita said.

"But—"

Mama Rosita waved her hand to cast aside Joline's confusion. "If I try to heal in English it makes me have to think too much. Not good for healing."

"But you speak English?"

"Who do you think taught Marco? But if I keep the secret, I don't have any conversation I don't want to have, right?" She giggled. "Tell me. I think maybe it is important."

"You are amazing." She kissed Mama Rosita on the cheek. "You feel hot. Are you feeling all right?"

"Don't worry. Forget about it. Tell me."

She thought back to the cold, the water, and tried to remember what had happened. An image began to poke its way through the cotton balls clogging her brain.

"I was at Lake Tahoe, this huge lake in the mountains near home, in California." She shifted sideways to watch Mama Rosita's face and make sure she understood her words. "I was with Bryce—he has a beautiful house that looks out over the lake." Images began to pop into her head, one after another. Maybe more had happened for her than she realized. "Yeah, I remember, we were swimming on the lake. See, he's got this big yellow dock way out on the lake. He's so proud of this thing he has built, like an enormous yellow lily pad. Anyway, he brings people who work with him there as a reward. He's kind of famous for setting up huge picnics on this dock, and people spend the day out there and swim. Do you understand?" Mama Rosita nodded, tiny beads of sweat outlining her forehead. The room still felt chilly to Joline, but that could be residue from her journey. "In my vision, it was me and him on his big yellow dock. And he set up this challenge." The images rushed at her, like she was watching them on a screen. "See, the top layer of the water is warm, but the lake is extremely deep, and as soon as you go six or ten feet down, it starts to get really cold. He rigged up a series of prizes for me, floating at different depths, colored bowls filled with marbles. The blue bowl had blue marbles, the red bowl had red marbles. I had to prove how far down I had dived by the color marble I brought back up. I've never even been a strong swimmer, but I kept going deeper, because I saw that beyond all the bowls of marbles, Dylan was down there. And it became this awful race to get to Dylan."

"Your son?"

"Yes. He was under the water. Really deep. And I knew that if I gave up I would lose him. It was so cold." The memory brought back a penetrating chill deep in her bones. She shivered. "But I couldn't stop. It got darker and colder the further I went. And he was always just out of my reach. So I stayed under. I was freezing. And then I blanked out. That must be when Marco came to get me."

"Was your son struggling? Was he in trouble?"

"No. He was happy, actually, but he didn't realize that he was sinking. And I could tell he didn't know he would sink to the bottom if I didn't stop him. He would never get out."

Mama Rosita nodded. "And this yellow dock. You feel the dock is a safe place for him?"

"It's Bryce's dock," she said. What was she going to do about Bryce? She had nothing without him. There was no other line of work she could imagine doing. But she was too tired to care. "Mama Rosita. I have to tell you something. I don't think Mr. Bryce is good for Casa Munay."

She nodded. "I feel that last night, too."

"He could ruin this community. I'm so sorry. I didn't know."

"I know, *mi hija.*" Mama Rosita stroked her hand. "But maybe he is not as powerful as you think."

"No, Mama Rosita. He gets what he wants. Always. He even asked for a ceremony with you on Saturday. As if he can demand that."

"I will do this," Mama Rosita said.

"What? Why would you do that?"

"He needs healing too, *mi hija*. I can feel that. Tell him Saturday at noon." Mama Rosita had no idea what kind of force she was dealing with. And why should Bryce be the one, of all people, to get access to Mama Rosita's gifts? But Mama Rosita had already moved on to the next topic.

"Your sister?" Mama Rosita said. "Last night was important for her. I think she is ready. Have Marco bring her to me in the roundhouse at three o'clock today."

"Really?" She grabbed Mama Rosita's hands again. "You think you can help her?"

"I will try, *mi hija*. I know you love her with all your heart. The *luna balsamica* rises this afternoon. Pachamama is at her strongest with the moon in the sky, the mother version of the sun. When both are in the sky, it gives strength, which your sister needs. And the last part of the moon is a time of release. This is a good time."

As Mama Rosita stood, she faltered slightly before leaning against the couch to steady herself.

"Are you sure you're okay?" Joline asked.

"Si, *mi hija*. Si. Just old."

She helped Mama Rosita down the stairs. Then she grabbed her phone off the couch and texted Bryce: "Sorry. Under the weather. We r on for Sat at 12pm."

Exhaustion and relief swept through every cell in her body. Mayu must have helped Ellie, made progress against the cancer. That had to be what Mama Rosita had meant. And Mama Rosita would drive that healing even further.

She looked at the clock on her phone. It wasn't even noon. Plenty of time. When Ellie got back upstairs from breakfast, she would tell her the good news. But she needed to rest. As she puffed up the pillows crammed into the crease of the couch and dragged the dense blanket up from the floor, her body yearned for a sleep as deep as the lake she had dived into the night before, but without any of the cold. She needed the dark and the quiet and the warmth. She slid the blanket over her head and slipped effortlessly out of consciousness.

TWENTY
Ellie

E llie ran her hands across the wood table in the dining room. The grains seemed more intricately woven this morning, and her fingers bumped along indentations in the wood she hadn't noticed before. The stamen of a large hibiscus flower painted on the wall behind Tess looked like it might reach out and touch her. Everything was more vivid, more acute today, and yet her memories of the night before were imperfect. She now understood why "journey" was the perfect word for what she had experienced, like she had gone miles away, to a completely different time and place, a different dimension.

"You look tired," Tess said, putting her napkin on her lap even though there was no food on the table yet.

"Sorry. Just thinking about last night."

Marco came out of the kitchen and placed a small tray in front of her with three saucers. One had a small pile of onions, one a mound of salt, and the other held four wedges of lime.

"It is important before you eat today, to get your system working again, get your enzymes back where they should be." His voice was quieter than Ellie remembered. "This should help. Just combine these, a little of each. Then you can have a simple breakfast."

Raw onions were not what she had in mind, but she understood that following his suggestion was the fastest way to get to a real breakfast. She squirted a couple of lime wedges onto the onions, sprinkled on some salt, and used the silver spoon that he had left, the size of a baby's. The taste was surprisingly appealing, the juices on her tongue prickling back to life.

"How is Joline?" He spoke gently, looking only at Tess.

"I think she's okay," Tess said. "Thank you. For everything." She said these last words slowly, looking directly into Marco's eyes.

Ellie stopped chewing on her onions. There was a wordless conversation going on between Tess and Marco.

"Arabella will bring you a proper meal shortly." Marco touched Tess's hand and let it linger there before leaving.

Ellie waited until he was into the kitchen before she spoke. "Wow. Go on a trip and miss a lot," she said, piling up another spoonful of onions. "What happened last night?"

"Is it that obvious?" Tess said, her head dropping to her chest.

"Are you kidding?"

Tess reached for the water in front of her and took a long gulp. "We had this amazing conversation that went on for hours. And then—God, if Joline hadn't gotten sick . . ."

"But Parker?"

"I know," Tess said, resting her elbows on the table. "This is what I mean. This is the problem."

Arabella placed a platter of scrambled eggs and a bowl of rice on the table. Her sister brought a glass of green pulpy juice for each of them.

"Maybe I'm not wired to turn off chemical reactions to other people. Ignore emotional connections," Tess said. "Marco said something to me last night that made a lot of sense to me. That maybe we don't need to expect so much from one person. We can get what we need from many sources in our lives. I adore Parker, I do. But why not live in the moment, give and take what's needed, when it's needed? Not put all that pressure on one relationship?"

"Look, I've thought a lot about this." Ellie couldn't wait to eat and ladled some of the eggs onto her plate while she talked. "And I think, well, for me, it's always about more than the moment.

For our lives to add up to something, it has to have more heft than that. What came to me was that you can't be with one person and love someone else, or you're not really there. It causes too much damage. But I do believe that commitment is a beautiful way of strengthening love, of making it something more than a romantic fantasy. It doesn't mean you have to expect everything from that one person, or that everything is perfect, God knows. But that sense of commitment does create a bond you share with no one else."

"Or is that what society tells us to stop us from running rampant?"

Ellie spooned some rice onto her plate. She had never seen Tess let food go cold.

"Remember what Gavin told you when you saw him? He was right," Ellie said. "Even though I technically broke things off with him, I didn't ever really let him go."

If she hadn't had to make a ferry that day to get off the island, she might have never left. She had purposely left him with only enough time to make it down Main Street and onto Straight Wharf, just enough time to step onto the boat. She knew the ramp would be removed in her wake and leave nothing between her and the dock but the foam kicked up by the engines and the sound of the anchor chain scraping against the hull. There would be no way to go back.

"I need to see him so he can understand that," Ellie said. "Will you come with me?"

"Understand what, exactly?" Tess asked, sounding frustrated.

"Please just trust me. I can explain it all in the car," Ellie said.

"Okay, but let's go now. Joline won't nap forever."

Ellie's stomach lurched at the thought of what would happen if Joline found out. She reached for one more teaspoon of onions and lime, the taste bitter on her lips.

Marco's directions to the hotel were flawless. As Tess parked the car on the opposite side of the street, Ellie began to feel shaky, worried what might actually happen if she found Gavin there.

The Santa Maria looked like a hostel, the metal and glass door nearly off its hinges, the peeling paint of the facade revealing layers of stucco from a different era. The sidewalk was cracked and tilted, as if a tree was trying to force its way through. She pulled open the door and stepped inside, the bright light of the sun disappearing. She blinked into the darkness of the lobby and saw that it was little more than a reception desk propped up in a hallway, manned by an old Ecuadorian gentleman in a polyester vest. She backed up into Tess when she realized that Gavin was standing there, wearing his L.L. Bean coat and loafers, a soft leather bag on the floor next to him, his wallet resting on the desk. He was signing something.

"You're leaving," Ellie said.

Gavin stopped writing mid-motion. "Yes."

Longing and resistance swirled in her chest. She took two steps forward but stopped again. She was conscious of Tess right behind her, an anchor to another world. Gavin hadn't moved.

"I didn't think you were coming." Was he angry? Or sad? He looked resolved. She wondered if her presence shifted anything in him, the way seeing him drew out an inexplicable part of herself. She turned around. Tess still had her left hand on the door as if reluctant to let it latch behind her. Her other hand clutched the strap of her bag, the strength of her grip visible along the edge of her forearm.

"I'll give you some time, Ell. I'll be right outside." Tess paused as if to record the full texture of the moment before backing out the door and then letting it close. Ellie felt her absence as soon as she was gone, her lifeline back to her other world, the only other person who had been to each place and understood that she existed in both.

She found herself unable to cross the space to Gavin, not with the receptionist standing there, his gold name tag glinting between them, his eyebrows half lifted in interest at the conversation he could tell was charged, even if he didn't understand their words.

"There's a sitting area," Gavin said. "Just over there." He rattled off a few lines in Spanish and put his luggage behind the desk.

He came to Ellie and took her hand, leading her past a lone

elevator and through an open doorway. Large planters flanked an L-shaped bench covered in a velvety fabric that looked like it had been scratched regularly by a cat. A skylight let in one square of light that hung at an angle on the far wall. Gavin kept hold of her hand as they sat on the bench. There seemed a deep sadness about him, a somber heaviness in his arms, in the hunch of his back, which she had never seen, not even on that last day on Nantucket.

"I always thought I could wait a lifetime to have you come back to me," he said. He opened her palm and traced the length of each finger as he talked. "I told myself that what we had was too special, that something would give at some point, and you'd walk by the Sconset house again one day, and we'd pick up right where we left off. Just like last time. I decided that I could wait as long as that took." He brushed the tip of her pinky and then reversed the pattern, drawing a line deeper into her palm after each trip to the outer edge.

"Last night, I had this dream," he said. "It was so real. The two of us laying out by your grandfather's cottage, at night, like we used to, looking up at the stars, telling each other that we would always find each other no matter what."

She looked at his face. Was that coincidence or had they had the same vision? Had they actually been side by side somehow, looking up at the universe from the same patch of earth?

"I was always waiting for you. Even when I was married, without really knowing it. And I've been fine with it. I could wait for you 'til I'm eighty if I knew you were alive out there somewhere. But knowing you were sick—"The word caught in his throat. "It made me desperate to know now. To hear you say that you were sure too, that we would be together eventually."

"Gavin—"

"No," he said. "Don't answer it now. I know it was crazy of me to come here. It wasn't fair. And I realized last night that needing to know the answer now is like accepting that you are going to die. That's not what I want. You shouldn't have to answer that now."

Ellie nudged the cuff of his jacket above the scar next to his wrist bone. She rubbed it lightly. She did love this man.

"I can answer it now," she said, and saw hope pool in his eyes.

How to explain to him what the plant had helped her understand? That while her love for him was real, it was a romantic, one-on-one, indulgent kind of love. Her love for her family was something more complete, and while the undertow of three kids and a husband was sometimes depleting, their love crashed over her in a way that nothing else could match. Her family was the real love of her life. And her family didn't exist without David, without the love that had been its roots, its nourishment. Carrying around the idea that Gavin was her soul mate, that she was making some kind of sacrifice to be with David, to keep the family whole, was what had begun to poison her from the inside. She finally understood that she had sacrificed her family to be with Gavin, not the other way around.

"Maybe if we hadn't gone separate ways when we were young, maybe it could have been different. But my heart belongs to my family," Ellie said. "I love them so much it hurts. Maybe it's cruel to tell you that, but I need you to know it's where I want to be. You and I, we had a love that was real, and we will always be connected. I know that. And we might find each other in another dimension, in another lifetime. But it can't be in this one."

He searched her eyes for something more and then dropped his head. He didn't say anything for a long while. An ache swelled in her throat.

"I will never stop loving you," he finally said, tears streaking his face.

She wished there was something she could say to take away the pain she'd inflicted, but there was no going back.

"Goodbye, Ellie," he said, and stood.

Slowly, she got her feet under her, failing to hold back her own tears. She needed him to go, but knew it would be for the last time. She would never see him again. He brushed his thumb across her eyebrow and then held her face in his hands. An uneasiness overtook her as he pulled her face toward his. She wanted to turn away, reject the need to be physically joined, but could see the devastation already dimming the beautiful blue of his eyes. It seemed cruel to deny a moment of closure for the love she was taking from him. And so she put her mouth on his and let him kiss her one last time. His tongue, smooth and cool, caressed hers, gently tasting the inside of her mouth, his thumbs tenderly rubbing her cheekbones. She tried to ignore the quiver at her abdomen, the desire that had not yet been fully extinguished. He slowly pulled away with one last brush of his lips and then wrapped her in his arms. She grasped him hard, closing her eyes against his chest. She breathed in the soapy smell of him, a scent she had once associated with first love and innocence, then lust and betrayal, now with a distant love that would stay forever in her past. After several long moments, she relaxed the clutch of her arms, and released him.

As he walked away, she put her wet face into her hands. No. She needed to watch him go. She needed to be an equal part of the physical break, to remember that she had been the one to finally let him go. When she turned around, she saw him, head down, take a step to the side to avoid someone before continuing past the elevator. Joline was standing at the door.

TWENTY-ONE
Joline

The scene in front of Joline clicked by in slow motion, and with each frame her shock increased. A strange man had just held Ellie with the urgency of a lover. There was no mistaking their kiss. As badly as she wanted a different story for what she had just seen, her heart already knew what it was.

It hadn't occurred to her to wonder what Ellie and Tess were doing in town when she'd raced down here with Marco to find them. She'd overslept. She was so worried that Ellie would miss her healing with Mama Rosita, with the moon in the perfect position, her only concern had been finding them in time. That Marco knew where they were seemed like a divine offering. Tess had been standing awkwardly at the entrance, and said something about waiting outside, but Joline saw Ellie just beyond reception, and needed to get her back to Mama Rosita. Her excitement evaporated ten feet past the door.

"Ell?" Joline heard the desperation in her own voice. Ellie looked like a ghost, a person so physically diminished by whatever had just happened, that the reality of the situation only sunk in deeper.

"Joline." Ellie reached out at the air in front of her.

Tess appeared in the doorway, but didn't say a word.

"I don't understand," Joline said. But her thoughts immediately went to David. David, who had clutched Ellie's blue and white head scarf through her nine-hour operation, refusing to put it down until he saw her alive again. David, who came to Monterey so Dylan could go on a father–son kayaking trip. David, grinning at the camera after Ellie went into remission, his arms stretching around the three kids and his wife, the joy back in his eyes, his shoulders broad with confidence again.

"I—oh, God." Ellie's voice was barely audible. She crumpled onto the bench.

Joline couldn't move. Tess hurried over to Ellie and put her arm around her in a motherly way.

"Who was that?" Joline asked. Her own voice sounded small in her head.

"Gavin," Tess said. "The one from before school."

How did she know that? Wasn't she rattled by this?

"Ellie didn't know he would be here, Jo. It was over," Tess said.

Her words pierced Joline's consciousness with the bang of a needle popping a balloon.

"What do you mean 'over?' What are we talking about here? How long has 'it' been going on?"

Ellie began to weep soundlessly, her shoulders shaking.

"And you knew about this? You *knew* about this?" Joline's voice bounced off the walls around her. "And what, you've been conspiring to hide this from me—" Her tone was biting, but didn't begin to approach the rage she felt building, didn't come close to expressing the confusion that was tilting her world at an unrecognizable angle.

Tess stood. "No, Joline. That's not—"

"You know what?" Joline's vision diminished to nothing but disconnected pixels. "I can't do this. I can't."

She backed away and ran through reception. She had to get out.

When she stumbled through the front door, Marco was waiting on the curb.

"Where's Ellie?"

"Mama Rosita. Shit." This wasn't happening. This couldn't be happening.

"But she's coming, no?"

159

She could see concern creeping onto Marco's face.

"I can't—" she started. "She's in there." She waved her arms but didn't quite have full control of her limbs. "Bring her back. I—" She let out a gasp. "I have to go."

Her head buzzed with confusion, her hands heavy at the bottom of appendages that felt unattached, her feet slapping the ground in front of her. She needed to find a quiet place. Somewhere she could come back into her own body, ground herself. She knew there was a small chapel a block or two away, off the square. The cold innards of the sanctuary, with its old wooden pews and stone floor, were of no interest to her. But there was a little garden on the side of the building, a patch of land that had been left undisturbed when the church was built. That was where she needed to be.

The iron gate was hard to open, the bottom of the fence stuck in the dirt. When Joline tugged hard, the gate scraped the road with a jarring squeal. The garden was even smaller than she remembered. Patches of grass ran through the center. Two stone benches faced the outer wall of the church and a small statue of the Virgin Mary. She cradled baby Christ to her bosom with one hand, her cloak falling off her shoulder, and held the other hand on her heart. A small bed of flowers surrounded the footing of the statue, separating Mary from her visitors. The stone seats were worn, the ground beneath indented by the thousands of feet that had rested there.

Joline turned away from the statue and ambled to the opposite side of the garden, in search of the small altar Anita had shown her once. She spotted it, partially hidden behind a spray of yellow flowers. She sat on the grass and gazed at the semicircle of stone, standing on its centerline like a moon half-risen above the horizon. Triangles of yellow ceramic outlined the circular edge, pointing outward, mimicking the rays of the sun. Several small flat rocks jutted out from the surface, cemented there as tiny shelves. Anita said the angle of each was designed to catch rainwater before letting it roll onto the next level, a kind of fountain in the rain. The altar had been erected to honor Yakumama, the mother spirit of water. The gardener had carefully planted yellow Ruda flowers, with their featherlike petals, as a tribute to Inti, the god of the sun. The altar was meant to honor the symbiosis between the two gods. It was the harmony between Inti and Yakumama that allowed tender crops to grow and thrive. Too much sun and a blooming flower would wither; too much water and it would suffocate in the mud. Balance was nature's true secret.

Joline closed her eyes and tried to locate that kind of balance. She didn't want her anger, or shock, or whatever surge of emotion might come next to overpower her friendship with Ellie, but confusion pulled at all her senses. She focused on her prana breathing, looking for the warmth of the sun within, the healing flow of Yakumama.

She had carried in her heart such a deep understanding of Ellie, as a friend, a mother, her brother's one love. Had she been wrong about her? Was she a different person than who Joline knew her to be? What about her family, her marriage? How much of her life had been a lie?

She felt the air move behind her. Tess sat on the grass next to her, very close. Joline could hear her steady breathing. Tess had lied to her, too. Was there anyone in her life who wasn't hiding something?

"Marco thought you might be here," Tess said. Joline focused on the altar. "I want you to know that I didn't know any of this until about forty-eight hours ago."

The knot in her chest loosened. She was way too tired to be angry with everyone she knew, and was aware at some inner level that she didn't want to be alone. A bee flitted in and out of the Ruda flowers, banging against each one, bouncing off and then moving on to the next. The bee hovered, changed direction, and dove in again.

"I almost slept with Marco last night," Tess said.

"You what?"

"So tell me." Tess's voice was contemplative. "Which side of 'nature supporting' is that? The one that dropped Marco into my life at this particular moment, or the one that made you sick last night and stopped me from going through with it? And which nature is the true nature? The one that put Gavin, literally, into Ellie's path, or the one that gave her cancer back before she had a chance to tell David she had screwed up?"

Her eyes were puffy. She hadn't gotten much sleep either.

"Or maybe," Tess said, "maybe we muddle around in this life trying to do the best we can given the shit that gets thrown at us. And maybe we don't always do such a great job of figuring out the right thing to do."

Joline leaned against Tess. She closed her eyes and silently asked Inti and Yakumama to give her the right combination—not too much sun to scorch, not too much water to drown—but enough of both to help her nurture understanding from the desolation in her heart.

TWENTY-TWO

Tess

Tess pulled Joline up off the dirt behind the church and coaxed her into going back to Casa Munay. As they drove up the hill away from town, she tried to imagine what Joline and Ellie would say to each other once they had a chance to talk. What if they were truly fractured by this? They had been friends for so long, such close friends, and they both loved David. Tess had to make sure they found a way to figure this out. It was an odd feeling for her, to be the one in the middle, the one who needed to hold them together. That was Ellie's role.

"I hope Mama Rosita can still help Ellie," Joline said, quietly, looking out the window as they drove. "It is such a good sign that Mama Rosita wanted to work with Ellie today. You have no idea how amazing that is. But I don't know if this stuff changes that. All this bad energy." Joline put her head in her hands. "Shit, this sucks."

"Here's what we're going to do," Tess said. "We're going to get you something to eat—you haven't eaten, have you? And we're going to let Ellie rest after her session. And then we are going to huddle up the three of us and work through this."

As soon as she pulled into the driveway at Casa Munay, she

saw Ellie pacing back and forth along a short line in front of the inn, her hand on her head. She looked even paler than she had in Otavalo.

"What's wrong?" Tess was out of the car practically before she could get it in park.

"Mama Rosita collapsed."

"What?" Joline rushed around her side of the car. "What happened?"

"I don't know. She was working on me, kneeling next to me. And she was moaning. And I thought it was part of the ceremony, but then she clutched her stomach and she passed out. Oh God, this is my fault."

"Where is she?" Tess asked.

"In the roundhouse, with Marco."

Tess ran down the hill and flipped open the tapestry at the entrance to the roundhouse. She was starting to hate that building. Mama Rosita was on the floor, on one of the mats from the night before. Her girlish expression was gone, her sparkling eyes clasped shut in pain. Small groans escaped her pursed lips. Marco was on one side holding his grandmother's hand, and Arabella knelt on the other, sponging Mama Rosita's forehead with a cloth.

"Marco, what happened?"

Marco stood and led her to the side of the room.

"She's very sick." Marco had the resigned posture of someone standing outside an ICU unit, having been warned of the worst possible outcome. Except there was none of the usual flurry going on behind a glass door, no team of doctors in scrubs doing everything they could to revive the patient. No one was doing anything. Joline barreled through the entrance and nearly collided with them.

"What happened?" Tess asked again.

"It came on fast. She says she has a pain like a knife in her belly. She is weak. She's coming in and out. It looks like it could be appendicitis."

"I've had appendicitis. Shit. Not something to mess with," Tess said.

She knelt next to Mama Rosita. Arabella dipped the cloth in a pail of water and wiped Mama Rosita's forehead gently. She pressed the back of her hand to the old woman's cheek.

"She's burning up," Tess said.

Mama Rosita held her hands to her abdomen and convulsed, rolling to the side with a groan that sounded like a defenseless animal surrendering, with no hope of fending off the predator.

Tess stood again. "Marco, we don't have a lot of time. If she turns septic, she could die within a few hours if we don't get her to a hospital."

"Maybe we should discuss this outside," Joline said.

She ignored Joline. Marco was staring right at her, but looked like he had stopped translating the English words in his mind. Nothing was registering. She remembered when Parker had gone into shock after a biking accident. His mind didn't function quite right. She was going to have to walk Marco through this.

"It will be okay. I have a number to call, Medivac. I'm sure they have a helicopter in Quito. They can probably get here and have her in the hospital in under an hour. Let me get the card and I'll call. You need to get Mama Rosita into the back of your truck."

She spun toward the door, but Marco's hand caught hers.

"Tess, my grandmother doesn't believe in surgery."

"What?" The volume of her voice startled Arabella, her eyes glazed with fear. Mama Rosita moaned again. Marco didn't move. "You can't be serious. What's the alternative?"

"We have already called the medicine man in Otavalo. He will prepare a healing ceremony for her. He should be here soon."

"And if that doesn't work?" Second after precious second ticked away. They didn't have this kind of time.

"Then she will accept that it is her time to move beyond this world."

"That's bullshit. That's what people with no options say." Tess felt the combination of impatience and adrenaline rip through her system. She had to inject some level of practicality into the situation or she would combust. "I can fix this. But we have to move. You have to tell your grandmother that I can save her life if you'll let me."

Mama Rosita's head moved to the side. She looked up at Tess. Was she understanding the gist of the conversation? She let out a long guttural moan.

"Tell her!" Tess pointed at Mama Rosita. Marco's eyes pleaded with Tess. He looked childish in that moment, bewildered by competing instructions. How had she been attracted to this man who was standing here doing nothing?

"Do you want your grandmother to die today? Do you?" Marco flinched. He had to understand the reality of what she was saying.

"Tess—" She shrugged off the hand that Joline put on her arm.

"Tell her."

Marco knelt on the floor, his back to Tess. His large hand caressed the top of his grandmother's head. Tess could barely hear the murmurs between them. How could she even be sure what he was telling her, what exactly he was asking her to consider? The conversation dragged on far too long. They had to move.

Marco kissed his grandmother gently on the forehead, placing a damp outline of his lips there. Was that a kiss goodbye?

"Make the call," Marco said as he stood. "I'll get the truck."

By the time she found her insurance card and called the emergency number—she hated that the one window in the tiny telephone room faced the wrong direction and she couldn't tell what was going on—Marco had rallied a group of men from the field to carry Mama Rosita to the pickup truck. Mama Rosita's body was barely half the length of the truck bed, and from a distance could be mistaken for a sack of barley.

"Tess, you ride in the back with Arabella. Help keep Mama Rosita steady." Marco jumped into the driver's seat.

Tess was relieved to see that someone had laid down a mattress for Mama Rosita and had found a blanket. Arabella looked terrified. She was still clutching the damp cloth. One of the men propped her up on the open hatch, and she inched toward the mattress, careful to tuck her skirt around her legs once she was safely beside Mama Rosita. Tess hoisted herself up and sat cross-legged on the other side of Mama Rosita. She covered Mama Rosita's legs with the blanket. Her face had faded to a khaki color, and she was shivering.

The truck began to move, each jerk and sway punctuated with a spurt of air from Mama Rosita. She was breathing like someone in labor, expelling her breath with the bumps in the road.

As they pulled away, she caught a glimpse of Ellie leaning against the wall of the inn, her hand still on her head. The men all turned from the dust kicked up by the tires and receded back toward the Casa in one denim wave. Joline stood alone.

Mama Rosita tapped Tess's leg. When she offered her hand, Mama Rosita grabbed it, each finger like a separate vine clinging to a tree. Tess closed her hand around Mama Rosita's with equal strength, a message to hold on.

Through the window into the cab, she watched the side of Marco's face. His jaw tensed, and she couldn't tell if he was fighting back worry for his grandmother or grinding his molars in anger. Had she unfairly pressured him? But Marco had to know it was the only real choice. How could he turn down a chance to actually save her?

Mama Rosita tugged on her hand. She was trying to say something.

"You carry much grief in you, my child." Mama Rosita's voice was strained, every word an effort.

"Shh, don't try to talk," Tess said, shocked to hear near-perfect English. Had she understood every word in the roundhouse?

Mama Rosita licked her lips, and then swallowed with a grimace. "Your heart, it is like a tight fist closed over a shard of glass." She held Tess's hand with both of hers and unfurled her fingers. She massaged the palm, digging into the knot of tension below her thumb. Tess glanced at Arabella, still patting Mama Rosita's forehead with her stiffening cloth. She didn't seem to be listening, or maybe couldn't understand.

"You must let the pain go. You suffered the greatest of losses, a long time ago, the loss of the first source of unconditional love you had ever known, but you have never let yourself grieve. You have never let your heart move on. But don't be afraid. She won't leave you." Mama Rosita rubbed her palm more gently, like the sweet caress of a mother. Tess felt a tide of emotion rise in her chest.

"Why do you say this?"

"I see her. She is with you now. She is always with you. Holding you. There is so much love there. It is beautiful." Tess reached up with her free hand to wipe her eyes. Mama Rosita grabbed it and held both hands in hers. "She has never wanted you to be alone."

Tess let the water run down her face. Was her mother really there? She hadn't let herself believe it for such a long time. Even when she most needed a mother in her life. But Mama Rosita could see her? Had she been there when Tess sprained her ankle in the marathon and limped the last four miles? Was she there the day she'd struggled to ease her youngest sister's grief after her miscarriage? Had she been there all along?

Mama Rosita closed her eyes again. She put her hand on her belly and let out a long, low groan that sounded beyond pain. Her agonizing moan seemed to echo in the sky, getting louder, stronger. Tess looked up as the helicopter dipped below a line of trees.

The truck turned past a fence into a huge dirt field, a rusty soccer goal at each end, a line of chalk in the middle long since kicked off. The helicopter inched toward the ground, tentacles of dust grabbing at the pontoons to pull it to earth. She lowered her head toward Mama Rosita's face.

"These people are going to help you," Tess said. She desperately hoped it was true, that they weren't too late.

Two EMTs jumped out of the chopper and ran toward the truck, hunched against the torrents of wind. Tess needed to get out of the way. She kissed Mama Rosita on the cheek and then released her hand, aware of a warmth in the center of her palm that hadn't been there before.

The pilot jumped down from the bulging eye in front of the helicopter and strolled toward them, papers flapping in his hand, his earphones stretched around his neck. His body was taut, commanding. He looked at Mama Rosita and then down at the form in his hands. Of all the stats about Tess they had likely printed out before lifting off, her birthdate was the one that made it most obvious that the woman groaning in the bed of the pickup was not Tess Whitford, not the one insured for emergency executive transport. The pilot's sharp eyes held steady on her as he spoke.

"*Tu eres la Senora* Whitford?" She nodded, wiping her nose.

"*Quién es ella?*" he asked, pointing to the truck.

"Mama Rosita," Tess said, acknowledging for the first time

the risk she had taken. The Medivac insurance was technically only for the insured or a member of their immediate family, and Mama Rosita was neither of those things. If the pilot refused to take Mama Rosita, she would have a disaster on her hands. Marco put his arm around her back and squeezed her shoulder hard, a message.

Marco and the pilot conferred in rapid Spanish. The pilot pointed to something on his sheet several times, to which Marco said, "*Si, si,*" and "Mama Rosita," followed by a jumble of words she couldn't begin to understand. Finally the pilot relaxed his military stance and handed the papers and a pen to her. For an instant, the pinpricks of his eyes turned soft.

"*Todo bien?*" he asked, nodding at her. "It's good with you?"

Tess had no idea what Marco had said, but knew better than to meddle in a negotiation that had already been won. She nodded and signed the form.

They transferred Mama Rosita onto a stretcher and secured her inside the cavity of the helicopter. Marco climbed in behind his grandmother. His hand went up in the window as the skids lifted from the ground. Less than five minutes after the helicopter had arrived, they took to the air and were gone.

TWENTY-THREE
Joline

After the truck lumbered out of the gate, Joline forced her feet to move in the direction of the roundhouse. She knew there was a log on a patch of grass nearby where she could sit.

Maybe this whole trip had been a mistake. The peaceful week, meant to be full of healing and sisterly love, was a mess.

Her stomach was beginning to turn from empty to sour. She needed some food. She changed direction and headed back to the Casa. With Marco and Arabella both gone, she wasn't sure who would feed them, but she wasn't beyond poking around in the cupboards to find some bread or crackers.

She found Arabella's sister, Mariana, sitting at the small table in the kitchen, huddled over a mug of tea. She stood when she saw Joline, then cast her eyes to the floor, perhaps embarrassed that she had been caught sitting on the job. Joline put her hands on Mariana's hunched shoulders. They silently exchanged worry for Mama Rosita, the shock of it still fresh. Mariana hugged her, then held out a chair, placed another mug on the table, and assembled a plate of cheese, fruit, and warm rolls. Joline was so grateful she wanted to cry. She ate slowly, careful not to overwhelm her stomach, but managed to finish three rolls, strength returning to her limbs a little bit with each one.

She had finished her second mug of tea when the back door of the kitchen creaked open. Arabella's arms hung at her sides like dead weight, her face streaked with tears and dirt. Mariana embraced Arabella, both of their bodies thick with sadness and worry.

Joline left them and headed upstairs, relieved to find Tess there, splayed out on the couch.

"How is Mama Rosita?"

"She was in a lot of pain. I worry her appendix may have burst already. But they wasted no time getting her in the air."

Joline sat on the other end of the couch. "God, what a day."

"Where's Ellie?" Tess asked.

"I don't know."

"So you guys haven't talked yet."

"We've been a little distracted." She never ceased to be amazed by Tess's need for action, her desire to create a plan and execute it as quickly as possible. Joline preferred to listen below the surface, wait for her true feelings to take shape beyond her initial reactions.

"Well, you guys have like a day to figure this out. You need to talk it through and move on. Because obviously there's no way she can tell David."

"Of course she has to tell him," Joline said.

"No way." Tess sat up, her elbows on her knees. "There's too much at stake here."

"More at stake than the truth?"

"What good does the truth do? Seriously, tell me. What good comes out of telling David?"

Joline hesitated. It would be devastating to David. But did that mean they would pretend that none of this had happened? How would that work?

"Isn't David dealing with enough?" Tess asked. "How can you add this?"

"It's not just David. The guilt, the secret, it's killing Ellie. Literally. Don Emilio said the first thing she had to do to get well was deal with the problem in her heart, remember? She needs to tell David the truth before—"

"Oh, fuck Don Emilio! We're talking about Ellie and David

here," Tess said. "He would be wrecked by this. How can you want that?"

Joline tasted acid at the back of her throat, the remnants of a sour thought that had taken root the minute she saw Ellie and Gavin together. The part of it she couldn't ignore.

"I can't carry this lie around for the rest of my life. This is my brother. Every time he talks about Ellie, comes to me for consolation, at some level, I'll be lying to him."

"This is about you now?"

"Oh, come on." How could Tess not see the complexity? The reverberations?

"No. You listen to me. You have to think about those kids. I know what it's like to lose a mother. It's like you walk around with half an arm the rest of your life, like you're gushing blood wherever you go and everyone looks at anything but at that and pretends like everything is all right. And the one thing I could hold onto was this ideal of my mother. Maybe it sounds stupid, but my mother was perfect to me, and of everything I had to question, like what was God, or whoever fucking runs things, thinking the day my mother's car crashed, I have never had to question that we were everything to her. Her family was it. Me, my sisters, my dad. Maybe you think that makes it harder to lose someone, but it doesn't. Because I have always felt lucky that of all the kids in the world, I was the one who got that mom." Tess cleared her throat. She never talked like this. "You can't take that away from these kids, or from David. Ever."

"Maybe it would be a gift to understand that there is no such thing as that ideal, that they don't have to measure themselves against something that doesn't exist." Couldn't Tess see how much of her life had been blinded by striving for impossible perfection?

"But it's not your choice," Ellie said. She was standing behind them, at the top of the stairs. Joline hadn't heard her come upstairs. Ellie surprised her by taking both of her hands in hers as she sat. The wildness in Ellie's eyes was gone. She looked serene.

"Jo, I have no idea what you think of me right now, but I have to ask you to leave this up to me. I hate lies. I should have told David a long time ago. But now, it doesn't make sense. I can't bear the idea that we might not have time to work through this—"

"But don't you see?" Joline asked. "You are sick with this guilt. You won't get well if you keep trying to bury the truth."

"All I ask is that you leave it up to me," Ellie said. "Maybe it's selfish to ask that. But David is my husband. I need you to respect what I decide."

Joline leaned back. Could she do that? Circumstances change. Who could say what David would need most five years from now?

"Can I ask you something?" She couldn't get the image of Ellie and Gavin together out of her mind. She had seen them touch. It was obvious how they felt about each other. "Did you ever consider leaving David?"

"Joline—" Tess interjected.

"No, it's fair. I have nothing more to hide." Ellie took a long, slow breath in her nose and out her mouth. "Gavin and I have a long history. He occupied an important part of my life, even when he wasn't there."

Ellie looked less innocent to her somehow, wiser. She was a woman with experiences far beyond the portion Joline knew about. She followed Ellie's gaze out the sliding doors. Clouds the color of steel rolled over the mountains in the distance, their gray fuzz stretched to the ground with rain. To the east, strands of sun highlighted a section of trees, making them look falsely tinted against the ashen sky.

"I loved Gavin deeply, I won't lie to you about that. And I let the idea of him too far into my heart for a time. But David is my life. We made a life together, and I never should have turned my back on that."

"Unless it isn't truly what you want," Joline said.

"No, you misunderstand me. A life with David *is* what I want. And the kids. I made that choice a long time ago. That's the point. It's about building something together and honoring what we've built. We have gone through so much together, and things haven't always been easy, but that makes it even more precious. I don't know how I ever let myself forget that. I'm not proud of what I did. But I never stopped loving David."

"Maybe you need to forgive yourself and move on," Tess said.

"Is that really how it works?" Joline got up and opened the sliding door. A burst of wind rushed through the door. "Remember when Jax came back after that year on the road, after Dylan was born? I had given him total freedom, but I assumed that what we had, we had a baby together, for Christ's sake, that it would mean something. And in he waltzes with some young groupie on his arm. Clearly, he happily forgave himself and moved right on. Is that really how it should be?"

"Jax was an idiot," Tess said, slouching back into the couch. "He never had any idea what he had in you."

"Listen to yourself. Parker pours out his heart to you and you're ready to jump in bed with the first Ecuadorian man you meet."

"I didn't jump into bed with him. I—we understand each other, we have a lot in common."

"And what about Parker?" Joline asked.

"Ultimatums don't work for me."

"Maybe this is about what he needs for a change. He's half the equation, you know, or has that not occurred to you?" The breeze turned cold, and Joline shut the door.

"I need to go for a run." Tess was already at the armoire, pulling shorts and a t-shirt off the shelf.

"Is that your solution to everything? If you could sit still for a minute, you might actually tune into how you feel." The sour taste was back in her mouth. She needed to meditate, something to ease the spike of adrenaline that kept invading her bloodstream.

"Oh, stop it with the 'tune in' bullshit already. Clearly it's not helping." Tess raked her hair back.

"Guys, don't do this." Ellie looked stricken.

Joline said nothing as Tess tied her shoes, downed the half-drunk glass of water on the table, and ran down the stairs.

TWENTY-FOUR

Tess

The fluffy dog picked its head up briefly when Tess scooted by, but settled back into a splash of sunshine beside Marco's desk. She hauled open the front door of the Casa and was surprised by the chill that forced itself inside. She considered going back up for a sweatshirt but decided against it. What she needed was a challenging route to keep her warm. Marco had said the waterfall was up a winding path. Steep was good. Could the dog actually get her there? What was her name? Cha-Cha? No, Chi-Chi. That was it.

"Chi-Chi?" The dog flipped onto its belly, all four paws at the ready. "Want to go to the waterfall?" Chi-Chi leapt up and shimmied through the partially open door. She began to whine anxiously, her wagging tail the only suggestion that she wasn't warning of a wild animal around the corner.

"Okay, girl." She stretched each of her quads briefly, hurried by Chi-Chi's guttural noises.

"All right, already," she said, and broke into a run. As soon as Chi-Chi was on the move, she quieted and raced past Tess in a direction she hadn't gone before. She skirted past a vegetable garden and onto a knotty path that headed vaguely west. The trees immediately closed over them, a verdant tunnel. When her eyes adjusted she saw Chi-Chi's tail disappear around a bend. She knew better than to match Chi-Chi's pace. The dog would tire, and the altitude required a measured speed. She reappeared, running back toward Tess to make sure she was coming, then darted off again. When Tess reached the bend, Chi-Chi was waiting several yards ahead, at the first suggestion of an intersection. Seeing Tess, she turned left and took off again.

Tess was completely frustrated by Joline. For someone who made it her profession to understand nuance in complicated situations, Joline was maddeningly sure in her own life that her way of thinking about an issue was the only valid choice, as if anyone with a different view was a less evolved human. It was infuriating. She knew how loyal Joline was to David, but shouldn't that make her want to protect him from all this pain? And why couldn't she entertain the possibility that staying single might be the best thing for Tess? She had a full life, and lived it under her own terms. She didn't think messing with that formula was a particularly good idea at this point.

The route began to steepen, tree roots forming steps across the narrow path. With each upward push, warmth circulated through her body, and she was glad she hadn't bothered with a sweatshirt. The canopy thinned overhead, but the sun was lost behind a thick cloud, thankfully eliminating any shadows that would normally mask small hazards. With the incline, she felt the pressure in her lungs immediately and welcomed the tension in her thighs and glutes. Other than the altitude, the route was a lot like Skegg's Point, where she and Parker sometimes raced to the top. He would ride his bike up the serpentine road, and she would scamper over tree roots and rocks straight up the inside. Running down was harder, nature's footholds on the way up becoming launch pads for a steep downhill fall on the return.

Chi-Chi waited at several more forks, each path looking exactly like the last, and Tess began to appreciate the fact that she wasn't trying to follow verbal directions. A bead of sweat stung her eye, and she didn't see the thorny branch that reached out and slashed her shin. She slipped on a pile of leaves and cursed, determined not to slow her steady ascent.

About twenty minutes after the uphill climb had begun, the path flattened out, and became quite narrow, with a severe drop-off to the right. Tess slowed to a stop and leaned over with her hands on her knees in an attempt to catch her breath. The trees on the left looked like they were crawling up a dirt wall, the bony tendons of their vast root systems exposed. A pebble kicked up by Chi-Chi's paws skipped over the ledge, ricocheted off a rock, and disappeared into a snarl of brush below. Veering toward the safety of the dirt wall as she walked, Tess heard a distant roar that sounded like the steady flow of traffic on Route 280 from the hills of Woodside. It took her a moment to realize it was the waterfall. She started to see hints of the river through the tangle of tree branches and leaves about forty feet down the slope. The path narrowed to less than three feet across, and the next fifty yards were extremely steep. She was amazed to find a handrail that had been dug deep into the dirt wall on her left, a series of wood knobs with a thick rope running between them, one like you might find on a walk through Sequoia National Park. Who had put it there, in the middle of nowhere? She held on, careful not to let her hand slide off the mossy sections. At the bottom, the path flattened out to the river. She was standing in a canyon of sorts, the source of the noise directly ahead.

The water crested over a huge rock formation, roughly a hundred feet above. The start of the waterfall looked deceivingly narrow, like a small stream barely able to cut through the bushes growing on top of the rock. But the volume and power of the water as it fell and then pounded the rocks below was impressive. Tess stood at the river's edge and let the cool mist kicked up by the churn blow over her face.

There were several flat-topped boulders in the middle of the river. Tess chose one with a manageable set of stepping stones reaching toward it. Careful not to slip into the water, she picked her way across and then leaped onto the dry platform. Chi-Chi went skittering farther along the bank, looking for her own fun. Tess closed her eyes and breathed in the mist. She could hear nothing but the driving rush of the water. It was relentless, pure power, pure strength. It surged through her. She dropped into a plank position and began to lower and raise her body. Eight push-ups. Sixteen. She braced for the vice-grip that usually clenched her shoulder, but there was none. Twenty-four. She still couldn't believe her shoulder could be free of pain. Strength was health. A picture of Ellie's muscles withering with cancer flashed through her mind. Shit. She had to change that thought to keep going. She pictured Parker's strong arms, holding him up on his handlebars. Thirty-one, thirty-two.

She leaned back on her haunches to stretch, and then cupped her hands into the water and splashed it over her head, letting the icy drops snake down her neck. She noticed for the first time how still the water was right in front of her rock, an eddy safe from the tornado swirling down the rest of the river. The rocks on the bottom were perfectly clear, as if there was no water covering them. Tess settled her breathing, but every exhale left her empty, confused.

Marco understood her. She did have lots of love in her life, her friends, her sisters. Why should she rely on any man, let alone one man, to make her happy? Marco was willing to share intimate conversation, and had been ready to give of himself physically without demanding any kind of commitment. Was there anything wrong with that?

The waterfall continued to pound, vats of water thrown over and over into a free fall from the edge of the cliff, pummeling the river below. The vibration bounded up to her chest, and the raw emotion that had snuck up on her in the truck with Mama Rosita surfaced. There had only been a few times in her life when she had let herself yearn for her mother. Like the day she received her acceptance letter from MIT. She knew she would never go far away from her sisters—they were entering their high school years and needed her more than ever—but she had secretly applied anyway, to find out if her mom had been right, if she could actually get in. She'd snuck the bulging envelope up to her room and read through the letter twice. But she found it held no real joy without her mother to share it with, and buried it in the bottom drawer of her desk.

And what would her mother say about Parker? Tess was sure she would have liked him, his smarts, his sense of humor. But would she advocate marriage for her independent daughter? Would she tell Tess that giving in to an ultimatum was a small price to pay if she really loved him? Or would she tell her to stand firm? Or maybe she would think her attraction to Marco a sign that Parker wasn't the right fit anyway? Tess wished she knew. She hated indecision above all else. It was a disease that infected everything.

Was it supposed to be this hard? It hadn't always felt hard. Like the time she and Parker had gone skiing in New Mexico for a long weekend. After two days exploring every run on the mountain, the headwalls and cliff jumps, they had started a playful debate over the fastest way to cover the most vertical feet, starting from the bottom, up to the top, and back down. It was the kind of disagreement that could only be settled with proof. They each picked their route and headed to opposing chairlifts, having agreed the deck of the Coyote Grill would serve as the finish line, the perfect place to toast the winner and enjoy the last of the afternoon sun. A race wasn't the smartest idea for the final run of the day—more accidents happened during the last run than the whole day combined—but she couldn't resist a chance to beat Parker at an argument he seemed too confident he would win.

When she popped off her skis at the bottom and raced up the steps of the Coyote, she was shocked to find Parker already lounging in the sun with a pitcher of margaritas and two frosty glasses on the table. There was no way he could have beat her that badly. When he started to laugh, she realized how blatantly she must have been wearing disappointment on her face.

"What the hell?" she asked, not yet ready to indulge him by accepting whatever ruse he was trying to pull.

He filled her glass and raised his. "I just figured, why do all that work, when you're going to win anyway?"

She swatted him with her ski glove and couldn't help but laugh at her own childish behavior, how she had thought of nothing else on the chairlift up and on the way down Blitz and Inferno other than how sweet it would be to win, all while he was lazily sipping his drink and basking in his own joke. They missed their dinner reservation that night. She found something erotic about being bested at her own game.

Chi-Chi barked. Tess jumped at the noise. The dog stood on the bank of the river looking intently at her, her tail low behind her rump. Tess straightened her legs and bent into a stretch, conscious of needing supple muscles for the descent back to Casa Munay. But Chi-Chi barked more continuously.

"What's the problem?" The river darkened as if dusk had come in an instant. Tess stood up as the eddy around her rock erupted with pockmarks. By the time she crossed back over the river and joined Chi-Chi on the bank, her salty skin had been washed clean. It was pouring, and she was already soaked. Every patch of sky above the rock walls was the same gunmetal gray. Chi-Chi scampered over a rivulet of mud and up the steep path they had taken in. She considered staying put until the rain passed, but Chi-Chi began to bark again from the crest of the hill when she saw Tess wasn't behind her. The branches along the bank hunched over against a driving wind, and the rain pelted her harder. Tess grabbed the rope and started to pull herself up the narrow passage, her sneakers barely finding purchase.

Once they reached the narrow section, the current of rain and mud shifted, now running off the dirt wall to her right and over the ledge on the left. Chi-Chi's back legs splayed out from under her every few steps. Tess clutched the skeletal tree roots climbing the wall beside her, conscious of each step forward. The water streaming down her forehead made it hard to keep her eyes open. She swiped at her face with the back of her wrist, but her hands were too wet, the rain too relentless.

Chi-Chi was about twenty yards ahead, and turned around, wagging her tail again, her tongue hanging over her teeth. Tess guessed Chi-Chi had reached the spot where the path moved away from the ledge, and thought Chi-Chi's enthusiasm might be premature. If the rain didn't stop soon, every path down the mountain would be washed away. Marco's story about his parents flashed in her mind.

Tess picked her way along the slippery path, fantasizing about carabineers and ropes and crampons and a hat to shield her eyes. Her ruminations were splintered by a deafening crash. A tree behind her snapped and toppled, its roots grasping at the air as it slid over the side of the ledge, taking a section of the path with it. Chi-Chi barked again, and she forced her feet to move toward higher ground.

When she reached Chi-Chi's spot, the dog broke into a run again, but not in the direction Tess expected. Instead, Chi-Chi ran through a small opening in the trees they must have passed on their way in. It looked like it went farther up into the mountain.

"Chi-Chi," Tess yelled. "This way."

Chi-Chi stopped and turned but made no move to retreat. Her bark was high-pitched and urgent.

"Chi-Chi, you have to show me the way." She cursed herself for running out without paying attention to the weather, for failing to pick a visual marker for every turn they had taken, for following a dog. Her sneakers were already buckets of mud. Rivers of water crossed and connected around her feet. She began to wonder if she should go back to the waterfall, where the rock wall was firm and stable, and wait out the storm. But the path was gone, darkness was coming, and without Chi-Chi, she would never find her way home. Maybe the dog had a different route in mind, one that was less steep, with less chance of a mudslide.

She ducked under a tree branch and followed Chi-Chi. The path was narrow, with dense vegetation on both sides, and the ground felt more stable. It was a fairly steep incline. Why were they heading up? The wind whipped through the trees, and hundreds of goose bumps erupted on her bare arms and legs.

Within a quarter mile, the path opened up to a clearing. A ring of rocks encircled what might have been a fire pit, but was now an enormous roiling puddle. Behind that, a stone wall curled over a small cave. Chi-Chi ran inside, tail wagging. Water pooled on the edge of the entrance, but several feet inside, the ground was completely dry.

Tess noticed the silence first, the layer above her head too thick to register the sound of the rain. The room was cold. She rubbed her arms. To the right side, two rectangular rocks flanked a third, set up like a living room made of stone. An odd selection of items were strewn on the floor in the center—dried leaves, wilted petals, multicolored pebbles, and a small pile of beads. She sat on the center slab, longing for a set of dry clothes to change into, wishing she was back at the fire at the Casa. Why had she ever left?

Chi-Chi leaned against her legs. Tess moved away from her wet fur, but Chi-Chi scooted closer, and lay down on her feet. She patted the dog's head, and wondered how long she had until the graphite sky turned to night.

TWENTY-FIVE
Ellie

E llie stared at the wall in the phone room for several minutes before dialing. She could picture everything going on at home—David peering into the freezer with his reading glasses on, studying the re-heating instructions for the lasagna or the enchiladas she had left for them, Hannah and Lilly at the kitchen table playing Uno while devouring a pile of Oreos, Connor hard at work on a term paper in his room. Would calling them bring the turmoil she was experiencing into the house, like opening a portal that shouldn't exist between two worlds? She didn't want her mood to infect them, but she needed to hear their voices, be connected to that more predictable place.

Lilly picked up the phone. "Mommy! I was right, Daddy, it's Mommy!"

Ellie rubbed the curly phone cord. "Hi Lilly-Lu. How'd you know it was me?"

"The caller ID is a really long weird number, so I knew it. But guess what, guess what? My team won the spelling bee today at school. We spelled 'continent' right, you know, as in one of eight big pieces of land, wait is it eight or seven? Anyway, the other team put an 'a' in the end instead of the 'e' and we got it right and

we won! Daddy's taking us to the Green Street Diner to cele-
brate, and Margaret invited me over after school tomorrow and
Daddy said I could go and I'm super excited because she just got
a new bike. An orange one, and she said she'd let me ride it."

Ellie looked at the glass of the small window. Ropes of rain
meandered down the window panes, blurring the vegetable garden outside into a jumble of greens and browns. Lilly's voice
sounded sunny. Maybe it was even warm at home. After Lilly
gave her a full report about how many eggs she had been able to
collect from the chickens that morning, the phone got passed to
Hannah while someone yelled upstairs for Connor to pick up.
Hannah was disappointed with a fifth-place finish in her swim
meet the day before, and Connor didn't say much other than that
everything was "fine," before blandly announcing that he should
probably get off the phone since they were supposed to be getting into the car to go to dinner.

"Sorry for the chaos," David said, the chatter of the kids muffled behind his voice. "You'd think we were going on a camping
trip with how long it's taken me to get these guys out the door.
How is everything down there?"

Where could she even start? How could she ever explain?
Would she ever? Joline finding out made everything infinitely
harder, which she hadn't thought possible. What she had finally
ended in the courtyard had taken on new life now that David's
sister knew her awful truth.

"I wanted to hear your voice. I miss you." She pressed the
phone against her cheek.

"We miss you, too."

A thin layer of fog coated the inside of the window. She drew
with her finger on the glass.

"Ell? What's wrong?"

She dropped her finger from the window.

"It's been a tough day. The medicine lady here, she collapsed.
She was working on me, and they took her away and we have no
idea if she's going to be all right or not, so . . ."

"That's awful, Dove," he said.

She swallowed before trying to say anything else.

"Anyway, I know you have to go. I'm glad everything is okay
at home. Everyone sounds good."

"We're doing fine. But tell Joline she better get you home safely. We miss you."

After they said goodbye, she kept the phone in her hand, letting the receiver drop to her chest. She finally placed it gently in the cradle, and leaned back against the wall. The heart she had drawn on the window was dripping from its edges. She drew a larger one around it, coloring in the inside to fix the streaks, and left the room before it started to slide down the glass.

"It's pouring out," Ellie said when she got back up to the room. "I hope Tess didn't go too far. She'll be soaked."

She wished Tess hadn't run off. She needed her there as a buffer. She had no idea how to apologize to Joline for cheating on her brother. Or if the apology should equally be for lying to her for so long. She didn't know what to say.

Joline was tapping away at her phone. Of all of them, she was the last one Ellie would have thought would be continually dealing with her email. She should have been turning the patter of the rain into positive energy or something.

"I have a serious problem." Joline continued typing, apparently wanting to finish whatever she was working on before saying more. Ellie looked out the sliding door. The entire mountain range was shrouded in menacing clouds.

"Bryce wants to meet again tomorrow. If he finds out that Mama Rosita is sick, I'm sure he'll accelerate everything. He'll use it to scare the neighbors into selling. I wouldn't put it past him to change the numbers."

"What do you mean?"

"As brutal as the current setup is, at least he's offering real money to everyone for their land. If he thinks he can cut that in half, maybe he will. He'll tell them that they can't survive here without Mama Rosita."

"Is that true?"

"I don't know. Maybe. Even with the small number of healings she does now, one hundred dollars for a healing is more than anyone makes in a month. It keeps everything going. There is no other source of income like that. If it were to end tomorrow, it would be a real problem."

"Just don't tell him she's sick," Ellie said.

"He's planning on a ceremony on Saturday with her. I already told him it was set."

Ellie walked over to the sliders. The weather mimicked her mood, tempting her to stand out on the deck and soak in it. She couldn't get the picture of Mama Rosita's face out of her mind, twisted with pain. She was sure Mama Rosita had used too much of her energy to try to help her. It was what had made her sick. If Mama Rosita didn't recover, she would never be able to forgive herself.

"Joline, can I ask you something? How much do you have riding on this? On Bryce?"

"Everything." Joline dropped her phone onto the table. "I wouldn't have agreed to drop my other clients if he hadn't made it worth my while with the salary. Plus there's a series of bonuses at key points, like breaking ground, signing a certain number of shamans onto the project, running the first session. Big bonuses."

"So if this location doesn't work out, all that gets delayed," Ellie said.

"That's not the issue. I didn't ever expect it to go as fast as he's trying to force it right now. But if I balk at his plans for the center, or worse, if he thinks I'm interfering with it, he'll fire me. At a minimum."

She sat next to Joline on the couch. "Then get your old clients back. You don't want to keep working for him if you guys don't see eye to eye on the right way to go about this, do you?"

Joline put her head in her hands. Her uncertainty seemed odd. Where other people might feel obligated to stay the course on something, Joline never hesitated to follow her intuition and change direction if something didn't feel quite right. It's one of the things she loved about Joline. A free spirit who was truly that, because she never let anyone else make the rules.

"Tell me you didn't sign a non-compete," Ellie said. Joline didn't move. "Oh my God, you did."

"It's pretty standard in the Valley, Ell. And Bryce has an army of lawyers that is not to be dissuaded."

"It's likely indefensible anyway. Judges don't like

non-competes," Ellie said.

"You try that against him. Too expensive."

"But non-competes are meant to stop people from stealing trade secrets. This work is *your* trade secret. You didn't actually sign off that you'd be restricted from coaching other people, did you?" Ellie asked.

"For two years. But I felt we had a strong partnership. I didn't put any energy into the idea that it might not work out. This was supposed to be my future."

"You should have showed it to me, Jo. That's what lawyers are for. To protect you from the stuff you don't want to think about." It made Ellie sad that no one thought of her as an attorney anymore. Half her friends at home didn't even know she ever was one. She hadn't practiced law in years, but it didn't mean her brain had dried up. And the basic principles of the law never really changed anyway. She could have helped Joline avoid this.

"Well, it's done." Joline sighed and leaned back. "And beyond the contract, I'm making twice as much as I ever made. I can't afford our new place without this job, even if I could get my clients back."

"Well, maybe David and I can help." David made the decisions when it came to helping Joline financially, and it was easier if she didn't know the details. But surely he would help her.

"Oh, Ell. I already owe David too much money. That's what the first bonus was going to be for. You can't imagine how much I've been looking forward to finally paying that back."

Ellie wasn't sure what to say. This is when Joline would probably insert one of her "nature will support" comments.

"How long ago did Tess leave?" Ellie asked. She looked at her watch. It was almost six-thirty.

"An hour ago? Or longer?" Joline joined her at the slider. "Shit. It's ugly out there."

Together they watched the rain wash across the deck.

"What do you think she'll do about Parker?" Ellie asked.

"I'm not sure, but I hope she gets out of her head long enough to listen to her heart, like Don Emilio said." Joline got up and walked over to the slider.

"Why isn't she back yet?" Ellie said to no one in particular. The sky was quickly turning black.

TWENTY-SIX

Tess

From the rock inside the cave, Tess watched the rain's relentless barrage. When it finally tempered to a drizzle, she walked back out to the clearing. Dusk was drifting quickly into night. But the wind had shifted, making the air much warmer, almost tropical. Chi-Chi hopped onto one of the stone seats around the would-be fire pit.

"Okay, Chi-Chi, let's go."

The dog sat.

"Let's go back to Casa Munay. Come on, Chi-Chi, show me the way. We don't have a lot of time."

Chi-Chi lay down on the rock, her ears at attention.

"Maybe you need me to go first and then you'll understand."

She walked through the clearing, her sneakers squelching. The first few steps into the tree-lined path were a steep combination of rocks and mud. A stream of water curled past the rocks on the left side, carving a small crevasse and further narrowing the passage. Her foot slipped off the first rock, and she had to grab onto a sapling to avoid a fall. The bark cut into her hands. She tested a different foothold before putting her weight on a new spot. Five minutes into her crawl down the hill, Tess had made little progress, and Chi-Chi hadn't joined her. Through the trees she could see the clouds pulling apart, unveiling a clear view of the darkening sky. She estimated that the light would be gone within a half hour, and at the rate she was going, it would take her well over an hour to get back. If she didn't get lost. If she didn't fall and break her leg in the dark.

Chi-Chi jumped up when she came back into the clearing, wagging her tail from her perch atop the rock.

"Okay, I get it." Tess sat on the driest spot she could find among the circle of rocks. Her stomach was completely empty, aching for food. She was starving and exhausted. But at least her clothes were almost dry. Even Chi-Chi looked dry. She fantasized for a moment about making a fire, but the pit was still just a pool of water, and the whole world around them was dripping. She rubbed her palm where the tree had shaved off a few layers of skin.

As the sky dimmed, a few stars blinked on, joined by a wedge of moon. Chi-Chi hopped off her rock and trotted into the cave. Not wanting to be alone in the growing darkness, Tess followed, pausing at the entrance to allow her eyes to adjust to the lack of light inside. Chi-Chi was lying on the longest rock, and she knew instinctively that huddling with the dog would be the only way to stay warm inside the cave. She shivered when her bare legs touched the stone, and she pulled Chi-Chi toward her. The dog fit perfectly into the inner arc of her body, and even gave her a soft place to put her head. She patted down the fur in front of her nose, and breathed in the musky mix of dirt and rain on Chi-Chi's coat.

A howl jolted her. A coyote? A wolf? But Chi-Chi didn't move. Tess told herself that if Chi-Chi wasn't worried, she shouldn't be either. The other animal must be far away, not interested in their plight. Her arm moved up and down with Chi-Chi's breathing, slow and steady. The dog was already asleep.

She hugged Chi-Chi and stared at the opening to the cave, outlined with hints of moonlight. Ellie and Joline would be crazy with worry. She pictured them pacing around the room, and hoped they would stay put and not try to find her.

She wondered what Parker was doing just then. Probably lighting his grill and cooking up a tenderloin for himself, opening a bottle of wine. Her stomach groaned at the thought. The simple things we take for granted.

Her right hip started to ache, but she didn't want to shift her position and disrupt Chi-Chi, risk losing her blanket and pillow. Instead she tried to match her own breathing to Chi-Chi's—long pulls in with equally long breaths out.

She thought about Mama Rosita's words in the truck. That her mother was always near her, protecting her. Was she there now? Mama Rosita had stated it confidently, and in that moment, Tess had felt something inside of her shift. But she had to be careful. If she gave into the tears that had surfaced in the truck, she might never stop. She might drown. And besides, if Mama Rosita was right, why did she still feel nothing but alone? She was undeniably trapped in a dark cave, on a cold rock, alone. In the end, she was always alone. Her self-reliance was what kept her moving forward, what made her strong. She couldn't ever forget that.

She clutched Chi-Chi tighter, hoping for sleep, hoping that sunrise would offer her a way to get back. In the silence, she felt a layer of warm air settle onto her back. It pressed against her with the weight of a blanket, enfolding her in warmth. She closed her eyes and let herself imagine, just this once, that the heat was emanating from her mother, that her mother was there, embracing her, keeping her safe. Would there be any harm in that?

When Chi-Chi picked her head up, Tess startled. It took her a moment to remember where she was. Deep purples and pinks streaked across the entrance to the cave. Was it morning? She released Chi-Chi and inched up slowly to separate her hip from the granite platform. Blood returned to her tingling feet, still damp and caked with mud. She rubbed the lingering drowsiness out of her eyes. She couldn't believe she had slept so soundly. Her body was surprisingly warm, which seemed impossible. And then she remembered the feeling of being cradled by her mother in the night. She looked around the cave to confirm that she was actually alone.

A crosshatch imprint of Chi-Chi's fur lined her thighs and

her forearm. She ran her fingers over the same pattern on the side of her face. She took the rubber band out of her hair and scratched her scalp before wrestling her sticky mane back into a ponytail.

Outside the cave, the pastel sky hovered above the dark mountain range, its slopes not yet touched by the morning light creeping up behind. The air was chilly again, the forest a murmur of chattering birds waiting for the official start of the day. When the sun finally glimmered over the tip of the farthest mountain, it painted the rocks around her in gold. How amazing that the same sky that had produced something ferocious and uncontrollable could then offer something so beautiful.

Chi-Chi panted and wagged at the edge of the path in what Tess now recognized as her ready stance. She looked out over the mountains again, grateful for whatever forces—chance, or fate, and even something less explicable—that had kept her safe. She worried for a moment about their trek down and hoped the path hadn't been swept away in the storm. But Chi-Chi seemed confident, eager even, and Tess realized there was nothing more to do but send her thanks into the sky and follow Chi-Chi home.

TWENTY-SEVEN
Joline

Joline opened the front door of the Casa and almost fell right into Tess.

"Oh, thank God, you're all right." She wrapped her arms around Tess. Her body was stiff with cold. Chi-Chi circled them, her paws the same muddy mess as Tess's sneakers. Dirt streaked her face, her hair.

"What happened? Are you okay?" Ellie came up from behind and added her arms to the group hug.

"You need a hot shower," Joline said. "You're freezing."

"I need food." Her voice was hoarse.

"I'll get something from the kitchen," Joline said, "but you have to get warm."

"How about a bath," Ellie said. "I'll get the water going."

Tess nodded and let go. Instead of going upstairs, she knelt on the floor. Chi-Chi immediately sat in front of her, their heads at about the same height. She stroked Chi-Chi's fur and held the dog's face, communing in a way Joline had rarely seen her attempt with most humans, let alone a dog.

"Find something for Chi-Chi, too," Tess said. Chi-Chi licked Tess's face from her chin to her eyebrow. Tess laughed. "I love you too."

Tess stood slowly, clearly stiff, and leaned on the railing as she walked up the stairs.

Joline wandered down the hall, slightly drunk with relief. She and Ellie had done nothing but worry all night. They had ventured out into the storm at one point, trying to retrace the path Ellie and Tess had walked the day before, but their flashlights illuminated nothing but a yellow curtain of water in front of them, and their calls for Tess were drowned by the deluge. They had nowhere to turn for help, and spent the night huddled in their room, every sound a possible harbinger of Tess's reappearance.

As she walked into the dining room, it occurred to her that Arabella and Mariana were probably still asleep in the kitchen. Tess needed real food, but she didn't feel right waking the sisters. Creeping up to the door, she was surprised to find them sitting at the small table by the stove, working on what she first thought was needlepoint. With a pile of materials between them, the two sisters were sewing tiny beads onto round pieces of white netting. Joline recognized the mesh discs as the covers used in the dining room to keep flies out of open jars of honey or carafes of juice, the larger ones used to protect bowls of fruit. The beads around the edges served as colorful weights mooring each veil in place.

Both women jumped up when they saw her, clearly not expecting a breakfast customer so close to dawn. Joline tried to communicate with her hands and broken Spanish that she was just looking for food for Chi-Chi and something simple and warm to take up to Tess, but both women were already in full motion, pans clanking, before she could explain.

Standing at the vacated table, she could see that the sisters had assembled sets of the finished mesh covers into plastic bags tied with a ribbon and a price tag. She guessed it must take twenty or thirty minutes to sew the beads onto each circle, allowing them to complete just two or three an hour, and they sold a set of four or five for just two dollars. The economics of that were astonishing. What would Bryce's plan mean to these two? Would the windfall of money mean they would no longer have to sleep on a kitchen floor and wake before sunrise to make goods for sale at the market?

Clearly in the way of the sisters as they whisked and chopped a path around the kitchen, she left them to their cooking and sat at the long table in the dining room, listening to Chi-Chi lap up water and crunch on a bowl of food. By the time Tess and Ellie came back downstairs, Arabella and Mariana had brought platters of fruit, pancakes, and eggs out to the table, their bright white aprons neatly secured.

Tess looked much more steady, refreshed even, as she pulled up her chair across from Joline. Chi-Chi sat at Tess's feet, forcing Ellie to pull her chair down the table a bit.

"How are you feeling?" Joline asked. "What happened?"

Tess heaped eggs onto her plate and described the hike to the waterfall and the storm and the mud and the cave. It sounded terrifying, but there was a quality to her story that was a bit like she was relating a dream, or as if the details were merely that, a tiny part of something vast.

"My God," Ellie said. "You're lucky to be alive."

"Without Chi-Chi, I might not be. And it was cold in that cave, but somehow I didn't freeze up there."

"You are an amazing woman," Joline said. "Nature gave you incredible strength to get through that alone."

For a brief moment Joline thought Tess might cry. Instead, she reached for the pancakes. Chi-Chi got up and wandered into the kitchen.

"Any word on Mama Rosita?" Tess asked.

"No. Nothing." Joline wished she knew how to get in touch with Marco, or had at least written her number down for him. It hadn't occurred to her in the midst of the crisis.

"She has to get better or I'll never forgive myself," Ellie said.

"How is this your fault?" Tess asked.

"It's like I'm so sick, I'm toxic. Mama Rosita wasn't strong enough to take it on." Ellie's eyes were raw, rimmed at the edges with pink. Of course, neither of them had gotten much sleep. Second night in a row. Tess pulled her chair closer to Ellie and put a hand on her arm.

"No." Joline took the time to pick her words and speak them slowly. "Listen to me. Mama Rosita has been healing people for over fifty years. She is highly practiced at not internalizing any of it. This has nothing to do with you."

"Except that everyone who comes near me lately ends up getting hurt somehow."

Joline knew this was an attempt to start the larger conversation. They had stayed silent on the topic of David while waiting and worrying for Tess, stepping around the huge pricker bush of emotions that would be increasingly difficult to avoid now that Tess and daylight had returned.

"Listen, Mama Rosita was already feverish when I saw her yesterday morning." Joline leaned forward, her elbows on either side of her plate. "Whatever was wrong with her started well before the ceremony. But she knew she could help you, and she wanted to do that."

"Which still makes it my fault. She shouldn't have tried to help me if she was sick." Ellie pushed a slice of peach around her plate.

"Not your fault. Her choice. Ell, this guilt isn't helpful." Joline felt a surge of impatience surfacing in her words. "And it's a cop-out. It's a beautiful thing Mama Rosita did for you. Appreciate it."

"A cop-out?" Ellie asked. "What do you mean by that?"

"It's easy to feel guilty," Joline said. "It's harder to face the truth."

"Are we talking about David? You're saying I should tell him?"

"I don't see how that helps," Tess interjected.

While she could never stop being David's sister, Joline wanted to get back to being Ellie's friend. She desperately wanted to help Ellie get through all she was facing, and she knew no other way than to speak her mind. Anything less would be disingenuous. She moved around the table and sat in the other chair next to Ellie.

"I think you're looking for forgiveness," Joline said, "but it's not me you need it from." Ellie's eyes shifted downward. "But maybe needing that is selfish. Maybe Tess is right. Maybe the price is too high."

"So you think I shouldn't tell him?" Ellie asked.

"I don't know, Ell. I'm not sure what the best thing is for David, but I think this guilt is literally making you sick."

Ellie pushed her chair back and put her forehead down on the edge of the table. Tess looked at Joline with an expression that accused her of being too hard on Ellie. She rubbed Ellie's back and tried to shoot back the message that she was just being honest.

"We need to find a way to help you through the guilt," Joline said.

She wondered what the future would look like for Ellie, David, and her. She couldn't control for every outcome. She could only do two things, keep working every possible channel to help Ellie get better, and help Ellie face the truth. She worried what the second of those would mean for her brother.

Bryce had asked to meet on a bench on the Jose Lopez Street side of the square. Otavalo was nearly empty given that Friday was not an official market day. The skeletons of a few booths stood stripped of their goods, abandoned by their owners. A Coke can rattled across the cement, propelled by the breeze. Joline brushed her knuckles under her nose, hoping her lavender hand cream would combat the smell of the dirty water pooled in the gutters. She watched an old man sweep the far corner of the square. A small bird pecked at the ground as if determined to dig up worms from the concrete.

Bryce crossed the street, sidestepped the broom, and walked with purpose toward her, his leather folder clutched at his side. He had on khaki dress shorts and a pale blue, perfectly pressed linen shirt. She wondered how he managed that in his tent. Maybe he had upgraded to a hotel in town, not that there were any that offered much luxury.

"Thanks for meeting again on short notice. I know you're supposed to be with your friends this week."

She nodded, reminding herself not to be intimidated this time. She had decided to tell him that Mama Rosita was sick, that they should postpone everything until she recovered. The community trusted their shaman above all, and proposing any kind of change while she was ill would be a mistake. Any successful plan would need Mama Rosita's and Marco's support; otherwise, it was too likely to fall apart.

She was taking a risk. If Mama Rosita didn't recover—she hated even having that thought—or if Bryce decided to use her illness as leverage, a way to frighten everyone into selling, she wouldn't be able to stop him from bulldozing his way forward. But if she convinced him that Mama Rosita could be a powerful ally, she might be able to slow things down long enough to come up with an equally compelling plan that wouldn't destroy Casa Munay. Everyone would win.

"Bryce, I don't think I was clear enough the other day—"

"I want to apologize. I was too hard on you." He leaned toward her. "You raised some significant points, and I should have listened better."

Joline studied his face. His eyes had softened again; the glint of the tyrant that had colored his features two days before was gone.

"You were right when you said that we didn't want to launch this center under a cloud of bad karma," he said. She relaxed into the bench. "I've been talking with people around here in town the last couple of days to try to understand things better, get a clearer picture of the lay of the land. And here's what I've decided to do. We're going to build a school as part of the retreat center. Well, not on the same property. The school will be down here, in Otavalo. I'll kick-start it with some funds to get it up and running, but then a percentage of our profits will go to keep the school running, so it can be free to the kids here. Free." His face broke into a grin. "It's unheard of. The people will go crazy for it. And it will be inextricably bound to the center. The size of the land at Casa Munay allows us to build a larger facility than we had originally imagined, so we'll be able to generate bigger profits. And the more successful the center, the more successful the school." Joline blinked at him, trying to absorb it all. "Awesome, right? We'll be helping a whole city of people. Oh, and I'm thinking that we let Mama Rosita stay in her house through the rest of her life if she wants. She's good for the story. She won't technically own the place—well, in reality she never has—but there's no need to ask her to move if you think that's a mistake. She should stay."

"Without her neighborhood, or any land to grow food on anymore."

"She can come eat at the center if that's what you're worried about."

Joline tried to get her mind around the added complexity of his new plan. Real people would surely benefit. A generational community would still be leveled, but the sound of that destruction would be muffled by roars of joy coming from a much larger crowd.

"And Marco? What happens to him after she dies?"

"Who's Marco?"

"Her grandson. That property is all he has."

"He's a grown man. I mean, you can't expect him to live off his grandmother his whole life, can you?"

"That's not exactly how I would describe it." Why did people always think moving away from home was a sign of success?

"Joline, let me give you some advice." Bryce put his arm on the bench behind her back. She sat forward. "Don't let your thinking get clouded by one subset of people. We're talking about doing something groundbreaking, investing in the future. It will help hundreds of families in this town, hundreds of kids. That kind of progress never happens without a few people's lives getting disrupted. But you have to see the greater good. The bigger picture. It's real progress. You can't let the emotions of a couple of people get in the way."

But I love those people, she wanted to say.

"Anyway, I want to announce it tomorrow. After the ceremony."

Joline hesitated. If she told him about Mama Rosita now, he would surely accelerate this plan, get all of Otavalo on his side before even alerting Mama Rosita and Marco to the tsunami coming their way. They wouldn't stand a chance.

"Let's put the ceremony off," she said. "It will give us a little time to think through all of this before you announce anything."

"What more is there to think through? Tomorrow is perfect. We should call in any of the workers that are around, and we'll tell them that we're going to build a school. They'll get to hear the good news first. And it will make your sales job next week quite a bit easier."

"Bryce, listen to me. You need Mama Rosita on your side. If she doesn't agree with the plan—"

"Won't matter. We'll already be heroes."

A gust of wind scattered the sweeper's pile of dirt and litter around his feet. He stepped out of the mess and started over. Joline knew that not telling Bryce right then that Mama Rosita was sick was lying by omission, and if he found out, she would pay dearly for it. But if she had a chance of scuttling his plan, she needed an alternate one that would be equally compelling to him. She needed time to work out what that was.

"I've gotta go," Joline said, standing.

Bryce tucked his portfolio under his arm. "Thank you, Joline. For pushing my thinking. I wouldn't have come up with this without you. It's the right thing to do. See you tomorrow."

She watched him stride away, his loafers clopping across the square, echoed by the bird still pecking at the barren ground.

TWENTY-EIGHT
Ellie

*E*llie took off her sweater and rested it on the deck railing. The sun was doing its best to pull the rain on the ground back into the air. There was a mild breeze, but all traces of the cool mist that had preceded the storm were long gone, and the humidity was beginning to make her curls unwieldy. She had tried to nap after breakfast but realized within a few minutes that nothing but a full night's sleep would help her feel rested. She folded her body into the hammock chair next to Tess's and swung in silence, sensing that Tess was deep in thought. She didn't want to interrupt.

A family of birds darted around a tree off the side of the deck. They flew so fast in swoops and swirls, it was hard to say who was in the lead and who was chasing, but their chirping suggested a happy game. She wondered if birds did such a thing, or if she was misunderstanding a turf war of some kind.

She thought about what Joline had said, that she needed forgiveness from David, and that the only way to get that was to tell him the truth. But it seemed utterly selfish to give him all that pain so that she could be absolved of it. She didn't think she could face that. But could Joline be expected to keep this secret forever? Ellie couldn't bear the idea of him learning about all this after she was gone, with no chance to talk it through with him. He would have no way to understand that their love, their family, was what had remained most sacred to her. Would he ever believe that? She didn't know what to do.

"Can I tell you something?" Tess asked. Her voice was unusually tentative, soft. "I've never told this to anyone before. I thought I was foolish, or maybe desperate in some way." Tess shook her head.

She turned her swing to face Tess.

"Ever since my mother died, I—" Tess paused. "It started right after the funeral, at the house. Our house was full of people and I couldn't find Lucy and Sara, they weren't outside in the yard, they weren't in their room. When I walked by the door to my parent's room I felt a hand on my shoulder guiding me inside. I looked behind me, but there wasn't anyone there. But I could feel that touch on my back, leading me into the room. I almost forgot about it when I found my sisters huddled on my mother's bed crying. We curled up together and fell asleep." Tess kept her hammock swinging, her eyes trained on the mountains beyond. "But I have felt her ever since. Well, I didn't know that's what it was. Like that feeling you get when someone walks into the room behind you, and you feel them before you see them, you know?" Tess glanced at her, mid-swing. "Or sometimes a thought pops into my head out of the blue, like someone whispered something in my ear that I wasn't thinking about. Do you ever have that happen?"

For the first year or so after Ellie's grandfather died, she would wake up in the middle of the night and think for a moment that he must be visiting, that he had made a sound to wake her up and he would be sitting at the end of her bed, ready to show her a special piece of sea glass he had found, or ask her to read his favorite Coleridge poem out loud. She would carefully open her eyes, hoping to find him there, but he never was. She had chalked it up to wishful thinking, a desire that never materialized.

"I told my father once, early on, that I thought Mom was still around, following me. He was still in really bad shape, and he said we didn't need anyone else in the family losing their marbles. So I was always afraid to tell anyone else. I never even told my sisters, I didn't want them to freak out. I tried to make it go away, to be normal. I figured that it was a weakness I had, you know? Because it was my job to get on with it without her. And yet every time I had trouble with something, or even had something good happen, I kind of knew she was there. It was embarrassing to me on some level that I had this need to conjure her up, and that I was desperate enough to believe that she might be there. And after a while I kind of forgot about it. I figured I grew out of it."

Tess dragged her feet on the deck, slowing the chair. She grabbed the sides of Ellie's swing so that they were facing each other.

"What I'm trying to say—part of me wanted to tell you this, even last time, and part of me thought it was the wrong thing to say. But maybe mothers have this ability to forever watch over their kids. That as a mother you will never really leave them."

Ellie had thought about this many times. Even in her darkest moments, those times when she pictured the black void that must be death, the flash of nothingness, total evaporation into a pile of dust, she couldn't help but hope that her soul would remain connected to her children by some filament of existence, on some plane that was beyond the human brain to comprehend. But it was too horrible a thought to fully contemplate. She didn't want to be ash in the ground. She wanted to stay with her children, to hold them, to talk to them, laugh with them, encourage them. She wanted to be the one to brush Hannah's hair, straighten Connor's tie, wave from the audience when Lilly danced. Those tender moments were what fed happiness, replenished confidence, filled her children's souls with love. That's what she was put on the earth to do.

"Mama Rosita told me that she could see my mother." Tess blinked over the droplets of water balancing on her lower lashes. "She said that my mother is still here." Tears were now rolling down her face. "You'll always be with them, Ell."

Tess was finally saying the unsayable. That she was most likely going to die. Disintegrate. Disappear.

Other than the long line of doctors who were practiced at looking her in the eye and telling her she was going to die, no one had yet had the courage to discuss death with her. Really talk about it.

But she wasn't ready to give in. She had come to Ecuador because she had to find a miracle, get back to being a mom. How could that be taken away from her now? From her children? Why would any force of nature want Connor and Hannah and little Lilly to be without their mother? Little Lilly. In her final days, would she know when to stop holding on and say goodbye? How could she ever say goodbye to her children? A cry erupted from her like a shout. She reached for Tess.

"I don't want to die." She clutched Tess. "I'm so scared. I'm so scared."

Sobs rumbled through her body, and for the first time in her life, she didn't try to stop them. Her chest heaved with an endless stream of tears. She couldn't die. She didn't want to die. *Please don't let me die.* The harder she shook, the tighter Tess held her.

"It's okay," Tess said. "It'll be okay." Tess swayed with her, letting her cry as the sun moved across the deck and the birds continued to circle and swoop.

Ellie heard Tess and Joline coming up the stairs just before dinnertime. She was stretched out on the couch, reading the opening page of the novel on her lap for the third time. All the crying had left her with a throbbing in her sinuses that was pushing across her forehead. Although she had to admit she would take a headache any day over the usual tightness on her side, and there was no such tightness today. She appreciated the reprieve from the cramping.

Joline fell into the chair, looking like she had been tossed there, barely registering the cushions that broke her fall. She explained Bryce's latest plan, how he imagined himself as some kind of philanthropic hero, and his belief that Joline's fingerprints were all over the idea.

"So you didn't tell him not to come tomorrow, that Mama Rosita isn't even here?" Tess asked.

"No. This whole school thing complicates everything. He's right. There are going to be a lot of people in Otavalo who will think it's a good idea."

"But he can't take this land away," Ellie said.

"I know." Joline sunk even deeper into the chair, melding into the upholstery.

When they had first arrived and Joline had used words like "sacred" to describe the place, Ellie had assumed it was a nod to local tradition, the way one might admire a Mayan ruin for its place in history. But now she understood the sacredness of the place as a living element, as integral as the scruffy trees, the winding rivers, and the craggy outline of the mountains. Did Bryce even have any clue what he would be destroying?

"The scary thing is that he actually thinks he's doing a great thing," Joline said. "That makes him even harder to stop."

"You have to be careful." Tess leaned on the slider, her long legs in silhouette against the glass. "You can't let him think you're playing him. I don't think you have any choice but to call him in the morning and tell him she's sick, cancel the ceremony, and hope he doesn't find out you already knew that today. If he thinks you're tampering with this—I know you don't like to think this—but he's the kind of guy who follows through on his threats. It's his best way to get what he wants and create a deterrent for the next person in your shoes. You have too much on the line to put yourself in that situation."

"But I brought him here. If he ruins this place, there's no one to blame but me."

"You didn't bring him here with that purpose, Joline." The wistful Tess from an hour earlier was gone. Ellie wondered when she might get a glimpse of that side of her friend again. "Sometimes things don't go the direction we anticipate. And it sucks. But I don't think there's anything you can do."

Joline sat still, her head hung in resignation, or maybe it was heavy with all she worried would unfold. Ellie wished she had some clever idea that would help, legal advice that would offer her real protection.

"Forget all this," Joline said. "I know what we have to do. We can't let Bryce's nonsense get in the way of what we came here for. We have to keep up the momentum of all the work you've been doing, Ell."

"Oh, God, now what?" Tess crossed her arms.

"I have this great meditation I brought with me. It's a sound meditation. I wanted to do it a few days ago, but this is the perfect time. No outsiders, no rituals, just the three of us. I think it will really help. Please?"

"Can I keep my clothes on?" Tess asked.

Ellie laughed. She reflected on how lucky she was to have been handed these two women as roommates so long ago, one that would push her thinking, the other who would have her back. She liked to think that, with them, anything was possible.

TWENTY-NINE
Tess

Joline put her iPod and a small speaker on the floor of the roundhouse, but didn't sit. "This is a standing meditation. A movement meditation really."

Tess was surprised that Joline wanted to go to the roundhouse for the meditation. As far as she could tell, nothing good had happened there all week. Fortunately, all signs of Mama Rosita's collapse were gone. There were straw mats on the floor and a pile of rocks in the middle. She took a tentative breath, bracing for any lingering stench from the ayahuasca ceremony, but smelled only the moss on the walls and an earthy scent in the air reminiscent of a hot-stone sauna. She let her shoulders drop. The room was a pleasant temperature, the thick stone walls having not yet succumbed to the heat of mid-day.

"I picked this meditation because it is about asking an essential question, which is perfect because I think we are all struggling with very difficult questions. And all the anxiety we have dealt with in the last couple of days can cloud our ability to sense the answer that is right for us. The music and the movement will hopefully help us put aside that anxiety, at least for a bit."

Tess stretched her calves. They were still tight from the steep climb up to the waterfall. Was that only yesterday?

"This meditation focuses on the seven chakras. The chakras are centers of energy that are associated with locations in our physical bodies, and each chakra is associated with a particular emotion. Some of them will make perfect sense to you, like the fourth chakra, or heart chakra, which is about compassion, forgiveness, and self-love. The third chakra, right here between your navel and sternum," she illustrated, putting a flat palm above her belly, "is where our self-confidence and personal power comes from."

Joline went on to describe each chakra in detail, the colors and emotions that went along with each one. Tess found herself thinking about self-confidence and personal power. Was that what had made her determined to get Mama Rosita to a hospital? Or was it compassion and caring? Maybe it didn't matter as long as it saved her. She looked back at the spot where Mama Rosita had been. What if she didn't make it? She couldn't help but wonder if Marco would blame her for forcing Mama Rosita onto a helicopter, out of her own element, even though it offered her the best chance of survival. This must be how Joline felt, convincing Ellie to come down here. Would David blame Joline somehow if it didn't work in the end, even though it would still be the cancer, not the attempt to cure it that was the culprit?

"I will warn you that you may find yourself wanting to move in some unusual ways. Let yourself go with your instincts. But it might feel strange at first, so I suggest we all agree to close our eyes, stay in our own journeys. This way we can move in the way the music hits us and not feel self-conscious. Agreed?"

Was there a choice? Ellie looked eager, possibly even excited. Tess figured anything coming out of an iPod was harmless enough. She could go along without objection. Give Joline a break.

"Great. I'm going to turn on the music. Close your eyes. Just let it flow. "

A female voice with a British accent spoke over music that struck Tess as dramatic, in a 'welcome to the gates of heaven' sort of way. String instruments held long, melodic chords, with chimes in the background. A male American voice joined the woman's. They talked in a steady stream, giving instructions, like paying attention to how their feet felt on the floor, and being aware of their bodies. The woman's voice asked them to let a question arise from inside themselves, something important that needed resolution or required guidance. Her accent wasn't British, actually. More like Australian. Or New Zealand.

One question? She had more like nine questions that kept her spinning in circles. Why did Parker think marriage was necessary? Why was she so confused? Why did his proposal make her angry? Yes, that was a good one. What about his insistence that they get married made her angry? What did that say about their relationship? About her? And if she didn't go along with it, would he actually walk away?

The music changed to some kind of bizarre didgeridoo with a strong tribal beat behind it. An orgasmic breath popped into the music every few bars. It sounded sexual, the woman's breath was erotic. Tess tried to quiet her head.

"Red is the color of the first chakra," the male voice said. "Let a bright red light shine on your question."

Tess tried to focus on the idea of her anger, but it was difficult not to sway a bit to the music. She let her hips move side to side, bending her knees to get into the rhythm. The heated breathing continued to punctuate the music, and she couldn't help but picture being in bed with Parker, laying on top of him and letting her hips do the work. Just the thought of it made her body yearn for his. But then why had she been drawn to Marco? She shook her head and tried to concentrate on the idea of Parker. She loved how they fit together. It made her feel free.

To her disappointment, the music changed. It had more of a techno beat than the first, a modern, swanky sound. The female voice said that the second chakra was the center of sexual connection. Tess smiled. She had jumped ahead.

The man said the color for the second chakra was orange. As the music kicked into full gear she found it increasingly difficult to stand still. "Fill your lungs with the color orange." She started to bob her head to the beat, feeling her ponytail swish back and forth behind her. She relaxed into the rhythm, letting her body move however it wanted.

"Feel the beauty of life," the woman said. Tess cracked her eyes open for a split second and saw Joline doing some kind of ape-like movement in a circle.

Closing her eyes again, she let the music take over her body and let her arms sway above her head, her feet and hips grooving to the beat. She remembered the night she had closed her first round of financing, securing the money she needed to get her company started. She had bought a bottle of champagne, cranked up the music in her living room, and danced with total abandon until midnight. She had been giddy with excitement, knowing she had sold a group of relatively conservative investors on her vision, on her ability to lead the company, on her sheer will to succeed. It was a major milestone for her. She couldn't quite remember why she had celebrated alone.

The music changed again, and the beat got even faster, like two hands in constant motion on a bongo drum. Grunts and calls in the music made it sound like some kind of tribal dance.

"The third chakra," the man said, "is all about your inner power, your personal will. Embrace your own power. Let it move you. Yellow is the color." The beat was too fast for her mellow dance. But it was great for push-ups. She got down on the ground, and thrust her body up and down, up and down to the beat. Tess began to breathe hard, trying to make it all the way through that section of music without stopping. Her shoulder showed no sign of pain. Awesome. Sixteen, twenty-four, thirty-two. She was nearing forty when she thought her arms might break.

"Bring attention to your yellow solar-plexus, and get into the power." Tess was heaving, having a hard time controlling her breath. A wild yell pierced the beat, like a savage call slingshotting through a forest. It kicked an extra burst of stamina into her arms. Up and down, up and down. Forty-eight. She had to stop. She lay flat on her stomach and clasped her hands behind her back to stretch her arms. When the music came to an abrupt end with a final whack of the drum, she was still breathing hard.

"Listen to you answer and then tuck it away." She had failed to ask her question again.

The next section of music was considerably slower. It was a wandering melody with a shaker behind it. Tess got her feet under her to stand again and worked to slow down her breathing. She opened her eyes to orient herself and catch her balance. Ellie was swaying to the music, with her hands over her heart. Tess shut herself away in the privacy of darkness again. A piano took up the melody.

As she listened to the flow of the music, she realized she had been asking the wrong question anyway. Her anger was no more than a thin layer of dust, easily swept away by the melody wafting from the piano. The soulful chords enveloped her and her throat swelled. She realized that heaped beneath the veneer of anger were layers of sadness.

"Bring awareness to your heart, the fourth chakra. Bathe it in green. Let your heart be open." The voice explained that the heart chakra was about love and peace, the power to forgive, the ability to trust. And then he said a word Tess didn't expect. Surrender.

Surrender to what?

Mama Rosita had said she carried a shard of glass in her heart. She had fought against that pain for so long. Did she need to surrender to that pain? To grief? If her mother had always been there, she had never truly been alone. Maybe strength had nothing to do with being alone. A tear dropped from her eye and skipped down her cheek for the second time that day. She let it drip down her throat. She began to dance again, slowly moving as each chord filled the room with sound. But this time Parker was holding her, and they were moving as a connected pair.

"Open your heart," the man said. "You are loved. You are at peace."

Was she at peace? Could she be at peace with Parker for the rest of her life? What was standing in her way?

"Ask your question from the core of your heart," the woman said.

Maybe that was the question. What was standing in the way of finding peace with Parker, being happy with him, saying yes?

"Let your heart get bigger. The color green is everywhere."

She held Parker closer in her mind. She moved with the music, imagining both her hands behind his back, his arms holding her tight. She could almost feel his chest lifting against hers with each breath. It was as if they were really together, moving to the sound of the piano, alone on a dance floor, the music joining them. She relaxed into his arms and imagined that he was what kept her standing. At first it felt risky, like she might topple forward and land on her face. But as she experimented with it, she realized that all she had to do was lean into him, let him know her weight was there, and he wouldn't let her fall. They danced.

Again the music faded sooner than Tess wanted. She reluctantly let go of Parker, her arms dropping to her sides. The didgeridoo was back. And the shaker.

"Move your awareness to your throat. This is the fifth chakra. This chakra is blue." Listening to the odd tone of the instrument, she realized that it was actually someone's voice making that sound. Full of vibration, singing out in an unusual key. She bounced to the beat a little, but missed the melody of the last piece.

"Hold space to speak your own truth. Let your voice be heard. This chakra wants to make noise, let the sound come free."

Tess wanted to be back in the melody of the heart. Making her voice heard was not her particular issue. She started to hear sounds from across the room, though. It was Joline, calling out in staccato bursts, completely uninhibited. Then she heard another sound, from Ellie's direction. She was holding a long, slow note in tune with the music. The longer she went, the louder it got.

"Listen for your answer."

The music shifted to a wavy synthesized sound. The voice asked them to focus on their sixth chakra, right between the eyebrows, something called the third eye, the center of intuition, insight, and inner wisdom.

They said to put the question into the purple light of the third eye. What was standing in the way of being with Parker? Maybe she had an inner wisdom about it that she hadn't been trusting. Was there a part of her that held the answer that she had never listened to? She felt the desire to raise her arms above her head and place her palms together. She stood on her toes, lengthening her body as much as possible. The sounds of a choir filled the room. Tess imagined a riser full of mouths in the shape of an "o."

"Bring your awareness to the golden light right at the top of your head. This is the seventh chakra, your portal to a higher source. Bring your question into that light."

She brought her arms down to her sides, lowered her heels to the floor, and asked her question again.

What was standing in her way?

The music progressed down the scale of a harp and a piano

joined in with the beginnings of a soothing melody. With each change of octave, the music reverberated deeper in her chest. "This chakra is our connection to endless possibility and divine perfection. What we fear is emptiness." Emptiness. Something inside her opened up at that word. Beneath the layers of sadness stood a gaping hole that hadn't been filled for a long time.

The voice told them to lie down, to just *be*.

Tess lay down on the straw mat. The sounds of an ocean and ringing chimes filled the air around her. The song took on the quality of a lullaby, simple notes on a piano. She listened to the chimes. They were exactly like her mother's, the ones that hung on their porch. Her mother was there. She was sure of it. She could feel it, not as a physical presence exactly, but as something all encompassing. It felt as if her mother's spirit was filling the entire room, like sunlight through a window. Tess let her hands fall open, palms up, and felt her mother gently removing shards of glass from her grip, her touch a salve. She caressed Tess's palm and kissed the spot where the splinter of glass had dug into her for so long.

The images ran through her mind one after the other. Most of the memories she had replayed of her mother—the Kimball's volleyball, her mother brushing her hair, the night on the porch when she was sick—were times when her mother had been taking care of her. After losing her mother, Tess had been so determined to drag herself to a standing position every day and prove that she could survive that she had never let anyone else play that role, never let anyone take care of her. She had never let someone hold her up and stop her from falling to the floor. And she was suddenly bone tired, like she had come to the end of an excruciatingly long run only to discover she was caught in the middle of a desert with no water, no shade, and no one to call to for help.

But she could call Parker. That's what he'd been trying to say that morning before she left. That all he wanted was to take care of her, for her to let him do that. She had always seen her independence, the fact that she didn't rely on anyone else, as a strength, but now she saw it as a wall that stood between them. She had never hesitated to take care of her sisters, her friends, but she had shut him out when he tried to do the same for her.

All because, from the time her mother died, she'd never believed anyone would be there to take care of her, unconditionally, ever again.

She put her hands over her eyes, the tears rushing out of her. Her shoulders bounced as she wept, her mouth stuck in the shape of a grin, baring her teeth in a way she couldn't control. Her mother's warmth cascaded over her, and she cried for every day of the thirty-five years she had missed her mother, for every day her mother's absence had taken up most of the space in her heart. For all the times she had felt heartbreak or disappointment and hadn't let anyone soothe her, for all the times she had chosen instead to go it alone. She let the waves of water wash through her, one after another, her heart finally surrendering the need to do it all on her own.

The chimes rang above her again, the piano striking cherubic notes over the sound of the surf washing on the shore. As her breathing came under control, the light behind her eyes started to move in the shape of a figure eight tipped on its side, a string of yellow and green arcing up and over before crossing itself and reversing course. She took her hands off her face. She must have been pressing down too hard. But the strands of light behind her eyelids continued to dip and swoop in the pattern of an infinity sign. She stopped fighting the vision, and instead let it swirl in her mind. She felt still by comparison to the movement against the darkness of her eyelids.

"Feel your own breath in your body." The man's voice was back. He told them to locate their seven answers and weave them together.

Tess didn't have seven answers. But she did have one, and was deeply grateful for finally understanding what it was.

When the piano struck its final note, and the sounds of the surf dissipated, she sat up and bent forward, stretching her back, and did her best to dry her nose on her sleeve. Ellie sat up slowly. She looked wiped out, but with the kind of triumphant exhaustion one sees at the finish line of a triathlon: energy expended in pursuit of strength.

"That was a beautiful meditation." Joline's voice was quiet. "Do you want to talk about it, Tess?"

Part of her wanted to share all of it, but she also wanted to hold it close, keep it dear.

"Not yet," she said.

"I understand." Joline's expression was like a hug from the other side of the room. Tess felt understood without having to say a word.

Joline folded into the lotus position. "Here's what I think we should do—"

A loud "hoo, hoo" floated in from outside the door, like an owl, or someone trying to imitate an owl. Joline jumped up and pulled the tapestry aside. It was Marco. Tess couldn't tell by his expression the tenor of his news.

THIRTY
Joline

"I'm sorry to interrupt, I waited outside until I heard the music stop." Marco seemed unsteady, hesitant. "I thought you would be anxious to hear."

"And?" Tess was already standing.

"She's going to be fine."

"Thank God." Tess looked like she was about to collapse. Ellie was on her feet then too, her hand at her mouth, her eyes misty. At least this was one bit of guilt she wouldn't have to carry home.

"They were able to remove her appendix before it ruptured. But they said it would have, and if she hadn't gotten immediate attention, at her age, the doctors said she could have died." Marco was looking at Tess. "My grandmother wanted me to give you this. It is a sacred symbol to our people." Marco held up a necklace, a leather strand with a hummingbird on it. He opened the clasp, and Tess stepped closer to let him put it around her neck. Joline thought Marco's cheek brushed hers as he worked the clasp. "With gratitude from both of us." Marco's hands lingered on Tess's arms, his eyes trained on hers.

"It's beautiful." Tess put her hand to her throat.

"Where is Mama Rosita now?" Ellie asked.

"She is still in the hospital. I am going back to get her

tomorrow morning."

"That seems fast," Joline said.

"She insists. She realizes the operation saved her, but she is not willing to stay there any longer. She needs Pachamama to help her recover. I hitchhiked back today to get my truck."

"Marco, you should have called. We would have come to get you," Tess said.

"No, it's better. This way, she has to stay there one more night and will rest up for the ceremony tomorrow."

Joline shook her head. "She can't possibly have the strength for that. I'm going to tell Bryce we need to postpone it."

"No," Marco said. "She was clear about this too. She said it must happen tomorrow."

"Marco, I need to explain some things to you about Bryce. You need to understand what's happening," Joline said.

She hadn't had any time to process all the answers that had come to her during the meditation, the powerful messages she had absorbed through her chakras, but at least one thing was clear. She wanted no more secrets from Marco or his grandmother.

"You need to know that Bryce has a plan to take your land," Joline said.

"Why?" Marco stepped back, as if he had been punched.

"For the retreat center. He wants to buy all your neighbors' property. Apparently you and Mama Rosita don't actually own most of this land. They do. And if they all sell, you'll be left with nothing."

Marco squinted. "Why would they sell?"

"It will be a lot of money to them."

She watched Marco's eyes dart around her face, trying to decode what she was saying by way of a hidden wrinkle line or hair follicle. Or maybe he was trying to figure out if she was actually the same person he had welcomed into his house as a friend time and again during the last year.

"But this is their home," Marco said.

"He plans to build a school, a free school, for all the children in Otavalo," Tess said. "That's how he gets everyone on his side."

Marco closed his eyes and then turned to Tess. "Why didn't you tell me this?"

She saw the energy that had swirled between Marco and Tess harden.

"I tried, I started to—I'm sorry, Marco." Tess reached out to put her hand on his arm, but he backed away. He leaned on the tapestry and slipped into the crack of sunlight at the door.

Joline followed him outside. "Marco, I want to help."

"I think you have done enough," he said, and walked up the hill, Chi-Chi wagging at his heels.

Joline took off her sandals to feel the grass under her feet. She needed to connect with the ground. They were sitting in the shade on a set of logs not far from the roundhouse. The logs had been carved and smoothed on top and were positioned to look out across the mountain range. The area was hidden from the inn by the slope of the land, which made it the perfect spot for quiet contemplation after a ceremony in the roundhouse.

"Bryce can't come here tomorrow," Ellie said. "It would be a disaster. You have to cancel the ceremony."

"No," Joline said. "Mama Rosita was clear about what she wants. And I don't want to interfere. Marco's right, I've already screwed things up enough."

"But you need to protect this place," Ellie said. "We can't let it be destroyed."

"It's out of my hands." Joline closed her eyes, trying to find her center. How did the wonderful energy from the chakra meditation get poisoned so quickly?

"But you can pick up the phone and call Bryce. Tess? Don't you agree?"

Tess was wandering behind the logs. Joline wasn't even sure she was listening. Tess seemed to be sorting through whatever had happened during the meditation. It was best for her to stay in that space, not be drawn back to plans and action. That would come soon enough.

"You know, there's something I figured out, one of the answers. It has to do with Dylan." Joline put her hands on the log. She knew it had once been a sacred tree. Before there was a roundhouse, generations of shamans had sat in its shade to learn from the masters before them. It had stood witness to the oldest ceremonies still remembered in local lore. She asked for its wisdom.

"I never used to care about money, you know? And a lot of the excitement of this thing, if I'm honest, had to do with the money—well, being able to pursue something that I have always dreamed of, of course—but to get paid serious money for it? But I realize that the money side was for Dylan, to show him that what I am doing is important, has value. And that I can support him. That you can do what you love and still live a good life. But that drive for, I don't know, accomplishment? Money as a measuring stick? It took away my strength in a way. It's trapped me in a future I haven't even paid for yet. And I've dragged Dylan along with me."

She spread out her toes, trying to get her whole foot in contact with the earth. She considered lying down on the grass, but didn't want to leave the log.

"But you've always supported him," Ellie said. "You've always given him a wonderful home."

"It was a ratty old place in a tough part of town," Joline said.

"I doubt he saw it that way, Jo," Ellie said. "His lyrics aren't about hardship. They're about love."

In her excitement about the new apartment, had she completely overlooked his feelings? He had lingered for a long time at the door of their old place before they left, but she had assumed he was memorizing the contours of the space for use in a song at a later time. But maybe he had simply been sad to leave.

She thought back to her ayahuasca journey, Dylan sinking through the lake with a contented expression on his face. Maybe he wasn't the one who needed saving. The mother, she reminded herself, isn't necessarily the wiser one. She moved her hands over the side of the log and pressed them against the bark.

"I hope I can fix things with Marco and Mama Rosita. I can't bear to have them think that I meant for any of this to happen." The greatest gift in all of her work with Bryce had been finding Casa Munay. It felt like a second home.

"I don't think Marco is too interested in talking to any of us right now." Tess finally sat.

"I know. But I wish I could explain to him how complicated this all is. I think he'll understand if I can walk him through the whole thing."

"No," Ellie said. Her face was tilted up, as if she was reading the sky. "He won't. All the explanations in the world won't matter. That's not what matters."

Ellie's voice sounded celestial, mystical. "I got my answer," she said. "I know what to do about David."

THIRTY-ONE
Ellie

Ellie looked up again at the tree above her. The leaves were uniformly green and taut. They waved at her with no hint of their brittle future, the eventual yellowing of their tips, the flash of orange that would be followed by a drop to earth.

"You know how we were supposed to ask a question?" she said. "Mine was, 'should I tell David?'" She noticed Joline clutching the edge of the log. She thought her hands must hurt. "I didn't get any answer at first, but I felt myself getting closer to him somehow, closer to his heart, so I could see how he feels, how he sees me." It didn't make a whole lot more sense saying it out loud, but she needed her friends to hear it all. "And then the most amazing thing happened. I finally understood it all at some deep level, before I could even put it into words, the answer became completely clear."

She looked out to the distant mountains. They were flush with green, the tree she had been examining replicated thousands of times over. It had been in front of her all along.

"So are you going to tell him or not?" Tess blurted.

"He already knows," Ellie said. She felt the truth of it even more strongly saying it out loud.

"What?" Tess glanced at Joline. "How?"

"I don't know why I didn't see it before," Ellie said, "but of course he knows. He knows me so well. Not that he has any details, but I realize that he sensed something was off for a long time. He was just as afraid to ask as I was to tell him. But he knew for sure something was wrong when I came home from that last trip and told him I wanted to sell Nantucket. That's when his fears were confirmed. I couldn't understand why he looked so upset. He had prodded me for years to consider selling the property. But on that day, he knew I was trying to keep myself away from something, from someone, on Nantucket."

She had buried that moment deep in her memory, but now she could smell the rosemary lamb in the oven, feel the stem of the wine glass in her hands, her throat still raw from holding back tears on the ferry and through the whole plane ride home. David was wearing his gray sweater, her favorite, the one with the frayed ribbing on the sleeves. He had popped an olive into his mouth, leaned against the counter, and asked about her trip. She had twirled the wine glass in her hand and tried to conjure a casual tone when she told him that she thought it was time to get rid of the cottage.

"What do you mean get rid of it?" David straightened up, the pit of the olive held hostage in his teeth.

Watching this scene from the present, Ellie realized that he had feared "getting rid of it" might mean she wanted to tear the tiny house down, and put up a larger one. Dig in deeper.

"I want to put it on the market," she said.

"Why now?" he asked. Something in his tone wasn't right, but she couldn't decipher the nuance over the clamor of her own heart thrumming away in her ears. So she started to talk. She told David how hard it would be to let go of that connection to her grandfather, but that she had to admit that it was becoming a bit of a drain to keep it up from such a distance, that things were changing on the island anyway, it wasn't the same place she remembered from her childhood, that this was probably the sensible thing to do.

David took a gulp of his vodka—he wasn't a gulper—and put his glass on the counter without looking at her. He made some matter-of-fact statement about how he was sure she knew his feeling on the matter. Lilly had skipped into the kitchen just then, asking her mom for a knee-hug, which required Ellie to get on her knees. She breathed in the lemony scent of Lilly's hair, reminded of what home smelled like. By the time she stood up, David had left the room.

A bee circled a patch of buttercups growing near the base of the log. It pecked at them, one by one.

"And then the meditation switched to a different chakra," she said, forcing her thoughts back into the present, "and I repeated my question, and I moved even further into David's heart. And this time, I saw his question instead of mine." She wiped at her face with the back of her hand.

"What he has been wanting to know is if I still love him, if I'm still with him because I want to be, or if it's because I'm sick, if it's only because it doesn't make sense to disrupt everything now. He isn't sure, with whatever time I have left, if he's the one I really want to be with." A whirlwind gathered in her chest. "And so what I need to do is go home and tell him that I chose him before I got sick again. That I chose him again while we were here. That I choose him now. He needs to know I still love him."

She knew what facing this truth would look like. For David it would be like staring at the surface of an ocean blazing with sparkles from the noonday sun, a glare he couldn't quite look at directly without searing his eyes. Her job would be to swim across the surface and snuff out each small explosion without getting burned and make the water safe again for him. She felt the arms of her friends converge over her then, giving her the strength her limbs would need to stay afloat.

After dinner, Ellie climbed the stairs back up to the room. She was pleased not to feel the fire in her chest on the last few steps, for once. She must finally be adjusting to the altitude. Or maybe her lung was stronger. Was it foolhardy to think that might be possible?

"His truck is still parked outside. He hasn't left yet," Tess said from behind her.

Marco hadn't made an appearance during dinner. Tess seemed

more anxious about it than Joline, who had apparently gone back to surrendering her future to the best judgment of the universe.

Ellie sat on the couch, sleep already beginning to tempt her. Her exhaustion felt pure for the first time in a long time, the kind that nudges you into a puff of slumber, light and airy and peaceful.

"Maybe he went to bed early," Joline said. "He's got to get up early if he's going to get all the way to Quito and back by noon tomorrow."

"It's only eight thirty," Tess said. "No, he must be avoiding us. I don't like it."

Ellie smiled. The old Tess was back, plotting and planning. That didn't take long.

"Tess, you're going to have to let it be. Nature will support."

"I don't want you to get blindsided, Jo. What if Marco is churning up all his neighbors right now?"

"Then Bryce will see the truth of how the community feels."

"And Bryce will know you told Marco the plan. He'll sue you, and make your life hell."

Ellie propped up the pillows behind her on the couch. She had to shake off sleep for at least a little longer. "So you fight him. I'll help you."

"I don't think he'd go that far," Joline said. "He's tenacious, no question. But he's not a bad guy."

Tess was pacing. "Remember ActiVision? Bryce was an investor. Jim Goodwin, the founder? He was diagnosed with testicular cancer, and Bryce forced him into a leave of absence, said they couldn't risk him being distracted. Essentially ushered him out of his own company. Hired a new CEO. That's so illegal it's not even funny, but Jim didn't have the resources to fight him. He ended up being fine, and Bryce still wouldn't give him back the CEO role. Said the company had moved on."

"Maybe Bryce saved his life. Maybe Jim wouldn't have recovered if he hadn't had time to focus on his health," Joline said.

"Really? That's the moral you're going to take from that story? How about that Bryce is only out for his own best interest and will crush anyone standing in his way?"

"Tess, the more we try to coordinate with Marco, the more it really will be interference." Joline did sound incredibly calm. The relief of knowing she didn't have to lie to her brother had probably helped her find her old sense of balance, a renewed faith that things would work out. Tess, on the other hand, was gunning for action.

"It would be hard for Bryce to prove Joline was responsible for the word getting out, anyway," Ellie said. "Think about it. Bryce's real-estate guys having been working this plan for weeks. Maybe someone else could have let it slip. It's not impossible that Marco could have heard about it from somewhere else."

"Unless Marco tells him exactly where he heard it from," Tess said.

"Well, I can't ask Marco to lie. What he says is up to him. I'm going to meditate. I need to surround myself with peaceful energy and then get a good night's sleep." Joline opened the wooden chest and brought out the mats and blankets.

Ellie's eyelids drooped. "I'm going to turn in, too. I'm beat."

Tess fidgeted and let out a sigh.

"Well, I can't sleep," Tess said. "I'm going to go for a walk."

Joline looked up from the box. "Please don't go up any mountains."

"No, I promise. I'm just going to wander the grounds. Get some air. Maybe find a llama to talk to. I won't be long."

Ellie set up her sleeping mat, not bothering to tuck the bottom sheet under the sides. She was tempted to crawl into her bed without even brushing her teeth, but she never let her kids get away with that ploy. When she came out of the bathroom, Joline was waiting and enveloped her in a hug.

"You know I love you, right?" Joline said into her hair and then stepped back. "I'm sorry if I wasn't more supportive about all this, I just felt stuck between you and David. It's a place you know I've never wanted to be."

"I'm so sorry, Jo. I don't think I've actually said that yet," she said.

"You don't have to. Just stay in your truth. That's all you can do," Joline said.

"What did I ever do to deserve you as my friend?" Ellie said.

"You taught *me* what being a friend is, Ellie B," Joline said.

As she lay down, she felt immense gratitude for Joline. Maybe she never should have questioned Joline's ability to understand her convoluted situation, to find a way to forgive. Love had a way of mending even the deepest fissures.

She remembered how Don Emilio had told her to breathe in those that love her and hold them inside. She decided to try it, deep breaths full of her kids, huge gulps full of David and everything they had shared. Admitting the truth would be the hardest thing she had ever had to do, but she had to believe that their love for each other would survive. As she lay there, the cloud of sleep that had been following her around since dinner reached up and swallowed her in its soft embrace. Floating there would free her from everything difficult. She released conscious thought and let the world fall away.

THIRTY-TWO

Tess

The sliver of moon in the sky was just bright enough for Tess to see without a flashlight. She wandered toward the spot where they had sat that afternoon. It was as good a place as any to sit and think. As the logs came into view, she could just make out the shape of Marco's back, and the movement of his hand as he stroked Chi-Chi's head.

"Your dog saved my life," she said. At the sound of her voice, Chi-Chi sauntered over and herded her toward the logs. Tess sat and brushed her hands through Chi-Chi's fur. "While you were gone. I asked her to take me to the waterfall, and we got caught in a storm. She showed me a cave and made me stay until the mountain dried out."

Marco looked at her then, and she could see the alarm in his eyes.

"I'm sorry. I should have told you never to go on that route if there is any threat of rain. It's dangerous."

"Your parents," she said.

"Yes." He caressed the smooth part of the log he was sitting on. The memory of his touch sent a tremor through her. She waited for him to say more, maybe ask her a slew of questions, or yell at her, but soon realized that he would do none of those

225

things. She felt the weight of him next to her, like an enormous boulder that had come to rest in a pasture and would sit still for a long time, immovable.

"Beautiful night," she said.

"Luna obscura. Dark moon. You would say waning moon? It is the time to let things go."

"You're not saying that you're actually thinking about letting go of this place, are you?" Tess had learned firsthand the power of nature. She wasn't convinced it was wise to leave everything in her hands.

"I have to ask you not to interfere," Marco said. She searched his voice for tinges of anger, but couldn't find any. "Our world here works in ways that you don't understand."

"And Bryce Gardner works in ways I think you might not understand. I can help you figure this out."

"Tess." He put his hand on her arm, his palm warm, his touch gentle. "Please."

She needed Marco to know she wasn't like Bryce, even though they were a closely related species.

"I'm sorry I didn't tell you sooner," she said.

"You know, a friend of mine followed you out of town the other day. He said there was an American businessman in town planning some kind of scheme and he saw you two with him. I told him he must have made a mistake. That I knew you weren't capable of any evil."

"And now?"

"Remember I told you a very old tree fell the night my father died?" Marco patted the log beneath him. "It is this tree. No matter how many rings are added to the outside of a tree for strength, its core forever remains. That's its essence."

"I don't understand."

"My feelings for you haven't changed." Marco tilted his head toward her and looked right at her. Tess knew in that moment that she could still have Marco. He understood her. They were similar in more ways than anyone would expect.

"You know how you told me that people like us are afraid of breaking other people's hearts?" she said.

Marco nodded, stroking Chi-Chi's fur again.

"Maybe that doesn't give the other person enough credit.

Maybe Anna would have done just fine."

"Maybe," Marco said. He didn't sound convinced.

"In fact, maybe we pride ourselves on being so strong that we don't leave any room for others to take care of us, to love us unconditionally. But we'll never know, is the thing I've realized, unless we stop being in control long enough to let them." She looked back up at the moon. She had never given much thought to how constant the phases of the moon were. It was in a different position in the sky with a different shape whenever she looked, and she had somehow mistaken that for unpredictability.

"Maybe loving someone is enough," she said. "And letting them love you back. Maybe that's all we should need."

Marco reached for her hand and laced his fingers in hers. His palm dwarfed hers, and she felt like a child placing her hand inside the paw of a bear. Such a gentle bear.

Sitting in the moonlight with Marco, Tess understood what Ellie had been trying to tell her. That not only was love not a guarantee against pain, but that a certain amount of sacrifice could make love stronger. That there would inevitably be obstacles in the way of any relationship, but a determination to move past them gave the relationship its texture and meaning, turned it from something ephemeral into something with girth and weight. Marco had helped her see that, too.

"You're a shaman in your own way, Marco. Don't let anyone tell you otherwise." She brought his hand up to her mouth and kissed his knuckles lightly. Then she let go.

"Good night, Marco." Tess finally felt the need for sleep. She left Marco staring at the moon, steadily tipped on its side.

THIRTY-THREE

Joline

When Marco's truck trundled into Casa Munay late the next morning, half the village trailed it in through the gate on foot. Joline rushed toward the parking area, anxious to see Mama Rosita, but couldn't get close to the truck. Fifteen or twenty kids sprinted ahead of the vehicle, the adults holding on to any part of the truck they could reach. The dusty carnival carried flags and flowers, and singing erupted in waves. A girl in a green skirt and lace top jumped onto the floor board next to Mama Rosita's window and leaned in to kiss Mama Rosita's cheek, yelling something afterward that was accepted with a whoop from the crowd. She had no idea how all these people had heard about Mama Rosita's illness, or the timing of her return, but their joy was contagious. A little boy in wool shorts down to his ankles jumped up and down clapping, while two men linked arms and spun in a circle, their rubber boots no impediment to their celebratory jig. Arabella and Marianna skipped past her and joined in a group hug with several women who looked like they might be relatives. Tess and Ellie came outside.

"What's all this?" Tess asked.

"Welcoming committee," Joline said. She should have known

that Mama Rosita's recovery would be celebrated. She wasn't sure how she would explain all the commotion to Bryce. He was due in less than half an hour.

Marco parked the car and walked around to the passenger side. His neighbors slapped him on the back while he smiled and nodded. Marco patted the heads of several of the children as he walked past. When he opened Mama Rosita's door, the crowd instinctively stepped back to give them room. Marco bent inside the car and lifted his grandmother's stout frame into his arms.

The color in Mama Rosita's cheeks was a relief, the burgundy of the scarf around her shoulders matching her ruddy complexion. She looked relatively strong, but Joline could see a tiredness in her eyes behind her wide smile. She winced slightly as Marco shifted his weight. She accepted another kiss from an older man standing next to Marco, his hair in a long gray ponytail.

Marco said something to the gathering and to Joline's surprise, carried Mama Rosita directly down to the roundhouse. She followed the procession down the hill and through the tapestry.

The roundhouse had been transformed. A throne of sorts had been constructed at the far end out of several sleeping mats, blankets, and a mountain of pillows. Marco and two other gentleman were busy helping find a comfortable position for Mama Rosita, her mouth pinching each time they moved her. Garlands of fresh flowers were strung along the walls and wrapped around the center trunk that supported the ceiling. Flower petals carpeted the floor, the brightest ones at Mama Rosita's feet. Mama Rosita eventually took in a long breath and Marco stood, apparently satisfied that she was in the best possible spot. Marco turned to the crowd and nodded his head before stepping aside.

The man with the gray ponytail kissed Mama Rosita's hand and gave her a small pebble. Behind him, a young girl bowed and whispered something to the old lady before handing her a daisy. Joline realized then that everyone standing in the roundhouse had silently formed a line. Each person in turn welcomed Mama Rosita back with a small token, a rock, a coin, a leaf. One little boy held out a marble, clearly a prized possession because his mother had to remind him twice to hand it over. Mama Rosita bowed her head at each person, the pile of items growing large in her lap. Her discomfort rose as the line shortened. Tess slipped a handful of petals into Joline's hand, nodding at the strands of flowers tied around the pole beside them. When it was her turn, Joline whispered, "Welcome back" into Mama Rosita's ear. When Ellie passed, Joline noticed that Mama Rosita held on to Ellie's wrist for a moment. Then Tess leaned into Mama Rosita, and the old lady grabbed Tess's face and kissed her forehead before placing her hands over her own heart. Tess glanced at Marco, blushing.

Joline's inner clock jolted her, urging her to look at her watch. It was after noon. She backed out of the crowd and hurried up toward the inn.

Bryce was leaning against his car, looking at his phone.

"There you are, I thought you'd forgotten about me."

"I was at the roundhouse. Mama Rosita is there." His elegant outfit of the day before had been replaced by jeans and a black t-shirt, and he hadn't shaved. But he still clutched his leather portfolio.

"I don't think you'll need that, though."

Bryce looked down at his hands, hesitated, and then tossed the portfolio into the open car window.

"Ready?" She was uncertain what was going to happen next and decided it was best not to say anything else. Let it unfold. As they walked into the opening in the stone wall, she saw that the crowd had fanned out against the walls. Marco rose from his seat next to his grandmother and came to greet them.

"Mr. Gardner," Marco said, "my grandmother is pleased you could come today."

"Please tell her I am honored," Bryce said, taking Marco's hand. "Thank you for gathering so many from your community for my ceremony. I think it is going to be a special day."

Joline tried to catch Marco's eye, but he bowed his head and led Bryce across the room. He asked Bryce to kneel in front of Mama Rosita. She was wearing a band of fabric around her head with feathers sticking straight up. It made her look taller in her makeshift chair.

She spotted Tess and Ellie and joined them against the wall.

"Did Marco say anything while I was gone?" she whispered to Tess.

"Nope. Everyone just stood here, waiting. Kind of strange."

"Mama Rosita says that we have gathered the community here today because you are an important man. This she knows," Marco said.

She could only see the side of Bryce's head, but it was enough to catch the smile stretching across his face.

"Please give her your hands."

Bryce reached out and Mama Rosita tugged on his wrists, nearly tipping him over from his kneeling position. She held her hand on the inside of his arm with her eyes closed for several moments. She then wiped her hand over his palms, first his right hand and then his left, as if she were petting him, or trying to rub something off his hands.

She spoke at a low volume and the room was completely silent, everyone straining to hear what she had to say. Joline hoped this wouldn't completely drain her. There was no question that she should be in bed.

"Mama Rosita says that you have healing hands," Marco said. "You have the ability to help many people, help them see deeper into what is central in their lives. You have been given this gift, and it is important work."

One of the young girls began to fidget. Her mother stroked her hair, and whispered in her ear.

"In our culture," Marco continued, "there are three sacred creatures, the snake who rules the underworld, the puma who rules the present state of the earth, and the condor who is our connection to the divine. You have condor in you."

Bryce's soul card. A bird of prey, but this one was revered.

"The condor soars high with great vision, but must also maintain his connection to the earth. Mama Rosita wants to know if you feel a flutter in your chest sometimes, like something is unsettled there."

Bryce nodded. His heart, Joline thought. His condition must be as clear as a signpost to Mama Rosita. He was transfixed.

"This is the condor unsettled. It is critical for your health that the condor find its place, the nest where it can settle in peace. It can hunt and kill and feed its family, but it must find the place it belongs, the place where it can best share its considerable gifts."

Mama Rosita waved Bryce closer. He bent toward her, and

she put her hands on his head, and then on the sides of his face. When she let go she looked grave. Joline hoped she wasn't in too much pain.

"Your condor craves the mountains, mountains like we are in today. The mountains are good for you."

Oh, no. There was no way she could talk Bryce out of all this if Mama Rosita told him these mountains would be a good place for his heart. He would operate his other businesses remotely if he had reason to believe it was the answer to the curse on his health.

"But your condor also craves water," Marco said. "Mama Rosita says that water is necessary for your healing power, your ability to heal yourself and others. Not a small river, but a vast reservoir, wide and deep. It is the depth of this water that gives you strength, that will make your condor fly."

Mama Rosita closed her eyes and began to chant.

"She says she is flying with the condor, searching for its nest. She sees very tall trees, sprouting up toward the sky, old trees that stand tall. As she swoops down, she sees thousands of people, hand in hand along the shore of this great body of water the condor wants to be near. All these people are filled with gratitude for you. You will help them heal in this place, beside this body of water. She sees you floating in the middle, on a great yellow raft."

Joline's head snapped up. A big yellow raft? Like a dock? Mama Rosita had remembered his dock on Lake Tahoe.

"Yellow is the color of peace. Mama Rosita says you would be wise to find this place. There you will do the work the universe has led you to do, and your heart will be at peace. Your condor will remain strong."

Joline covered her mouth in shock. Mama Rosita was sending him away. She had planned it all along. She couldn't help but smile under her hand.

"She has asked Pachamama to grant you this," Marco said.

After an awkward pause, Bryce got to his feet, realizing the ceremony was over. He shook Marco's hand vigorously.

"Thank you so much. Please thank everyone for coming." Bryce reached down to Mama Rosita and squeezed her hand. "Thank you, Mama Rosita."

Bryce turned to the crowd and took a deep breath. Joline watched him closely. Would he still announce his plans for a school?

Bryce said, "Well, I guess I'll head out. Joline, can I see you for a moment?"

As Joline followed him out, she turned back toward Mama Rosita, and saw her expression settle into a satisfied smile.

Bryce was moving at a slower pace than his norm, as if his feet were waiting for direction from his brain.

"You weren't kidding about her, were you?" he said. "Obviously, she sensed my heart condition. But did you pick up on what she said about the lake?"

"The big body of water?" Joline's pulse kicked up a notch.

"She didn't use the word lake, exactly, but the yellow raft?" he said. "Do you think that could be my dock?"

"Wow. It could be," she said, careful to keep a straight face.

He stopped moving. "Wait. Have you ever mentioned my heart attack to her?"

"No, never," Joline said. "I never said a word to her about your heart. That's her healing gift." Thank God he wouldn't have any reason to ask about the dock.

"Wow. That's incredible. She totally got me. And all those people? Standing on the shore? Do you get it? The retreat center should be in Lake Tahoe."

"Lake Tahoe?"

"I'm really sorry, Joline. I know you've worked hard to find us a South American location. I know you think the vibe down here is important, authenticity and all. But you said yourself there are a lot of issues with building down here that I probably didn't fully understand at first. I should have thought of this earlier. It will be like the Canyon Ranch of the West Coast, only better. We can bring the shamans there. We can fly them in. We'll have special guest healers that no one else will have."

"Oh, I don't know if they'd come to—"

"And none of our clients will have to travel too far. Whole

management teams can come together right in Tahoe. Clients can stop in after a ski weekend. It's much more forward thinking, and more responsible. Instead of bringing Americans to Ecuador, we'll bring Ecuador to them. The real estate will cost a fortune, of course, but the revenue opportunity is enormous."

"What about the school?"

"Right. It's a good thing we haven't told anyone about that yet. I hate to go back on my word."

Joline couldn't help but feel guilty that the one thing that might actually benefit the community in all of this was about to disappear with Bryce.

"You should still do it," she said. Bryce looked at her quizzically. "Think about it. It would be great incentive to get the best healers from around here to travel north. Give them a way to help their own communities." She cringed at her next thought, but knew it would help push the point home. "And it would probably be good for business."

"You're right." He started walking again, his hand massaging the scruff on his face. "Giving back to a needy community. Another feature Canyon Ranch doesn't have. Brilliant."

She had to admire his ability to make decisions on the fly. A person's greatest strength and greatest weakness were usually the same thing.

"When can you get me a new programming plan? Next week some time?" He was already trying to wrap up their conversation. She was just getting started.

"So much has changed from our original vision, Bryce. I need to think about if I'm comfortable going forward."

"What?" He actually looked wounded, and more than a little floored. No one ever thought twice about working with Bryce Gardner. Most people assumed it was an opportunity they couldn't afford to pass up. She had already made that mistake once.

"I'm going to need a new contract, Bryce."

He sighed. "You know how my lawyers feel about customizing employment contracts."

"I know, but I don't care how your lawyers feel. This is about how I feel. This is about two people who need to see eye to eye and be able to work together, not a bunch of attorneys stuck in the middle. And"—she cut him off before he could interrupt—"you can't give me the precedence or fairness arguments, either. This is a venture that has nothing to do with your other companies, and I need to know I can trust this relationship to keep working with you."

"Of course you can trust our relationship."

Was he actually surprised that the last few days had given her pause? God, he was dense.

"Then the contract shouldn't matter that much in the end," she said. "But I still need it. And I think you know you need me." She bit the inside of her lip. She was getting close to combustible territory, but she had to stand her ground.

"Are we talking about my kids, now?" He took a step backwards up the hill, exaggerating the height differential between them. "Doesn't that feel just the slightest bit nasty to you, to wield something personal as leverage?"

Was that what she was doing? Was that how she wanted to negotiate? She believed that there was still love there to be rekindled between Bryce and his kids, and she did want to help make that happen.

"I'd like to separate the two topics," she said. "I'm only concerned about the contract for my work on the retreat center. I will continue to work with you and your family for my regular hourly rate for as long as it takes, even if we can't work out the details on the center. You have my word on that."

His facial muscles shifted, some part of his veneer melting in front of her. He had spent a lifetime developing a poker face, but on this topic he couldn't hide his emotions. He was truly relieved.

"Good. Send me your terms and we can get together when you get back."

"I will," she said, crossing her hands over her chest. "Safe travels."

She stood still and watched him go. She may have given away her leverage, but the concept of having the "upper hand" only worked if you were willing to strike with it. She knew herself better than that. Honesty and good will had to be enough.

As Bryce walked up the hill, the peak of Imbabura towered above him, and Joline thought he had never looked quite so small.

THIRTY-FOUR
Ellie

llie repositioned herself on the stool in the phone room.
She took several long breaths. She wanted her voice to be
in control so she would be able to get through what she
needed to say.

He picked up after barely one full ring.

"Dove, are you all right?"

She put her hand on her heart. She knew she should do this
face to face, when she got home, but she didn't want to wait
another hour, let alone another day, to tell David how she felt,
for him to know the truth of where she stood. Given the layers
of pain she now understood he had been living beneath, she at
least owed him that.

"Yes, I'm fine," she said.

David exhaled. "Since you called my cellphone, I. . ." He
trailed off. She hated that, because of her, he had to live his life
braced for bad news.

"I needed to talk," Ellie said. "Just to you."

She heard quiet shuffling on his end. Was he moving across
the room to close the door? Where was he? In his study? In their
bedroom? She hoped he was tucking into his old leather chair
with the faded arms and the cushion covered in corduroy. It was

his favorite spot.

"What is it?"

A reservoir of emotion crested at the back of her throat, and she knew she wouldn't be able to keep her voice steady after all.

"I called to tell you . . ." Her words came out in small bursts, riding on her tears.

"Dove?" David's voice quivered.

She took in a gulp of air and pushed it back out in a stream through her lips. "I love you. I know now. . . . I realize you might not always have been sure about that. About us. But—" Her words were tangled in tears. "I never stopped loving you, David. It will always be you."

She leaned over, her elbows on her knees. She could barely breathe. She waited for him to speak, her anxiety growing with every second of silence at the other end. What if he hung up? Walked away? What if he had no idea what she was talking about? What would she say then? Had she been wrong?

Then she heard the small puffs of air on his end. David was crying.

"Oh God, David. I'm so sorry." She desperately wanted to be able to touch him then, hold him while he cried, weep together for everything she had damaged and everything they would need to rebuild. All she could do was clutch the phone and wait. She heard him take in a huge breath, his exhale slow and wobbly.

"I need you, Ell. Please come home."

She nodded as she spoke. "I'm coming home."

They stayed on the phone quietly for a few more minutes, gently ending the conversation that had only just started.

After hanging up, she didn't move. She pictured David alone in his study. He wouldn't have long before one of the kids would come looking for him, knocking on the big oak door. And he would find a way to regain his balance somehow and let them in.

Her homecoming would be more somber. There would be no way to wait a day, or a week, or for just the right time to tell David everything. But in many ways, that was a relief. She wouldn't have to paint on a smile and pick through her memory of the trip in search of the safest and least important details to share. She could simply start from the beginning and tell him the truth.

Of course, the kids would sense the mood, even though they wouldn't be able to quite put their fingers on it. That was the hardest thing, the persistent reality that she might not have enough time left on the earth to share with her children the vast lessons she had learned from these shamans, and her friends. Would she be granted the chance, years from now, to be with one of them at the brink of a major step in their lives, or in a dark moment of need, or on some random Tuesday in their adult years and offer even a token of wisdom she had taken from this distant land? Would she ever have that opportunity? Had these shamans done that for her?

She thought of Mama Rosita, so old, and yet so strong. Watching her summon the energy to deal with Bryce, on top of everything else, had been astonishing. Ellie hoped some of that strength had rubbed off on her somehow.

Yes. Strength. She had to start summoning her own strength. She sat up straighter. Marco had said the celebration would continue that night. The Casa often opened its doors to the neighbors for dinner on Saturday nights, but this evening would be more festive than the norm, including a local band that would come play and a troupe of girls who wanted to perform a special dance. Ellie realized with a bit of surprise that she was actually looking forward to it, and she hadn't looked forward to any kind of party for a long time.

As she stood up, she noticed that the moon had risen, a tiny crescent slice in the blue canvas of the sky. By the time she got home, the moon would be completely invisible to the naked eye, taking a short break before starting over from the opposite side of the orb.

THIRTY-FIVE

Tess

Tess wished she had brought a skirt that she could wear to the dinner, which would have been more celebratory. Instead, she tentatively packed all her hair clips away and wore her hair down. By the time she walked into the dining room, it was brimming with activity. Many of the men and women who had come for Mama Rosita's arrival were there, chatting in small groups. Tess admired the women's multicolored skirts, their lace tops tight at the elbows, puffs of cotton cascading down to their wrists. They all wore a different version of the same bright scarf, a long swath of blue, red or green cotton embroidered with flowers.

Joline was talking to Arabella at the corner of the room. Mostly hand gestures, as far as she could tell. Ellie was at the side table, pouring wine. She was wearing a coral knit dress with a twist of silver chains around her neck. She glowed. Tess wondered if it was the relief of finally coming to terms with what to do about David, but she couldn't help but hope Ellie looked vibrant because her health had improved. The color of her skin was pinker, the whites of her eyes a little bit brighter than six days earlier. Or maybe it was her "aura" that was all polished and shiny. Tess chuckled. Did she really just have that thought?

If she were being honest, she still didn't know if she believed any of it, that a group of medicine people, with no actual *medicine* at their disposal, could hope to cure the incurable. But she couldn't afford to write it off entirely. They would find out soon enough. Ellie would retake every test she could, David anxious to convince her to submit to chemo if only to give them a few more months, Ellie desperate to avoid it. She bristled at the possibility of Ellie, after all this, hearing yet another diagnosis no different from the last.

Ellie walked toward her from the wine table, holding out a glass of red.

"Thanks," Tess said, and they clinked. The wine warmed her throat. She realized that she had barely had a drink all week. An ice-cold martini with a stuffed olive was something to look forward to.

The band began to play. The age of the musicians had to range from twelve to seventy. The men and the boys alike wore perfectly pressed white shirts tucked into jeans or cargo pants. The instruments came in twos; standing drums, recorders, guitars, and one ukulele. The man with the biggest belly played that. The oldest one among them still had a full head of black hair. Their music was happy. Repetitive tunes that relied on the high notes of the wind instruments for their melodies. Tess was tapping her feet to the music when a warm hand touched her arm. It was Marco.

"May I ask for this dance?"

She took his hand. Ellie raised her eyebrows as Tess handed back her glass. There were two other couples dancing in front of the band. The musicians played a little louder with each additional person that took to the floor. Marco's strong arms guided her to the other side of the room. As they faced each other, he glanced at her throat.

"That hummingbird is perfect for you."

"You said it was a sacred symbol, but you didn't tell me of what."

"Well, first of all, hummingbirds, as you know, are very busy. They never stop moving." Tess chuckled. "But they use their constant movement to find stillness in a way, which makes them special. And many do not know that the pattern their wings make is like the infinity sign, you know, a sideways figure eight?" Something in her mind popped to attention. "They teach us about the immense power and strength it takes to be still, and how important that is if we are to find the nectar of life."

As they spun across the floor, she tried to imagine what would have happened had they not been interrupted that night. The combination of his physical strength and gentle demeanor was incredibly appealing. And it would have been the easy way out of her dilemma with Parker. But instead, Marco had helped her understand, perhaps more than anyone else, how she truly felt. As Joline often said, everyone has a unique way of helping.

"I didn't get a chance to ask you," Tess said. "What did you tell the pilot that convinced him to take Mama Rosita?"

Marco led her around the floor as he spoke.

"He knew who she was, once you said her name. I told him that you were too distraught to handle the paperwork yourself, but since we both heard you call her 'mama,' we could be assured that she was a relative."

"Never did I do so well by keeping my mouth shut," Tess said. "I don't think my Spanish would have impressed him."

"Won't the company refuse to pay when they find out?" he asked.

"I'll talk them into it. It would make a great PR story for them." She was already gearing back up for life at home. Action. Determination. She couldn't let all the voodoo make her soft.

"I'm sorry to see you leave tomorrow," he said. "You'll miss the breaking of the ground, I think you would call it."

"The what?"

"A truck arrives tomorrow with supplies for the first artist casita. Everyone will come back tomorrow, and we will start building it together."

"Your dream," Tess said. "Congratulations. Your father would be proud."

"I feel that he is," Marco said, nodding his head. Then he lowered his voice, and his steps slowed almost to a halt. "Tess, there's something I need to tell you."

She concentrated on her left hand perched on his shoulder and tried to quell the tremor in her chest.

"Mama Rosita told me when she was in the hospital that she

had a strong vision about your friend and her condition. She saw a big river, is how she said it. It was clogged when she came, but Pachamama has cleared away much dirt and silt since she has been here. It is now a strong river, running clear, which is very good. She's sure the plant helped a great deal with this. But my grandmother said there was one rock that had remained stuck to the bottom of the riverbed. It needed to be loosened. She put all her energy into making sure that happened right before she collapsed. Yesterday, she said, she saw that rock rolling away."

Tess stopped moving and pulled back to look him in the eyes.

"Are you saying that Mayu and Mama Rosita may have saved Ellie?"

"I'm just telling you what she said. But if she's right, I think you all may have saved her. *Ayni*, remember?"

She hugged him, and kissed him on the cheek.

"You know," Tess said, "your Anna was a fool to let you go."

"Perhaps I'm the one who has been the fool," he said, and winked, before bowing his head slightly and stepping back into the party. She shook her head and laughed. She was consumed by an urge to thank someone or something for Marco, for inserting him into her life for the briefest of moments, like one drop of iodine that colors a whole slide.

Tess retrieved her wine glass from Ellie.

"What was that about?" Ellie asked.

"He was just filling me in on Mama Rosita." She considered telling Ellie what Marco had said, but she didn't want to make promises she had no control over fulfilling. She would let the trained professionals back home make that evaluation. Instead, she put her arm around Ellie and kissed her on the cheek.

"You're cheery," Ellie said.

"Well, how much crying can a girl do? Seriously, this place brings on the waterworks."

"Joline should have put Kleenex at the top of her packing list." Ellie chuckled. "Any news from the office today?"

"No. They're still plugging away. I won't know anything until I get back."

"I know this trip was terrible timing for you," Ellie said.

"First of all, you know I would never have missed it. But in a way, the timing was actually perfect."

"What do you mean?"

Tess held up her left hand and wiggled her ring finger.

Ellie gasped and exploded in a hug. "You're really going to do it! Oh my God. Joline!" she practically yelled, and dragged Tess over to where Joline was standing. "Guess what?" she said, and held up Tess's hand for Joline to see. Tess couldn't help but admire the sparkle of the ring.

"Wow. Now I've seen it all," Joline said. "I'm proud of you, Tess."

"Both sides of the equation, right?" Tess hugged Joline, and held on through a full breath. "Thank you."

"When can we expect the invitation?" Ellie asked.

The possibility of a wedding without Ellie there jolted her.

"Parker and I had talked about taking a vacation the first week of July. So the last weekend of June would be perfect. You guys free in about six weeks?"

"Only you," Ellie said, "could pick a wedding date without even talking to the groom."

She gave an exaggerated shrug, and couldn't help but smile.

"Or maybe Parker will beat you to it and organize a surprise wedding," Joline said, poking her. "Although I don't think he could pull that off this time."

"What do you mean, this time?" Tess asked.

"Oh, come on," Joline said. "You always knew Parker set up that surprise party, didn't you? So he could meet us?"

Tess put her hand to her mouth and then burst out laughing at her own idiocy. How had she been that blind?

They fell into each other, Ellie's deep laugh rolling over, filling the room. She snorted, but didn't cough. Tess looked at Ellie again, and was sure she hadn't imagined what she had seen before, that glow. Ellie was beaming.

"To Casa Munay," Tess said, raising her glass. "A very special place."

They clinked their glasses one last time, to something bigger than they could master, and to something so simple it sat right in the palms of their hands.

Tess sipped her champagne, alone in seat 4A. Joline had decided to stick to her original plans and stay at Casa Munay for a few more days. She wanted to help Marco take care of Mama Rosita and figure out how she felt about continuing to work with Bryce. While Tess had been sorry to say goodbye, she appreciated being able to take full advantage of her upgrade. Letting go of Ellie at the airport had been particularly difficult. She was able to pull herself away only with the hope that their next reunion would carry some good news. Could Marco possibly be right about that?

The plane rose above Quito and pushed up over the mountains, all a shade greener than the week before, less snow piled in each nook. The volcanoes looked regal in the afternoon sun, and Tess considered that they were perhaps not as hardened and immobile as she had originally thought, rather were choosing to conserve their immense energy within.

As the plane banked to the north, she spotted a waterfall and realized they were about to fly right over Casa Munay. She squinted down to see if she could spot the cave, or the roofs of the casitas. Instead, just beyond the waterfall, she saw a long steep slope that angled off a tall and narrow peak. A swirl of grass and dirt a deeper hue than the rest of the hill looked as though it was formed into the shape of a heart. It seemed too perfect not to be man-made, but she couldn't imagine any humans tilling the land on such a steep incline. Given its position, she thought they'd have seen it from their deck at Casa Munay. Perhaps she'd been too stuck in her head to notice it then, not able to perceive anything other than fields and trees. Or perhaps she just needed a different perspective. Whatever the reason, she took it as a good sign, a welcome message from a land that had loved them well. Pachamama. Mother earth.

Tess stepped onto the escalator at SFO, hemmed in by other passengers. As she descended, she saw expectant faces and drivers holding name cards, but couldn't find Parker. She had been sure he would be there, the kind of guy who was courageous enough to come to the airport and hear her answer either way. He had asked her not to contact him while she was gone. Surely she couldn't be too late.

Tess shifted to the other side of her small step, and finally saw him. He stood about twenty feet back from the other greeters near a bank of arrivals and departure screens. He was leaning on a column, his white oxford tucked into his jeans. She studied him, this beautiful man, as he checked the monitor, glanced at his watch, and then ran a hand through his hair. When he finally spotted her, his eyes locked on hers, but he didn't move, as if frozen by the question between them.

She had played this scene out in her mind a hundred times on the plane, but hadn't counted on all the people and bags blocking her from running down the steps toward him. Instead, she held up her left hand, so he could see the ring on her finger. His eyes widened, and she let out a laugh. A grin erupted across his face, sending a wave of warmth through her. He broke into a jog, pushing his way through the crowd, his gaze on her the entire time, as if she might disappear if he looked away. When he reached her, he enfolded her in his arms. She hugged him tightly, and then, with deep gratitude, leaned against him and let him hold her.

ACKNOWLEDGEMENTS

My first order of thanks must go to GrubStreet, which has been instrumental in every step of this writing journey. Thank you to Eve Bridburg, Chris Castellani and the whole Grub crew for taking every writer seriously, for rigorously teaching us craft, and for giving us the tools to dream big.

I have immense gratitude for Michelle Toth and the entire team at SixOneSeven Books, including Andrew Goldstein, Whitney Scharer, and Eliyanna Kaiser. Michelle, you were the first to see the full potential of this work, and I will be forever grateful. Your keen editorial insights, entrepreneurial spirit, and boundless creativity have done wonders for this book.

Thanks to the unstoppable NIP group of Susan Bernard, Michele Ferrari, Louise Harland, Marina Hatsopolous, Rebecca Leeb, Stephanie Thurott, Judy White, and our fearless leader Ben Winters. The earliest version of this work was nurtured by your thoughtful critiques wrapped in steady encouragement. It made all the difference.

My thanks to Michelle Hoover for giving me your unvarnished feedback just when I needed it most, and instilling in me the courage to start over. Thanks also to Masie Cochran and Dawn Dorland for your wise editorial counsel. You both helped take this novel to another level.

I am ever grateful to a host of willing readers who offered their feedback along the way. Thank you to Lucy Atkins, Lisa Baffi, Roland Merullo, Sinead O'Connor, Molly O'Connor, and Rick Tetrault.

For critiquing this manuscript through multiple iterations and spending countless hours offering invaluable insights and suggestions, I am particularly indebted to my fellow writers Susan Bernard, Michele Ferrari, and Jessie Manchester Lubitz. I have been blessed with your friendship and counsel. I would have collapsed well before the finish line without you!

Bottomless thanks to Nora Speer for your reading and re-reading of this book, and for your relentless support of me and this project. Your friendship means the world to me.

Beyond reading the manuscript whenever I asked and giving me deeply considered and helpful feedback, deepest thanks to Lynn Tetrault for your unwavering conviction that this book would be a success. You have always supported anything I have ever attempted, and if I hadn't been born your sister, I would have chosen you!

Thanks to Cardiff Dugan Loy for believing in me, and opening doors, Sally Willcox for the NY introduction, and Michael Carlisle at Inkwell for loving this book from the first reading. Your enthusiasm for the work fueled me. Many thanks to Caitlin Summie Hamilton for your creative promotional work. I can't wait to see what we are able to do together.

This book would not have come to life were it not for some very special people in my life. Buckets of thanks to the original Pachamama Sisters: Lisa Baffi, Sally Everett, Nancy Harrington, Janet Kraus, Michelle LaCharite, Elizabeth Napolitano, Krista Anderson Ross, Laura Stone, Lynn Tetrault, Sherry Vogt, and Mimi Welch. Thank you for giving so much of yourselves without reserve on this amazing journey. Special thanks to Lisa for leading us down this path, and to Janet for our incredible partnership and the amazing experience that was Circles.

My thanks to the many wonderful shamans of Ecuador and Peru for generously sharing your gifts, especially Wayra, Don

Esteban, Mama Concha and Marijuanna.

There is no sufficient way to thank my parents for raising me to believe that anything is possible and giving me every opportunity to stretch my wings. I miss you, Mom. Thanks also to John Apruzzese, Don Apruzzese and Barbara Yeager for your belief in my creativity and supporting your little sister without reserve. The extended Apruzzese and Sherbrooke clans have been a powerful cheering section for me and I am appreciative of you all.

My world would not be the same without my sons, Henry and George. You amaze me every day and fill me with more love than I thought possible. I hope witnessing my transition from business to writing has given you some measure of encouragement to pursue your dreams, no matter how far fetched they may seem. Thank you for putting up with my endless hours staring into a screen. We're even!

Final and boundless thanks to my husband, Patrick Sherbrooke, for your continued faith in me, never questioning my decision to take a left turn and walk down this path. This book wouldn't have come to fruition without having you on my side. As you said to me once, "I'm here now, I'll be here then." I love you.

ABOUT THE AUTHOR

Katherine A. Sherbrooke received her B.A. from Dartmouth College and M.B.A. from Stanford University. An entrepreneur and writer, she is the author of *Finding Home*, a family memoir about her parents' tumultuous and inspiring love affair. This is her first novel. An avid supporter of the arts, she was a long-time member of the board of directors of RAW Art Works in Lynn, MA and currently serves as chair of the board of GrubStreet, a leading national literary arts organization. She lives outside Boston with her husband, two sons, and black lab. To learn more, please visit www.KASherbrooke.com.

CPSIA information can be obtained
at www.ICGtesting.com
Printed in the USA
LVOW11s1948081216

516411LV00005B/851/P